PROPERTY

OF

DJKRIMMER.COM

This one is for me and you - the ones yearning for the hot, older, tattooed lumber jack.

You're welcome.

Contents

Trigger/Content Warnings

This story contains the following possible triggers
- Off the page death of a parent
- talks about abuse from parent - off the page
- explicit language and adult sexual situations

I do my best to present this content in the gentlest of lights but please, take care and make sure to check in with yourself. Only you know you well enough to decide if you should proceed.

Remember to always put your mental health first and you matter.

PROPERTY OF HEL'S INK

Prologue

I WOULD ASSUME that in every person's life, there is that one moment in which you feel like you have finally made it. That all the sacrifices made could be justified. Despite all my unfortunate circumstances, I have finally made it to the top.

I am one of the best at what I do, and that is not cockiness. People travel from all over to come and sit in my chair and let me permanently mark them. I love what I do. And I love who I do it with – my family. The men I work with are all serious, well-known artists that could go off and each open their own very successful shops. But we don't; we stay at the famous Hel's Ink for one man - Tony.

Tony, the owner and founder of Hel's Ink over thirty years ago, was my close friend and mentor. Yes, I said "was" because he died four days ago. Sixty years old, the man was active, a non-smoker, and didn't drink – a lot of good it did him. He was so health conscious and still died early.

"Fuck I think I'm going to hurl again." Atlas, one of the other Hel's Ink tattoo artists and my annoying best friend, groans while he doubles over as if this hungover fuck is

1

going to vomit right here on my shoes. I shake my head, both disappointed in and embarrassed by this asshole.

"Atlas," I growl through my clenched teeth. "We are at Tony's fucking funeral. Get your shit together." My tone turns into a hiss as I smack him upside the head. I look from Atlas to the other two men standing next to us. Ash and Derek are the other two that make up our "foursome," as Atlas likes to call us, no matter how many times I've threatened physical violence to get him to stop.

Ash is our newest addition to the shop. He started working at Hel's Ink roughly two years ago and is a master with his Traditional Japanese work. And then there is Derek. Derek has worked at the shop for nearly as long as I have. He moved here from Northern Virginia and is our "mysterious, broody, grump," as Atlas would say. Derek doesn't have long-term clients; he only tattoos one piece on a person and has gotten into multiple arguments with both Tony and clients when he would flat out refuse to do another tattoo.

"Every shop has one prima donna." Tony would always say before rolling his eyes at Derek and moving on.

I look from my group to see Tony's girlfriend, Liza walking into the chapel, her two wannabe tattoo artist sons on either side of her, keeping her steady. Tony had been nice enough, or gullible enough, to allow them to work at the shop as shop hands. They took care of scheduling if we were busy, inventory and whatnot. They couldn't show up on time or sober, so it didn't last, and we went back to doing everything ourselves shortly before Tony passed. I shake my head before looking away from the spectacle to the closed black coffin.

Why is it closed?

I would've thought for sure it would be an open casket.

Tony was all about the afterlife traditions and taking things with you when you go. Several people in this growing crowd, including myself, will want to add something for his safe travels.

Liza leans in and wraps her arms around my waist, and I have to fight every urge I have inside my body not to shove this gold-digging shrew off me. Liza and Tony started dating less than a year ago; she is around my age, forty or so, and known for latching on to the more significant artists in our industry. It took all of us by surprise when Tony walked into the shop with her on his arm.

Tony had never been one to do relationships. He was very much the "love 'em and leave 'em" type. So, when Liza showed up trying to get purses, vacations, and jobs for her sons out of Tony, we thought he would throw her out. Shockingly, he kept her around and paid for the purses and vacations, but he made one thing publicly clear to her.

Tony only had two loves in his life. One was Hel's Ink, and the other was –

"Fox," Atlas' elbow digs into my ribs, making me wince. "Is that Janie?"

My gaze follows his and lands on the petite redhead walking into the chapel, Janie Pierce. Twenty-five years old, slim, with pale, freckled skin, long wild red hair, blue eyes, and Tony's daughter. I smirk when I notice her black pumps. Janie is short; most people are short around my six-foot-four frame, but Janie might hit my chest barefoot, maybe.

Jesus Christ, there she goes with her phone again. It's her dad's fucking funeral and Janie, as usual, has her phone out to chirp or what the fuck ever it is that an influencer does. What a crock of shit. The girl sits there and cons people into believing they will look like her if they use

3

whatever she holds in front of her camera. It's one of the many reasons we don't mesh well despite our close relationships with Tony.

"Yeah, that's her." I mutter as I fix the sleeves on my suit. I hate wearing suits. It's not that I don't have the money for nicer clothes, but I am more of a jeans and t-shirt guy. Comfort over fashion. This suit was expensive when I bought it three years ago. But I was a little trimmer back then, and since I had been on a bender up until yesterday, I didn't get around to going suit shopping before the funeral.

I turn toward Atlas, realizing I completely missed his question. "What did you say?"

"I said, I haven't seen her in years. When did she get so fucking hot?" I roll my neck as I try to ignore the uncomfortable urge I suddenly have to break my best friend's nose. This emotion must be due to this being Tony's funeral, right?

I stare at him in disgust and shake my head. "Fuck off, man. Don't be disrespectful to Tony like that."

I watch as Janie quickly moves out of the chapel, and I feel compelled to follow her. I walk down the hallway to see her leaning against a wall.

"Hey Torch, long time no see." I say as I stuff my hands in my pockets and lean against the wall opposite her. I allow myself to scan the redhead's appearance. Janie looks objectively attractive in her black belted button-up dress. Although, I am not sure that the lace fringe falling just below her ass constitutes proper funeral attire. What do I know, though?

"It's Janie, you dick." She all but spits in my direction, "And it hasn't been nearly long enough." I can't help but laugh. I have never been a fan of hers, but Janie's hatred for me would leave outsiders believing I ran over her dog.

4

I put my hands up in defense as a smirk pulls at my lips. "I apologize. I just thought I would check on you."

Her blue eyes roll so hard I'm in shock they don't get stuck. "I already told you, Fox. You can have the shop, okay? Just leave me alone." She pulls out her phone and starts tapping on the screen. Each *tap tap* is like nails on a chalkboard.

Deciding that I need to get this over with and ask the question on my mind, I clear my throat and cock my head, gesturing to the chapel. "Why is the old man's coffin closed?"

Her body visibly stiffens, and I see her hands tremble around her phone. She straightens to look at me and places her hands behind her back. "Because," She clicks, her voice holding more than venom. "As his daughter, it was my decision, and I found it more pleasing to look at the coffin than a dead body."

More pleasing.

Dead body.

I'm utterly shocked by her heartless words, and I watch mutely as she pushes herself off the wall and heads back into the chapel.

"Enjoy that shop, Fox. Hopefully, it doesn't steal your life like it did his." Her voice is distant, and I don't respond to her as she disappears behind the doors. My fingers run over the coins burning a hole in my pocket. The service will start soon, and I have no idea if the funeral director will allow me to place these coins in with Tony, but I will find out.

Chapter One

"THIS IS AMAZING FOX." Lauren squeals and gives me a massive smile before staring down at her hip tattoo in the mirror. Lauren – or "Ren" is my preferred client. She knows what she wants but is open to artistic changes. She never cancels, and she isn't bad company. It's just a shame that she has her brown eyes set on the dumb ass sitting at the station across from me.

"Atlas! The fuck are you doing man?" I call over to the idiot tattooing his calf on his table. Atlas looks up and gives me the dumbest fucking grin.

"Stay away!" He yells like a child. "It's almost ready."

Lauren walks over to him before I can cover her hip, and when she peers over his shoulder, she busts out laughing. I watch her double over and snort at whatever Atlas is tattooing on his skin.

"Ren," I growl as I stand up and walk over to them. "Tell that fucker he has a client in twenty minutes, and he needs to get – you've got to be kidding me." I am unsure what emotion I am supposed to be feeling when I look down at

7

the newest addition on Atlas' leg. Shock? Embarrassment? Honor?

The tattoo is an American Traditional style that neither of us would dare say we are proficient in. That was Tony's area, not ours. Atlas is better at it than I am, but most of my clients know me for my hyper-realism.

"Don't break my heart, Fox." Atlas' hand flies to his head dramatically as he lets out a sigh. I roll my eyes and shake my head. I can't help but chuckle; now, I am the no-nonsense "old man" of the shop. Even when Tony was alive, I was known as "Papa Fox" around the shop. I believe in having rules, in working hard and not straying from the path.

Atlas is the free spirit of the shop, always spontaneous, flirting, doing dumb tricks, showing up late, and partying. I am confident that his ability as an artist and just general good nature is the only reason Tony never fired him.

"No, man, it looks great." Another laugh escapes my lips as I sit on the stool next to him and admire his work. It's a black and gray fox tattoo with the phrase "For Fox Sake" written around the head. He's an idiot with an obsession for puns, you can't help but love Atlas.

I punch his shoulder playfully before turning my attention back to Ren. My eyes soften and I look at her standing next to the table, trying everything to get Atlas to notice her. But as always, he's as dense as they come.

"Come on Ren." I let out a small groan as I stand up, earning me shit from the other artists.

"Need your cane, old man?" Ash grins broadly as Derek snickers and mentions something about a "Life Alert".

"Yeah, yeah, someone answer that fucking phone so that I can wrap Ren up." Atlas rolls off the bed and launches himself at the shop phone in a way only he can because he's in his thirties and spends his downtime engaging in rock-climbing and CrossFit.

"Idiot." I mutter as I smooth the *Saniderm* bandage over Lauren's hip. I glance up and notice that the look on Atlas' face is darker than before. An unfamiliar scowl and scrunched brows have taken over his usually goofy features.

"Sup?" I ask once he walks over to me, all previous joking gone.

"That was Tony's attorney. You are supposed to go to a meeting with him and Janie tomorrow morning?" His usually upbeat and confident voice sounds uneasy.

"What? Why?" Janie and I haven't spoken since the funeral, but Tony's attorney said they would have Janie sign everything over to me, I would pay her and that would be that.

"If you're taking over ownership of the shop," Ren speaks casually as she wiggles her black sweats over her hips before tucking her blonde hair behind her ears. "Then you need to meet with them to fill out the paperwork." Ren just graduated from law school a year ago, and even though we should probably consult with someone a little more seasoned, she's been my go-to since Tony's passing.

"You should go with him, Atlas. The shop's manager needs to be a part of it. You *are* taking over a multi-million-dollar store, Fox, and I really think you should call Frank." Atlas and I both let out a loud groan of displeasure. Richard Franklin, better known as "Frank," is the shop's actual attorney. He is *the* attorney to the stars, and Tony kept him on retainer. I don't like him, so I haven't been contacting him over Tony's death and the transfer of ownership. But maybe Ren is right.

"Alright," I nod as I usher her to the front. "I will call

Frank today. Now deduct your legal fees from your total and pay the difference."

I STAND in front of my mirror wearing only a towel, my eyes search my large, tattoo covered body. The designs run from my neck down, in multiple styles of ink. I need a free place to put something for Atlas – it only seems fair after he got one for me. My left arm is covered in American Traditional style tattoos, most from Tony. The right arm along with my chest and stomach is all grayscale realism. Skulls, clocks, gears, roses, and the Norse deity, *Hel*, cover the rest of me – minus the stupid anime cat that sits happily on my ribs. But it's best not to think about all the memories of my tattoos right now.

I run a brush through my shoulder-length, dark blond hair and wrap a hair tie around it before beginning my beard care. I'm not like some guys with their obsessively manicured beards, but a good brushing and beard oil can make all the difference between looking well-kept and looking like you belong in the wild.

I'm no longer one of those guys with a six or eight pack. In my twenties and thirties, sure – I was all over the extreme workouts and the hard body. Now, I have muscle definition in my arms, chest, and back. But if I smack this gut, he wiggles, and I like it. It's a comfortable body, and I have had no complaints from those I allow to see it.

A beep pulls me out of my thoughts, and I look at my phone to see a text message.

Atlas: Fox it's too fucking early and I am
hungover AF *sick emoji*

Me: If you're not waiting outside my
building in 15 minutes, I am firing you.

Atlas: YOU CAN'T FIRE ME! I DON'T
WORK IN THIS VAN!

I roll my eyes at his *"The Office"* reference. That show is my "comfort show" as Atlas put it, when everyone found out that I would binge watch the show whenever I felt overwhelmed. Maybe it is my comfort show. Who knows. I do feel better when I have it playing. Speaking of, I am going to need it tonight.

Feeling like I need to make a good impression with the lawyers, I put on my one and only suit, the same one I wore at Tony's funeral. The heaviness of the loss washes over me again and closing my eyes, I inhale deeply. God, I miss him, I keep waiting for it to get easier, for the wound to fucking heal, but every time I have a moment of calm, it smacks me again.

My phone beeps, and I am thankful for the temporary distraction. I look down, expecting it to be Atlas, but instead it's from a number I do not know.

Unknown: FOX FUCKING SIMMONS

Unknown: You fucking brought in Frank?!?

Me: Who is this?

I watch the three dots appear...disappear...appear again...what the fuck? Just send the fucking text!

> Unknown: Who is this? How charming. It's Janie Pierce. Tony's daughter? You know the one that is GIVING you her father's company, and you decide to bring in FRANK??? Like I am some criminal?

I smack my hand over my face as I walk through my apartment and out the door. I can't wait to walk in there, sign this fucking paper and have Janie Fucking Pierce and her annoying, whiny ass out of my life for good. Every time this woman is around, I age by five years, she's exhausting on *every* possible level. I try to shake off my agitation, and possibly some nerves as I get in the elevator and save her number to a new contact before responding.

> Me: Frank is there so that I* ME* MYSELF* don't fuck anything up. It's not all about you, Torch, as much as those stupid followers of yours like to make you believe it is. Also, you are not GIVING it to me. You are giving me the first right to BUY it from you. Shit maybe you're the one that needs Frank.

> Torch: Fox, I swear to God, if you don't stop calling me Torch, I will castrate you! And leave my fans out of this! You're just jealous that I have a fan base and you are like 50 and still tattooing hearts with MOM banners around them.

Her roast is definitely a good one and when I see Atlas sitting in the back of an Uber, waving at me, I am still left speechless. I choose to ignore the brat, knowing that will piss her off even more. I slide my phone into my pocket, a smirk pulling at my mouth as I walk up to the vehicle.

"You fucking made it." I muse as I slide in the back of the sedan, scrunching some to fit my larger frame into the seat. Staring at Atlas, I see he is in a similar position, given that he and I are about the same height. I begin to wonder why Atlas didn't get an SUV to pick us up over the Prius, but that would've meant that I think Atlas was capable of planning and forward thinking. As much love as I have for the guy, those are not his strong points.

"Actually," I watch Atlas stick his pointer finger up. "We've been here for five minutes. You're late. So, I should theoretically fire *your* ass." I roll my eyes and flip him my middle finger

"I'm dealing with a pop." *Pissed off Pierce* or 'POP' was our code word for when Tony was on a rampage, and we all needed to act straight so that the usually kind man didn't have a reason to break something or someone. Apparently, his petite daughter inherited all his anger and is focusing it on me during the most stressful day of my life.

"God damn Fox, no wonder she hates you. She said to stop calling her Torch, so you make it her contact's name?"

I shrug as I pull my phone back just in time to receive another text.

> Torch: Oh, did that one hit a little below the belt? Well, when you're done crying, get your giant ass here. I have a product meeting at 2 that I cannot miss.

> Me: So feisty...don't worry Torch, you'll be in front of your camera telling the world that they too can have glowy skin if they buy some bullshit product you've never used.

> Torch: ...you think I have glowy skin?!?!
> *excited emoji*

I thank whatever higher power is up there as the driver parks the car outside The Office. Walking into the main lobby, I see Frank pacing outside a set of double doors while talking on his phone.

"Aurora, I promise," He sighs and runs a hand over his long face. "I promise, I am out on the next flight. Just make sure if he wakes up, he keeps his mouth shut." After hanging up his phone, Frank gives Atlas and me an overly confident smile.

"Women." He scoffs. "My niece is all up in arms about some guy she traveled across the country for, but that's a story for another day." He rubs his hands together and gives us a small smirk.

"Now, we're waiting for them to finish a couple of things up, and then Janie and you will have to fill out some papers, and the process will begin. It will probably take about a year to pay her completely and for everything to run through probate. Janie is fine with the deadline, of course. Though there was a bit of a surprise."

I look towards Atlas with a raised brow before looking back at Frank again.

"Surprise?" I ask. Frank nods and lets out a small chuckle as he moves closer to us and lowers his voice.

"Yeah, apparently, Tony wrote in the will that Janie could co-run the shop with you if she wanted during the transition year. But, of course, the girl instantly said no to that."

I let out a sigh of relief and a small laugh. "That would probably kill me."

"Kill you?" Atlas snorts. "It would kill the shop! Could you imagine – little Miss Insta-star in charge of Hel's?"

"Yeah, it would end in her blowing the profits on some bullshit purse so she can get some extra likes. Hel's Ink deserves better than that." The two men nod their heads in agreement as Frank walks us into the boardroom. I take a seat as the lawyer at the end gives me a wary smile. Glancing around, I realize Janie isn't in the room.

"Where's Janie?" As if on cue, the small redhead comes walking through the doors we just entered. Her long curls bounce as she walks, her expensive heels clicking loudly against the tile. As she sits across from me, I glance from her black pencil skirt to her olive-green top with almost no sleeves and – fuck, when did she get those tits?

My mouth feels as dry as the fucking desert as I reach for a water bottle and uncap it. Chancing another glance at Janie, I notice the red rims around her bloodshot eyes and the streaks in her makeup, causing her freckles to start peeking out from under God knows how much makeup.

"Alright, Ms. Pierce." The weary lawyer says as he slides the papers in front of her.

"Would you like to start signing these forms while I –"

"Actually, no." Her cold, defiant tone takes me by surprise, and I choke on my water. This fucking brat hands the papers back to the lawyer as I watch in horror. Her chin juts out as she leans back in her chair and stares at me with such a heated, challenging gaze that I'm bound to burn up with her.

"No?" Atlas scoffs. "But you said –"

"No one is talking to you, Compass." Janie retorts and I notice her body trembling slightly. Is this 'tough woman' thing an act?

"It's Atlas." His deadpan tone and her use of that name would have me rolling in any other situation, but not now.

"No, what, Janie?" I say softly. A sickening wave crashes in my stomach as her deep blue eyes fix on me.

"No. I will not sign, Fox." A perfect eyebrow arches as she crosses her arms over her ample chest and stares down her nose at me.

Your move, she silently taunts.

Do I kill her? I mean, I understand how one might think that murder is a little extreme. Hell, usually, I would be the guy who says that there might be a better way. But right now, at this moment, this woman holds my dream and my future in her freckled hands, much like a baby bird. And she is strangling my bird to death.

I let out a small laugh of surprise as I look at her. "Janie, you told me this shop was mine. I have texts to –"

She holds her hand up to silence me, then looks at her nails and winces before showing them to me. "Red nails, and I wore a green shirt. It's summer, Janie. What the hell, right?"

Yeah, I'm going to have to kill her.

Chapter Two

JANIE

THE SMIRK on my face may never leave. I was ready to give my father's tattoo shop to Fox. I mean, I still will. But he doesn't need to know that, yet, he is going to have to suffer for it first. Fox has no idea that I overheard the conversation between him, Frank and Atlas. I left the meeting to answer a call from my boyfriend and heard them talking when I was heading back in. I hid behind a wall and listened to the comments they made. I would be lying if I said they didn't hurt. Not necessarily because I thought those guys were my friends. I rarely ever spoke to them, and when I did, it was barely more than a *hi* or a grunt. It hurts because I really am seen as a dimwitted content creator with little to offer anyone.

I know what people see when they look at me. They read me like a dating profile, mainly because every part of my life has been on social media for the better part of a decade.

Janie H. Pierce

25 years old - Leo
5'3" - slim build – minus the boobs
unmanageable red hair and blue eyes.

THE REST DOESN'T MATTER. *What do I like?* Whatever is trending right now. *My dislikes?* Whatever is trending.

Most would define my job as a content creator or influencer. Fancy words for dancing on apps for likes and promoting products to my followers. What I genuinely like or enjoy is irrelevant, and it always has been. My dreams, ambitions, and goals have always been on the back burner because it's not trending or... because of that shop.

That shop - no I don't like referring to it by its name - is my dad's favorite child, the sibling I can never measure up to. Whatever my wants or needs were, the shop came first.

My dad was not a bad father, and I will take on anyone that dares to speak of him in a negative light. My mother died while giving birth to me, and he was single with a newborn. Having no family of his own, and my mother's side wanting nothing to do with a tattoo artist with a criminal record and a motorcycle, or his baby that was the cause of their daughter's death, dad took a risk and opened the shop within a few months of my birth. He used the tiny amount of money that his artist buddies had given him to help us financially and threw it at a broken-down shop so that he could continue to work and have me there.

I grew up in that fucking shop. Seven days a week, fourteen hours a day from birth until I turned fifteen. At fifteen, I was the shop hand in the back. Always the back. I rarely ever saw the front of the shop because dad said it *"wasn't appropriate."* So, I stayed in the back, making sure we had supplies, cleaning, restocking and whatever else needed to be done, along with starting my social media channel.

The channel originally started as a way for me to stop feeling so lonely. Friends have always been hard for me to come by. The kids in my school had parents that were doctors and lawyers – not tattoo artists. That, plus unlike the other kids, I was expected to leave school, go straight to the shop so I could help clean and restock the supplies. But also, so Dad didn't worry about me.

Then there was the dating scene, or lack thereof. I had almost no prospects for a boyfriend because my dad was massive, he rode a motorcycle and owned a shop full of other huge tattoo artists that would gladly beat or intimidate someone if he asked. So safe to say, no one wanted to risk dating me.

When I was fifteen, my dad tattooed some actor that ended up landing their breakthrough movie the next day, and the guy said later in an interview that dad's tattoo was his good luck charm. Seemingly overnight, the shop went from a decently busy, small tattoo shop to the fully booked place where the celebrities went to get their work done. I had thought that my dad was overworked in the shop before it blew up. But it was nothing compared to the obsession he had for his business after it blew up.

After the success started, he was rarely around – constantly tattooing the rich and the famous at all hours of the day and night. Some weeks, he would just sleep in the back of the shop because an A-Lister would be booked to come in at four in the morning.

At my sweet sixteen, I remember sitting at my reserved

table at this new restaurant I was dying to try. It would just be me and him, and then he would take a vacation for a week, and he and I would go to Maine. I was so excited, I sat at that table in my special dress and birthday sash, waiting for him for three hours, he didn't make it. One of his clients went longer, he forgot and no one at the shop told me, so I sat at the restaurant alone, looking like an idiot as I cried into my birthday cake.

After that, I rarely went to the shop. I made my dad let me stay home, there was fighting, but eventually I won. I had always been a well-behaved kid until the night I was stood up by him. After that the fighting and tantrums to get my way started.

That Halloween, I went viral for dressing up like a very famous cartoon Irish redhead movie heroine. Once that happened, my social media persona became another monster whose needs had to be fed before my own. What I wanted, liked, disliked, no longer could matter to even me anymore. No one wants an authentic you one hundred percent of the time, regardless of what is portrayed out there on the internet. Instead, you become entertainment to the viewers and fake to the real world. You are a puppet, and your viewers hold the strings. You will do what they ask, and if you don't, you will be canceled. From the time I blew up until now, I have accumulated well over one million followers, and I can say without a shadow of a doubt that I am lonelier now than ever.

YAWNING, I slip my green pajama bottoms and black hoodie on after toweling off from my shower. I walk through my sparsely decorated apartment to the kitchen to grab a drink. The number one question that company asks when I invite them to my apartment – which is so rare it is almost embarrassing – is, *"Oh, did you just move in?"*

No. I have been living at Oasis Apartments in apartment 13G for the better part of five years. But I understand their line of questioning. My apartment has none of the staples that make a dwelling form into a home. No pictures, no decor on the walls. I still have the blinds up that came with the apartment, never bothering to purchase my own curtains. The furniture is laughably non-existent. I have a coffee table that holds my laptop and the tools I need for posting on my social media platforms: a ring light on a tripod, and a gray floor pillow that has a tapestry hanging behind it that I use as a backdrop, and that's it. I am just as sparse in my bedroom, except I have clothes, shoes, and bags laying around.

I've never been one that could commit to anything long-term. Not that I didn't want to, I just didn't want to feel stuck with anything. What if I don't like the decorations? What if I despise a new haircut? What if the couch ends up being made by a company that dislikes baby seals, and my followers find out and think I support them and, in turn, cancel me? Shuddering at the thought, I put the bottle of wine to my lips, taking a long swig before heading back to my bedroom. I need to figure out what I will do with the tattoo shop for the following year. I don't want it. I have zero interest in co-running some shop with a man who is suffering from a god complex. Along with his *"bromancing"* buddies that are all equally as full of themselves.

Also, I don't really understand the whole tattoo trend.

How can you be that committed to something that you are willing to permanently mark on you? And getting someone's name tattooed on you? I cannot begin to count the number of pissed off customers dad had removed from the shop due to his refusal to do that.

I lean against my pillow while scrolling through my social media apps – ignoring the comments, likes, follows, and shares. It's not that I don't appreciate them, but when I am in an overwhelmed mental state, I don't want to be reminded that **Sally4040493** thinks that I *live a spoiled life* or that **Matt69694life** knows *a great cream that is sure to make my skin glow*. So, I click on the comments and like the first ten, adding random emojis so that my engagement stays high before turning the "do not disturb" feature on so my notifications will stop. Going to my text app, I frown in annoyance when I see that my boyfriend, Brody, still has me on read. Rolling my eyes, I quickly tap him out a text.

> Me: Hey B, I am calling it a night earlier. Guess you've been extra busy. I g2g2 my dad's shop tomorrow. I need to see u soon! I have things to tell you. Big changes…Xx

My lip curls as I hit the send button. Who in their right mind thinks that texting that way is cute? But I did it because – "*giggle* I am Jai, and I am as deep as a tablespoon! *Kiss kiss*"

"God, I am annoying." My online persona – Jai, is the doe-eyed pouty-lipped airhead that swings her hips and giggles.

I hate her.

This life is not the one I wanted growing up. I thought I was – well, it doesn't matter what I thought. The plans, dreams, and aspirations I might have had when I was younger are lost now, and I've learned to accept the life that I've fallen into.

Looking back at my phone, I see that Brody sent me a *"Kk,"* and I let out a scream in frustration. Why couldn't he be a normal person when the cameras weren't on? Brody is my male social media counterpart. About a year ago, I came across one of his thirst trap videos, you know, the ones that blow up because a guy licks his lips and stuffs his grey sweatpants – yes, they are stuffed. When I saw said video, I think Brody was somewhere around twenty thousand followers. I thought he was cute, so I made a duet video with him, something I rarely do because if I start doing them, everyone wants me to. I made an exception for him, and Brody became an overnight icon, and now he has about a million followers. Our followers liked the idea of us together, so we met and hit it off somewhat. After our second meeting, I think it was just decided that we should date because we get more views, and here we are. He is the closest person and only "friend" I have, as pathetic as that is, and it would be nice if he could give me some comfort.

Growing up, I had to be strong – the one that Dad didn't need to worry about. Mean attitude, smart mouth, and no feelings to hurt. My dad would joke that I hadn't shed a tear since I was born. A false assumption for sure. I did cry, and I still do. I just don't show it. I have yet to find someone I am comfortable enough around, my father included, to be that vulnerable with.

I look at my phone again and see I have another text. Opening it, I expect it to be Brody, saying I was being rude, not texting him. Ironic, right? But it's not Brody; it's Fox.

> Fox: Your dad and Hel's mean everything to me, Janie. Do NOT burn this down just because you have a bug up your little ass.

I read the text a few times as I try to ignore the pounding in my heart. Fox has always pissed me off. From the moment he came into my dad's shop with his giant stupid lumberjack build, his ear gauges, and that cocky attitude. I didn't like him then and I hated him after my dad took him under his wing, stealing what little time and affection I had with the man.

Placing the phone down and closing my eyes, I put those thoughts back into their special box. Thinking about Fox and my dad only adds stress, and stress worsens my condition.

I have *Essential Tremors*, which is a neurological disorder that causes different parts of my body to shake involuntarily. My medication helps to ease the symptoms I have. I feel grateful because I've seen people with this condition that are far worse than I am. My head and voice are typically only affected if my stress is unmanageable, and I have become a master at camouflaging with my movements, filters, and crazy hair. But my hands...

I sigh softly while gazing at the shaking appendages. I don't have an issue with my looks. I know I'm an attractive woman, even though the social media world loves to tell me I'm not. But my condition is something I've been able to keep off social media. It's my dirty little secret, not even Brody knows about it. Which has been easier to keep hidden than one might assume. Brody is not into hand holding or cuddling and the very rare times we've been intimate, he thinks he is just *rocking my world*. Gross.

I was diagnosed at twelve and found out through my

dad that my mother had it as well. Though hers was apparently far worse than mine is. Dad and I were the only two that knew about my ET, and now it's just me.

Rolling onto my side, I reach for my phone to plug it in and decide to send Fox a quick text before going to sleep.

> Me: Hey, you don't call me "torch" for nothing. *fire emoji*

Chapter Three

JANIE

LOOKING at the back of the shop, I take in a steadying breath as I try to calm my tremors down.

"It's okay," I whisper to myself as I walk towards the back door. "You are the boss. You got this, Janie." Truth is, I want to cry or vomit. Or cry *and* vomit, I'm not sure. All I want to do is forfeit and give this damn shop to Fox and run the fuck away. With the money I'm going to receive, I could leave the city, quit social media, and get a dog...maybe. I like dogs, I think I would like to have one, but it's that commitment thing again.

"Focus," I growl as I open the door and slip in. Walking through the back door of the shop, I am hit with the familiar aroma of ink, green soap, and disinfectant. Instantly I feel a burning in my nose and pricks at the backs of my eyes. *Fuck. How have I missed this smell? I used to hate it.*

"Well, look who finally showed up." Fox's rough, smug, rich, stupid voice announces. Nah, rough and rich make his voice sound sexy and while he and his little nearly naked fan club may think he's a gift from God, he is **not.**

I walk up front to the waiting and merchandise area to

see Fox and Atlas turning on music and the point of sales computer.

"We don't open until noon." Shit, my voice is shaking, that's not a good sign. Usually, my voice is one of the last things my disorder affects. I stare at the two men from behind my sunglasses. They are both the same ridiculous height. Atlas is younger than Fox by several years but still close to a decade older than I am. Fox's muscles have changed from when I saw him as a teen. When he first started here, Fox had an extremely tight athletic body, much like Atlas does. Atlas is the ideal gym body type. Bulging biceps, a firm, tight six pack with a very sculpted V. His massive, sculpted chest and Japanese dragon tattoo is on full display as he changes his shirt and – *OH MY GOD!*

"Are those nipple piercings?" My voice is much higher and louder than I meant for it to be. Both the men stare at me, and then Fox looks at the silver-colored balls on either side of Atlas' nipple.

"Well, god damn At, you done got metal through your titties." I shake my head at his stereotypical, an atrocious "hillbilly" accent while he makes his witty ass remark. Atlas gasps dramatically and puts a hand to his mouth.

"Oh my! Please don't tell anyone! I wouldn't want them to think I'm a slut!" He rapidly blinks his eyes at me. I give him an unamused look.

"Don't worry," I mutter as I hang my purse up. "Your Instagram ratted out your slut tendencies a long time ago."

"Now, Janie." Atlas smiles overconfidently, green eyes sparkling with far too much excitement. Is it too early to punch him?

"Don't go cyberstalking me and then falling in love." I gag at him before sitting on the bar stool and pulling out my phone.

"No worries there, you aren't my type." I hear an annoyed laugh come from Fox.

"Thirty seconds and you're already on your phone." His remark charges me up and I am ready to attack him, but as I lift my head to give him a verbal beatdown, I am silenced by Fox...shirtless. He's bigger than Atlas, but Atlas is tight, like the muscle you know came from gym workouts. Fox has those big, thick worker muscles. Like he moves logs for a living. Is that a job? Log mover? I would have to look that up later. His stomach is strong but has a softer layer over his abs that I, for some reason, can't stop staring –

"Did you decide to work here to gawk at us all day?" Fox's mocking voice snaps me out of my trance, and I feel my chest and face warm with embarrassment.

"Yeah," Atlas huffs, feigning outrage. "I mean, workplace sexual harassment can happen to men too, Janie. I am more than eye candy." I curl my upper lips and stare at the two men in front of me.

"So, you two just take your singular brain cell and rub it together to get your shared wit?" I ask while fighting the smirk forming at the slight scowl tugging at Fox's face.

"I mean," Atlas shrugs nonchalantly. "I'm down for some rubbing. It's been a little dry recently." He gives me a look that I am assuming he uses on the ladies to get them to drop their panties. Obviously, I have to save womankind from these imbeciles. Grabbing a bottle of tattoo aftercare cream, I throw it at him before looking back at my phone, begging my hands to stop shaking so hard. The last thing I needed was for them to notice and have something else to make fun of me for.

"So, just wondering," I say slowly, trying to hold my composure. "What did I interrupt when I got here? Are you two in a secret relationship? Is this some weird sex thing?"

Fox lets out a dry laugh before giving me the finger. "It's T-Shirt Thursday." He states as he slips on a shirt with the Hel's Ink logo on the front and graphic of the deity Hel on the back. I stare at the black and white drawing of the half skeletal woman while forcing the ache in my chest to go away. I can't think about this shit now.

"Fuck, you guys still do that?" I force out a snort before going back to my phone, trying to find something, *anything* to center me.

"*Everyone* in the shop does." Fox's voice takes on a serious tone like he is warning me to tread carefully. But I've never been one to heed warnings, and I sure as shit am not going to start now with Fox.

"Well, good for you guys." I give them a quick thumbs up before turning back to my phone. Brody hasn't texted me. I was hoping to at least talk to him before he had his photoshoot.

I jump as a black shirt lands in front of me, covering my phone's screen. Raising my head, I glare at Fox who has his massive arms crossed over his chest. I mean, seriously? Why are all these men so freaking big?

"Put it on." I raise my brow at Fox's demanding tone before staring back down at the shirt. I grab the shirt and chuck it back at him.

"Nah. I'm good. Thanks though." I flash him a smile so big I am sure my molars are showing. There is zero amusement on his face as he throws the shirt at me again before splaying his hand over the counter that separates us and leaning over to glare at me.

"It wasn't a request." He grits out through clenched teeth.

I stand on the footrest of the stool to meet his gaze and

reply in his same tone, emphasizing each word. "You are not my boss Fox."

I watch his right eye twitch and an honest to God sneer appears on his face. I'm ready, come on, give me your best shot. This was the most alive I've felt in...damn I don't know how long. Out of the corner of my eye, I see movement as Atlas forces himself between Fox and the counter.

"Okay, let's take a breath kids." Atlas' laugh is nervous as he pats Fox's shoulders. Fox shoves him off and points his finger at me.

"No shirt, no counter work. Either put it on or march your ass to the back room." I flinch as I think back to the hundreds of times I was told to stay in the back room by my dad. I take a deep breath and give him another smile.

"Do you have any with long sleeves?" I ask innocently.

Fox's anger is rising, and if the reddening of his neck is any indication, so is his blood pressure.

I am SO winning this battle.

I watch as he growls and runs his hands through his beard. "Torch, it is August in southern California."

I ignore the nickname; he's grasping at straws and trying to irritate me in any way possible. Not happening old man.

In fact...

I inwardly grin and toss the shirt back at him before going back to mindlessly scrolling on my phone. "No sleeves, no deal, Papa Fox."

I hear Atlas yell, "Oh no!!!" While doubling over in laughter. *Papa Fox* was my nickname for him, and he hates it. When Fox was just starting out here, sometimes my dad would have to leave the shop and I would be in the back. But when I knew the coast was clear, I would sneak out front and bug artists or steal snacks. On several occasions, patrons asked if I was Fox's daughter. And after the fourth incident of it happening, I started going around calling him *Papa Fox,* despite his protesting.

The intensity in Fox's glare sends fire and tingling energy through my entire body. Well, I think it's actually the *ET*, but still.

Come to think of it, my tremors are terrible today. Did I take my meds?

I think back, replaying my entire routine. Definitely took them. I look at my half-drunk iced coffee, and the corners of my mouth tick downward.

Did the barista give me regular instead of decaf?

"Wow, are you even listening to a fucking word I say?" Fox glowers. God, he is annoyingly tall. I am going to need to get a massage with all this neck craning. I wonder if my massage therapist is back yet from her vacation.

Okay, I am everywhere. This definitely isn't decaf. "Sorry, my coffee isn't decaf. I am kind of everywhere. What did you say?"

Fox huffs and throws the same shirt back at me again.

"I said, put it on over your long-sleeved shirt if you are that desperate. I'll pull one from storage for next week...If you make it that long."

I crack a grin as I stare at him. "Oh, don't worry, I will. You are stuck with me for the next fifty-two weeks buddy. Hell, I might enjoy it so much I'll just stay on as your part-ner." I watch as his witty smirk falls, and the light vanishes from his eyes. Smiling triumphantly, I hop off the stool and head to the backroom, shirt in hand.

Yep, I totally got this.

Chapter Four

FOX

YEARS AGO, I read something about how time spent in hell moves differently. A day on Earth is decades there or some shit. I never really paid it much mind... until now. Now, as I stand in the supply closet, listening to Janie drone on and on to one of her "sponsors" over the phone about her weekly numbers after casually telling me that she canceled my ink order, I realize that I am genuinely in Hell.

Two weeks – that is all it's been. I am sure I've aged ten years in this time. The brat fights me at every turn. Every. Goddamn. Turn. Every suggestion I make, she has an opposing opinion. I want to move merchandise to the left side, and she says right. I suggest turning the thermostat to sixty-eight degrees, and she – well, initially, she suggested sixty-nine, but after Atlas and the guys started in with the jokes you would expect from a group of immature men, she decided that sixty-seven was the preferred temperature and proceeded to wear extra layers.

"Torch, I don't care!" I yell from the closet. "I only use that brand of ink! Why in the fuck would you cancel my order?"

I walk out with the last bottle of my preferred black ink, clutching it like it's the last snack cake known to man – fuck, what a tragedy that would be. Janie is on her perch out front, resembling the harpy that she is.

I watch as she rolls her head to the ceiling before sighing loudly. Wait, is *she* exasperated with me? "I already told you!" She growls. "The brand I ordered is trendy in the tattoo world. It's cost-effective, highly pigmented, and vegan!" My deadpan stare doesn't seem to faze her as she continues to smile that stupid fucking shit-eating grin.

"I don't care about the cost," I bark out. "It's worked into my hourly rate. No brand is as pigmented as the one I use, you have no idea about the tattoo world, and finally – a girl who just ate a chicken burrito that was easily as massive as their big ass head can't talk to me about vegan versus non-vegan products." I smirk as I see her neck and chest turning pink, her tell sign that she's pissed.

"I'll have you know that I am very – Hello!" I watch her demeanor change as a man in his thirties walks in. The fact that Janie keeps things professional when clients or customers are in the shop is probably the only thing that I can appreciate about her.

"Yeah, I need to talk to someone about getting my girl-friend's name on my arm." I inwardly roll my eyes, and I watch as Atlas – who is working on a sketch at his station, laughs silently. We don't do couples' names. We have signs out front stating that; it's on our website, and there is a sign above Janie's massively irritating head saying that we do not tattoo names as well.

"Oh, I'm sorry," Janie's voice is kind and patient as she speaks to him. "We actually don't tattoo names unless it's like your kid or something like that. But maybe you could do something el –"

"I didn't ask your opinion." The man snaps and I instantly stiffen. "I said I needed to talk to someone about getting tattooed. And if you won't do my girlfriend's, that's fine; it's my daughter. Now go get one of the men who actually do the work."

I stand to go up front and tell him to fuck off. Janie may not be my favorite person or even my tenth favorite person, but no man should talk to a woman like that, *especially* Tony's daughter. Janie's voice stops me from walking to the counter, grabbing the douchebag and slamming my fist into his face.

"Okay, great! Well, I will go and grab one of the artists for you. I just need to know your daughter's name and see the birth certificate so we can verify that she is your –"

"Girl, shut the fuck up with your shit and go get your boss."

"Hey!" I bark, walking up behind Janie. An overwhelming sense of protectiveness fills my body to an uncomfortable level. I notice Janie's entire body is trembling horribly and now I'm starting to see red.

"Excuse me." She whispers in a quivering voice before pushing past me to walk to the back of the shop.

"Finally." The guy says and stares at me. "Okay, so, I'm leaving for a business trip, and my girl..."

I wave my hand in front of him and shake my head in disbelief. "I'm sorry, are you under the impression that you are going to receive a tattoo from us?"

The man blinks and then lets out a laugh. "Well, yeah... I'm a paying customer."

"No, actually, you're not." I stare at the slender man down in his beady eyes. It would be so easy. *So fucking easy.* One hit and this dickless fuck would be down. How dare he disrespect Jan– I mean, the shop.

34

Rolling my shoulders, I am becoming more uncomfortable with the betrayal of my brain. Hel's is number one. I'm only upset over Torch because she's Tony's daughter.

Right. Just keep riding that horse to freedom, Fox.

"Here's the problem bud." I state, trying to end this without bloodshed. "You just waltzed in here, disrespected the shop's policies and did so to my boss."

He blanches as he looks behind me to where Janie had run off to and then back at me. "Y-your boss?"

I nod. "Yeah, so if I were you, I would fuck off." I hear something hit the ground, followed by Janie letting out a string of curse words. Fuck, what now?

"I won't repeat myself," I growl as I nod my head towards the door.

Walking back into the tattoo area, I see Janie on her hands and knees with Atlas who is frantically trying to calm her down. Janie is completely red and nearly in convulsions as she tries to clean up — son of a bitch.

"Fox, I'm so sorry." Her voice is shaky as she looks up at me with watery eyes. Oh god, is she about to cry? "I – I stumbled and h – hit your tray, and the ink went everywhere."

"It really was an accident, man." Atlas says quietly while helping the ink-covered girl clean the floor.

I inhale slowly, "Okay, it's alright. At, can you get this? Janie, come with me." I usher Janie to the break room, and once inside, I close the door and turn to talk to her, but she instantly starts stammering.

"F-fox! I s-swear! It w-was... please I –" I place my hands on her shaking shoulders and lower my head to look her in the eyes. Keeping my voice as calm and soft as possible I try to talk to her, the girl needs to calm down before she passes out.

"Are you alright?" I watch her full bottom lip quiver as she looks at me with round, watery eyes. *Ouch.* That is an uncomfortable feeling in my chest.

"Yeah. I just – I don't do so well with yelling." I grab her shaking hands, and as soon as we touch, she rips them from my grasp as if I burned her. I give her a quizzical look and go to speak but she beats to the punch.

"Sorry," She gives me an uncomfortable laugh before sitting on the couch. "I don't like people touching my hands."

Raising a brow, I grab some wipes from the utility closet and hand them to her as I sit in front of her on the coffee table. She won't stop shaking. "Did that fucker really make you this upset?" I snarl while grinding my teeth. I know I need to be professional, to not lose my shit but I can't, won't let someone upset her this much.

The red color floods her neck and cheeks as she gives me the saddest smile I've ever seen.

"Fox," My name comes out more like a plea. Like whatever she is unveiling is something painful, and it makes her uncomfortable to do so.

"I have –" She's staring directly into my eyes and it's almost too much. I can see it all in her. The anxiety, sadness... maybe loneliness? No, it can't be that. How could someone with all those followers be lonely? She breaks eye contact and lets out a short breath while running her tongue over her lips in agitation.

Nope. Put that image in a box and set that fucking thing on fire. I will *not* replay that image.

"God damn it," She groans. "I'm going to tell you and you will make fun of me." I watch as her gaze lifts to the ceiling and she shakes her head. What kind of asshole does she think I am? Sure, we hate each other and are constantly bantering but I'm not a monster.

"Listen Torch, temporary war aside, if there is something you need to tell me, I will give you this one. Though, honestly, I'm sort of insulted that you would think I would make fun of you over something that is causing you *this* much stress." I watch her nod slowly and her reluctant gaze falls to mine.

"Fine," She lets out a deep breath. "I have a disorder called Essential Tremors. So, I can't control this." She gestures to her tremoring body. "It's why I wear layers and stay back so no one can tell. It only gets bad like this if I'm upset or have too much caffeine – No, stop, don't!" She smacks my forearm, causing me to wince and look at her.

"What the hell, Janie?" I rub my arm while glaring at her. For someone so tiny she sure knows how to cause pain.

"I didn't tell you this so you would look at me like that! I don't want your pity!" I blink, staring at her in confusion.

"I'm not giving you pity. Jesus! It's called being nice." Staring at me, she's silent as if trying to catch my bluff.

"No one knows." She states softly and I nod, understanding her unspoken words.

"It's nobody's business." Fuck, what is that look? Shimmering icy pools of blue are pulling me into a trance. I blink and shake my head. Why does she look so....... happy?

"Thank you, Fox." She smiles softly. A genuine smile and I have to swallow a lump in my throat. This is getting uncomfortable, and I feel the sudden urge to put us back on opposing sides.

"Nope, you are not thanking me. You are my nemesis, and you spilled all my good ink." It's getting too hot in here, and I am starting to have difficulty getting comfortable.

Sixty-seven degrees, my ass. I make my way to the door before the room steals all the oxygen.

"Yo, Janie!" Atlas' booming voice makes me cringe. Why can't that fucker just walk back here instead of screaming? "There's a Brody here!"

"Brody?" I give her a questioning stare as she gasps.

"Shit, my boyfriend!" *Boyfriend?* I don't know why her having a boyfriend makes me feel... whatever this is. But I don't like it. I feel constipated and irritable as Janie shoves me out of the break room so she can calm down and change before coming out to see her *boyfriend*.

***

"Am I missing something?" I ask as Atlas and I stare in bewilderment at Janie and her purple-haired boyfriend – Brody. Snickering, Atlas shrugs before going back to work on his client.

Brody has been here maybe twenty minutes. It took Janie over ten minutes to calm down enough to change her ink-covered clothes and come out. Apparently, when she said nobody knew about her condition, she meant nobody. It makes me wonder how close they can be if he doesn't notice her tremors. I also wonder why I really care about their level of "closeness".

I roll my eyes as he makes her take several photos of him standing next to different flash art frames and paintings that myself, the guys or Tony had done.

"What is that on your shirt?" Brody sneers, catching my attention. People ask about the shirts; all have the Norse goddess Hel on them considering the shop is named after her. But the tone he is using, like Janie has on a trash bag, it's irritating me, especially since that design is one that Tony did himself.

"It's our logo. You know, the goddess Hel?" I watch as

her long shiny curls fall to one side as she cocks her head. How does she manage that mane? Well, she doesn't by the looks of it. Her hair is as wild and stubborn as she is. Brody presses his purple eyebrows together in confusion.

"Is that like the Hades thing that is trending?" He asks and my body deflates. *The Hades thing that is trending?* All my mind keeps screaming is why is she with him. Better yet, why did Tony allow it? I get that she's a grown woman, but I never once heard the old man complain about this boyfriend and I feel like this would've been at the top of the list of things to bitch about.

"This guy is too stupid to breathe." I mutter as Atlas air high fives me from his station.

"Sort of," Janie says softly. Why is she so patient with him? Fuck, if I were asking her that question, I would be scraping my pride off the floor already. "It probably wouldn't interest you." She flicks her wrist, waving the subject off and I can't help but feel even more annoyed at her behavior. I've watched her in the short amount of time she's been here, having lengthy conversations with customers over the deities. The girl knows her goddesses. So why is she pretending like it's boring now?

"Yeah, I don't get the symbolism. But you may want to have a graphic designer do a new logo. That drawing is a little dated. If you want, I can give you the girl's contacts who did my graphics. I'm seeing her tonight at the meet and greet."

How much can one person dislike another? I am being forced to co-run a shop that is supposed to be mine with a woman that I cannot stand ninety-nine percent of the time – that other one percent is reserved for moments like the break room, or when she is late to work, and I get more time without her. I am literally in hell with the short, freckled red headed demon, but I think that even Janie hasn't hit the lowest level on my hate list. However, with his neon purple hair and *suggestions*, Brody is quickly plowing his way there.

Janie's mouth twitches slightly as she looks up at Brody. "Oh, you're going to that meet-up?" Is that disappointment I am hearing in her voice? I can't for the life of me imagine why. If I were dating that wannabe know-it-all, I would be ecstatic that he chose to do something without me.

Brody scoffs as he rolls his eyes. "Uh yeah Jai, this is important. Just because you don't take your career seriously doesn't mean I don't. I have to network and see my fans."

Wow...Brody really believes he's a big deal. How adorable. I watch the two of them go back and forth for a few more minutes before Brody proclaims that Janie is gaslighting him because she wants to hang out tonight, and he leaves.

Janie, avoiding eye contact, marches to the break room and shuts the door.

Fuck I'm exhausted, and it's only been two fucking weeks.

Chapter Five

JANIE

STARING AT MY PHONE, I am in disbelief. Ten minutes ago, I took a selfie in front of this new gourmet donut shop. It just opened last week and getting in here is next to impossible unless you are willing to wait nearly an hour in line, which I was today. But after posting the selfie of me in the line stating I am waiting for my sugar fix, the comments started rolling in. And while the occasional hate or troll comment is normal for someone with a social media following like mine, these were mostly negative.

"She's been kind of off the last couple of weeks."
"I heard Brody was with Gemma."
"Ah, she is getting old anyway."
"Like ??? You're 30 GTFO here grandma!"
"Here comes the binge train."
"Ugh, it wasn't cute to be this dumb at 15 and still not now. You are why we make less than men."

MY PERIOD HIT me like a train this morning, and even though my bed was singing the sweetest siren song, I came up with this fantastic idea late last night for the shop and I'm chomping at the bit to talk to the guys about it and get their opinions. In order to function while having cramps though, I am in desperate need of donuts. The fastest way to win me over is to give me baked goods – not that anyone ever tries to win me over. While waiting in line, I stare at all the different types. My eyes land on one called *'You won't regret this'* and I laugh. It was about twice the size of the other massive donuts, made of a chocolate cake donut, with thick peanut butter icing, fudge drizzle and pieces of broken Reese's cups.

As much as I like sweets, I'm not a chocolate fan. Fox is, though. I found this out yesterday when the man was throwing a temper tantrum over wanting a Reese's cup. He had been a total baby all day because he had back-to-back to back clients and the store on the corner was out of Reese's. Which I mean, yeah that is such an odd item to be out of, I'll give that to him. But it's not like they didn't have the thin version. When I came back with those, you would've thought I wrapped a turd up and handed it to him by the face he made. It was childish...even if the little pout he had on his face gave me butterflies. Well... maybe not, I did start my period this morning so probably just pre cramps... *not* butterflies.

Chewing on the inside of my cheek, I begin to have an internal struggle. I try to be thoughtful and give people things just because, but Fox and I are arch enemies. He is the Voldemort to my Harry Potter, the Magneto to my Professor X.

No! Worse than that, he is the Toby Flenderson to my

Michael Scott. A Toby who took care of me when I had a freak-out last week and didn't make fun of my condition.

NO! Janie, this is how Toby wins! He gets inside your mind!

But God, he was so freaking sweet when I told him. I fully expected my Torch name to be retired for "Shakes" or something like that. But he didn't, he listened, he respected me, and he didn't say anything to the guys. It makes everything that much more annoying because I need to stay adamant about my loathing of him.

"Can I help you?" The feminine southern drawl pulls me out of my thoughts, causing me to look up and smile at the woman. She looks around my age, maybe a little older and she is adorable. An aqua green long bob frames her soft face with black lowlights peeking underneath. A black ball decorates either side of her face accentuating her dimples that match the black ring hanging delicately from the middle of her nose.

"Hi," I say softly and point to the chocolate and peanut butter donuts. "I'm going to need a pretty big box."

BALANCING the absurdly large box of donuts, my iced decaf coffee, my bags, and the packages that were delivered to the back door that the guys apparently decided not to grab, I kick the door several times with my heel before Atlas opens it.

"Hey Red, what's cracking?" Is he serious? Does he not see me balancing everything?

"Help me, you ass!" I growl when he stands in front of me, just... staring. "My god! Did your mother not teach you manners? You help a lady struggling!" Atlas takes the package and donuts while holding the door open for me to walk through.

"My mom taught me that women should be equal to men. If Fox was carrying all that in here, I wouldn't help him either. See? Equality. I'm basically a feminist." He beams at me, and I roll my eyes.

"Spell 'Feminist'." Atlas frowns as I set my purse down as I walk into the tattooing area to see Fox sitting over his tattooing table, sketching.

"That is rude!" Atlas scoffs and looks around as if I just slapped him. "I don't get paid to spell, Red. I'm an artist." My face falls and I see Fox shaking from silent laughter out of the corner of my eye.

"You are a freaking tattoo artist!" I yell in disbelief. "Half the shit you do is lettering!" Atlas shrugs.

"I use spell check and then the client approves it." I shake my head in disbelief at the man.

"Okay, so I'm only recommending Derek and Ash to customers then." My response pulls a huff out of Fox as he leans back in his chair to look at me before speaking.

"And what about me? I know how to spell." Arching my brow, I am about to deliver back an insult – you know, something about Neanderthals and what not, but the drawing he is working on catches my eye and I am momentarily silenced.

"Wow, that's beautiful." I whisper while staring at the portrait of the 1950s pin-up-looking woman.

Fox chuckles. "Careful Torch, you're getting close to a compliment there." Shaking my head, I decide to let the banter go...for now. After all, I need to talk to them, and I would rather everyone be in a pleasant mood. So, I give him a small smile before dropping the donut bag in his lap. I then snatch the box out of Atlas' hands, who has already managed to stuff two donuts in his cheeks like some sort of hamster.

"Atlas, you eat all of my donuts and watch what I do to you." I warn.

Atlas waggles his eyebrows suggestively. "Don't threaten me with a good time, Red."

"What is this?" Fox inquires, his tone a little more forceful than I think is necessary. I notice his cold stare resting on Atlas. What is that look about? Are they fighting?

Fox opens the bag and pulls out the donut and I'm suddenly very aware of the increase in my hand tremors. Why on Earth do I care if he likes the donut?

"Um –" I tuck a curl behind my ear, only to have it go right back where it previously was. "I know yesterday you wanted Reese's cups, and the corner store was out, and umm – I saw it at the donut shop. If you don't want it, I'm sure Atlas will –"

"Oh, fuck yes!" Atlas yells excitedly at the exact time Fox barks out a "No!"

Fox's gaze lands on mine, and I feel like a deer caught in the headlights. Then, oh my god, he's smiling at me. He never smiles at me and fuck... Enemies or not I can appreciate that panty dropper smile. I rub my hands on the front of my leggings, God my palms are sweaty.

"Thank you, Janie. That was really nice." There is no sarcasm, no animosity, just genuine happiness in his voice and I feel this odd sense of satisfaction. Wait, I *like* when he's happy with me? No no... it's the period hormones.

"I hope it's good. I mean, I'm sure it's good, that's dumb. But the girl at the bakery said it's a shop favorite." Jesus Janie, stop rambling. "I'm going to go in the back and lay down for a few before the other guys get here. I am not feeling the best today, but I want to get your opinions on something once everyone is here." I take the donut box - despite the whining from Atlas - to the break room and sit on the couch, trying to ignore the cramping in my abdomen.

"OKAY." I say while sitting what is left of the donuts down on Atlas' station, ignoring his noises of delight. I pull the black folder out from under my arm and hand it to Fox while trying to calm my nerves.

"Listen, I know how you all feel about me, and I know how you all feel about my social media job." Choosing to ignore the snorts and chuckles at the mention of the word *job*, I continue. "But one thing you can't deny is, I know how to market. I know how to take something and make it big. And I was thinking; maybe I could start running a social media account for the shop, showcasing you guys and your work."

"We already put our portfolios online," Atlas says as he looks over Fox's shoulder at the folder I previously handed him. My heart does a weird flip flop when I watch Fox reach in his station drawer and pull out his black-rimmed glasses.

Snapping out of my trance because I DO NOT find Fox putting on glasses to read my papers sweet or enduring in any way.

At all.

Not even a little bit.

"I-I know about the shop website and that some of you

use Instagram to upload your work, but it's not uniform. The website is glitchy and outdated; there are zero talks about any awards or conventions that any of you have gone to or are planning to go to, which is unfortunate. I mean, Fox, you and Atlas are so well known–"

Atlas grins and elbows Fox's bicep. "Fuck yeah we are, the ladies love us, the guys want to be us."

Fox's scoff and eye roll fill me with discouragement. I look towards Ash and Derek who sit behind Atlas and Fox. Ash specializes in traditional Japanese tattoos. He's a few inches shorter than Fox and has the darkest eyes I've ever seen. Ash is about thirty – give or take and shows up every day getting dropped off by a different girl.

Derek is...well, a mystery. He doesn't talk much, and he only takes walk-ins. According to Atlas, the man used to argue with Fox and Tony because he refused to showcase his work or take repeat customers. It's a shame because his black and grey work is truly unmatched. But Derek just sits there, cleaning his already spotless area, as if he is not a part of this conversation.

Neither one of them are going to be of any use to me in this discussion. I swallow the hard lump in my throat. My presentation is going worse than I thought it would.

"If you look at the hashtags I printed out on page four, you can see that clients do advertise you, '*Hashtag Fox Hel's Ink*' is massive, and Atlas isn't far behind. If I streamlined this and got you guys more organized and in the public eye, your success –"

"Are we not successful?" Fox finally speaks while he drops the folder onto the tattoo table. "I mean, I make plenty of money, I own a famous shop."

"Co-own." I mutter, receiving a glare from him.

"Listen Torch, this is cute, I can tell you worked really

hard on it." Fox's patronizing tone causes my irritation level to shoot up. He takes his glasses off to look at me as he continues to speak. "But we are tattoo artists. Nobody here wants to sell skin creams or diet pills to make a living." My neck and face begin to heat up as a wave of embarrassment, thanks to his oh so sweet words hit me like a slap across the face. I had pretty much expected this outcome this morning when I was getting all the information together so I'm not sure why I am as affected as I am.

Forcing a smile, I give them a nod.

"Okay, yeah just forget it." I force out a tight laugh as I feel the heat going up my neck. "It was just a stupid suggestion, you know...something to do to waste time while I'm here." Putting my hands behind my back, I excuse myself to go to the bathroom.

Bypassing the bathroom, I walk into my dad's old office and shut the door. Dad may have had an office, but he rarely used it. He felt that being out there on the floor was where he belonged. So, The Office was usually mine. I would do homework, social media or just hide in here to get away from the sounds of the machines, the music, and the people.

Sitting down on the loveseat, I notice it smells like old books and pipe tobacco. My dad didn't smoke, but he loved the smell of pipe tobacco, so he would often puff on a pipe so that the room would fill with the aroma.

Burying my face into the arm of the loveseat, I inhale deeply while trying to ignore the painful ache in my chest. I try to hold off for as long as I can, but the dam is finally breaking and for the first time since I got that call that my dad had passed, tears begin to freely spill from my eyes.

Chapter Six

FOX

"ASH and I were going to go grab burgers. You want to come?" Atlas asks while putting his machine up. I look toward the back of the shop where the break room is. Derek had left to go God knows where and Janie had been in the back for five hours now.

"Nah, I'm not hungry. Those donuts were more than enough." Laughing, I smack my stomach and watch as Ash and Atlas leave. The truth is, I want to check on Janie, as much as it annoys me to admit. But I know I need to wait until it's just her and I. She will blow me off if the guys come in. Guilt fills my gut as I think back to this morning.

I was probably too hard on her. Not probably, I definitely was being a deliberate prick. Her charts looked impressive, I guess. I couldn't understand ninety percent of it. The charts and graphs – I have never been able to comprehend that kind of shit. When she handed me all those papers, she might as well have given me engineering principles, but I wasn't about to admit it in front of her and the guys. I'm the old man, the owner, I couldn't allow her to make me look stupid, intentional or otherwise. So, I pretended to look at it, understand it and tell her it wasn't happening, because I'm a dick.

What I hadn't expected was the fact that she chose not to argue with me. Or that she looked so dejected and embarrassed. I expected her to fight me, question my intelligence but when she said it was just a stupid suggestion for her to waste time, after she clearly came in like a businesswoman on a mission....

"Where the hell is she?" I mutter while scanning the break room, trying to stop myself from the mental beatdown I am giving myself. I walk over to Tony's old office and tap on the door. I wait a few seconds but get no answer, so I open the door and walk in.

Janie is asleep on the loveseat, her slight frame curling around a pillow in the fetal position. Her curly copper locks are wild and laying every which way. I kneel in front of her face, and instantly my gut twists tighter. Her mascara and makeup have run from the tears she must've cried.

"Hey," I say softly while placing my hand on her arm. "Janie, come on, you've been back here all day."

She groans but opens her eyes to glare at me. "What Fox? Am I bothering you back here?" I deserve the icy snap.

"You've been back here all day. I wanted to check on – what's wrong?" Janie doubles over and hisses out a breath before shaking her head.

"Nothing," She groans. "It's just cramps."

"Can I get you some medicine? I think I saw a hot pad in the break room. What?" She's staring at me, eyes wide, jaw lax.

"I said I was cramping, I am on my period, and I don't feel well. Why are you being so nice to me?" Shrugging, I sit on the floor so that my knees will stop screaming. Fuck, getting old sucks.

"My mom and sister would rise from the dead to kick my ass if I didn't offer to help you." The change in her demeanor isn't lost on me.

"Oh," Her tone is gentle and the look of sympathy on her face is making me itchy. "I didn't know about them. I'm so sorry –"

"Torch," I interrupt, my voice stern, "How do you feel every time someone says they are sorry when they find out about Tony?"

Her full lips form a thin line as she is silent. Wait. Full lips? They are lips, Fox! You are not adding adjectives! We aren't thinking about her lips, that wild mane of curls, or that fucking scent of hers. With my specialty being hyper-realism with a strong focus on colors, it is my job to describe life in general through colors. If Janie's scent and overall self had to be described as colors, it would be the green of tropical leaves, the blues of the ocean, and her presence in the warmth of sunshine. She smells of orange blossoms and tea, and it reminds me of cruising in the car with the windows down on that first warm day.

It's intoxicating in every fucking way it shouldn't be, and it pisses me off that I can't stop obsessing over it.

"You're right." Her voice startles me, causing me to flinch. Had I been that deep in thought?

"Are you okay?" She chuckles lightly.

"Yeah, just thinking," I mutter while trying to ignore the heat rising in my cheeks. What is this? Blushing? Men in their forties don't blush. I look around the old office trying to distract myself from the uncomfortable feelings I'm fighting. Tony hated The Office unless he was having an off day, then he would come back here and puff on his pipe and listen to music. Though never confirmed, I firmly believe that he came back here because this was where Janie stayed when she used to come to the shop and Tony enjoyed hanging out back here and talking to her.

"I'm sorry if I hurt your feelings this morning." I watch out of the corner of my eye as her jaw tenses, and she avoids looking at me.

"You didn't." She says quickly. "It would take a lot more than the opinion of some old man to hurt my feelings."

"Hey." I half fake being insulted. "No need to be nasty about it."

"Oh, you mean saying I sell diet pills to make a living isn't nasty?"

"So, you *are* upset!" I point my finger at her as she crosses her arms, the red blush creeping up her neck.

"I'm not upset!" She yells as she stands up, walking towards the door. I stand and follow her out to the main area.

"You are too! You're upset that you didn't get your way! What did you think? You could win us over with a box of donuts like you didn't completely fuck us over?" My mood is turning fast at the way she is acting. As usual, Janie goes into bratty temper tantrum mode whenever things don't go her way. I can't even begin to count all the phone calls I overheard Tony take with her yelling on the other end. But I shouldn't have to deal with her tantrums, this should *not* be my job, yet here lately, I feel like I'm doing a lot more talking her down than tattooing and I'm sick of it.

She looks at me, her glacier eyes looking crystal clear with the tears welling up in them. She blinks, and one single tear falls, taking all my anger with it. I cannot handle women crying. When my mom or sister would start crying, I instantly went into protector/fixer mode.

"I brought you –" She clears her throat as what sounds like a sob tries to escape. "I brought you that donut to be nice. Not to win you over. I'm on my period. I wanted a donut. I saw that one and thought of you. Trust me; it won't happen again." Another tear escapes, and I watch as her trembling hands go to brush it away. Is she really crying over the donuts?

"And I didn't fuck you over!" Her voice is loud and shaking as she glares at me, the hot tears flowing freely. "I heard you guys!"

"Heard us?" I manage to get out, my throat feels parched, and Tony's voice is screaming in my head, damning me for daring to hurt his daughter.

Janie laughs sarcastically as she rolls her eyes. "*She would end up blowing the profits on a new purse for some extra likes. Hel's Ink deserves better than that.*"

My stomach drops and my jaw falls open as her familiar words hit me. *My words.* The words I said to Frank and At before seeing the lawyers. Before Janie told me she wasn't selling her half yet.

"Janie I –"

"No!" She yells through her tears. "Nobody understands what I have gone through. I was going to give you this place, not because I wanted the money, but because I thought you would keep it thriving! I grew up here! This was my home. That man was my father! That logo is mine! The shop's name is mine!"

I blink and stare at her. "What?"

"Janie. Hel. Pierce." She enunciates each word through her clenched jaw. "Hel's Ink is named after me, you idiot. This is my shop, Fox. **Mine.** And just so we are clear, I was trying to be nice and include you and the guys in on my idea, put this enemy thing to rest because hey, you were nice to me, and I thought maybe we could actually get along. But I will be here for a good long while, and I **will** do whatever I damn well please to this shop. You can join in, or I will buy you out at the end of the year, but those are your only two options, old man. He might've been your mentor, but he was *my* father. I outrank you and I always will."

The low, almost growl in her threatening voice snaps something in me. I close the distance between us, towering over her short stature, not that it seems to phase her. Janie has "little dog syndrome." You know, where the chihuahuas think they are the toughest fuckers in town and like to assert their dominance. That is her.

"I have spent most of my tattooing career in this shop. Tony was like a father to me, and you will not come in here like a damn child and talk to me that way after everything I've done for this shop. You aren't the only one who lost someone, Janie." I try to remain calm, but her words lit a fire in me. How dare she say that to me? How dare she give me an ultimatum?

We stand toe to toe, so close I can almost hear her heartbeat. I stare in her eyes and momentarily glance at her mouth, she has this one freckle on the top point of her cupid's bow that is becoming an unhealthy obsession of mine.

Jesus Christ what is wrong with me?

Janie's eyes turn to slits as she snarls at me. "You said it yourself, *like* a father."

I smack my fist on a tray of supplies next to us in hopes to release some of this anger. "I was more of a child to him than you ever were!" I bark out. "You were never around unless there was a problem he needed to fix!"

"Shut up." Her voice is barely above a whisper, and I choose to ignore her completely as I continue to yell at her.

"Too fucking busy staring at your phone, hoping some random fuck out there taps the like button while your father sits in here, waiting for you to throw him a damn bone!"

"I hate you!" It comes out as a hiss between her clenched jaw.

"The feeling is mutual." I growl back. We stand there in silence, daring the other to break the stare first. Our breathing is heavy, and the entire room is charged with the electricity between us.

I don't know who initiates it, but suddenly her lips are on mine. There is no sweetness, no kindness. This kiss is primal, angry, and rough. I hoist her off the floor without any effort before slamming her against a wall. She lets out a loud moan before digging her nails into my shoulders, causing me to hiss in pleasure and my already hardening cock to twitch. Her tongue tastes like the sugar from the donuts. Her smell is intoxicating. She's soft and small, and fuck! My dick is painfully hard now.

I whisper a "fuck" as she bites my bottom lip before running her tongue over it. I press myself closer against her to pin her to the wall so that I have both hands free. My left finds its way to the base of her head, and I tug a fistful of her thick mane while my right hand runs over her breast.

I feel her hands run over my button-down flannel shirt. She's trying to undo the buttons, but her hands are shaking too much. Crying out in frustration, Janie grips my shirt and rips it, the buttons go flying, and with it, whatever control I have left. I rip off her sweater, revealing her pale, freckled skin and dark green lace bra that was doing the most fantastic job boosting up her ample tits.

I mean...

"My fucking god." I breathe out before pressing my face against her chest and breathing in that intoxicating scent. I run my tongue down her chest to her cleavage and fucking hell, she's so soft and delicious and I want to bite every part of her.

"More!" She rips my rubber band out and digs her fingers into my hair. I groan as I feel her rock against my throbbing erection. She lets out a loud gasp and I pause momentarily. She grinds against me again. "How fucking big are you? Holy shit, it feels like a forearm down there."

I can't help but bark out a laugh before pressing my cock against her center as I kiss the top mound of one of her sweet, soft breasts before giving into my animalistic urges and biting down. Her cry and moan send a current through me that runs straight to my cock. I need more of her, all of her.

I hear the chime indicating the front door is opening, and in an instant, Janie shoves me off her, grabs her shirt, and runs to the back just before Atlas and Ash walk around the corner. I stare at them, hair wild, panting, shirt ripped, and a bulging dick trying to burst through my jeans. Atlas blinks and looks around at the empty room.

"Ummm...Fox? What are you doing bud?"

I adjust myself, run my hands through my hair, and straighten my shirt that still has one button hanging on.

"Felt like working out, mind your business."

Chapter Seven

JANIE

FUCK. *Shit. Fuck.*

I slam my apartment door shut before sliding down the door and resting my head in my palms. What…in the **actual** fuck did I do?

I know what I did. I nearly had a fucking orgasm by grinding against Fox's massive erection! I groan as I rest my head against the door. Fucking hell. I was so hormonal and angry and…well it's obvious what else I was. But when he grabbed me and slammed me into the wall… when he bit me, marked me.

I am getting turned on again just thinking about his warm, wet tongue running over my breasts. Looking down, I peek under my sweater and see the reddening mark on my breast. *Fuck.* I have never been so equal parts embarrassed and turned on. The worst part of it all? I'm not embarrassed that I allowed my enemy to bite my tit and grind his *massive* erection against me, I'm upset because of Brody.

Brody.

I am such a fucking asshole. One of the things I am

57

actively talking about online are the men in my DMs that have a girlfriend or wife, yet here I am.

Sighing, I pull my phone out of my pocket to send Brody a text. I need to talk to him about this, I am not a cheater, I believe in being honest.

> Me: Hey! Can u come over? Xx

Shockingly, I don't have to wait an hour before getting a response out of him.

> Brody: Y? Arent u on ur period?

You know, would it kill him to just clean up his texts a little. I'm willing to give on some, but this? And then am I on my period? What does that matter? Fox was ready to fuck me period or – No...Janie...bad. We are not comparing the two.

Is there even a comparison though?

> Me: I need to talk to you.

> Brody: U R

I growl in frustration and hit his stupid profile picture with my finger to call him. It rings three times before his annoyed voice comes over the other end.

"Jai, babe, I don't do phone calls. But hey, you wanna talk to me over live? Maybe we could get some views in." There was a time, not all that long ago, I would've said yeah. I may not have enjoyed it, but I would have agreed to go live with him and try to get some extra money and followers. Now, I just want to scream.

"Brody, I need to talk to you. Just you." I hear him sigh and it sounds like he's getting up and walking. Brody lives in a "creator house". Basically, he and twelve other people, all social media creators, live together in some massive house and do trends and play pranks on each other. It's very annoying.

"Okay, I'm alone." He states and I hear the familiar ripping sound of his vape. Taking a steadying breath, I summon the courage to come clean.

"Brody, something happened today at work between Fox and I." I start and I hear him exhaling his pull.

"Which one was Fox?" I roll my eyes at his question.

"The one that was supposed to take over the shop originally." I wait.

Silence.

"He has longer, dark blonde hair and a beard..." Come on, he's the only one with lighter hair and a bigger beard.

Crickets.

I smack my forehead. "The older one."

"OH RIGHT! The one old enough to be your dad!" He says and it's now that I realize the dick measuring that was happening. Brody reminding me of our age difference is him trying to put himself higher. And while I am trying to come clean and work things out, I can officially say that Fox *definitely* has a bigger dick. So much bigger.

"Yeah," I clear my throat, focusing on the task at hand. "Anyway, Fox and I were arguing, and things got heated and...Brody I am so sorry but he and I..."

"You fucked him?" His voice is almost bored.

"What?" I sputter, "N-Noooot exactly. There was just... We kissed and –"

"Okay so what's the deal? Are you guys wanting a third? Because I am not into "daddies", no offense."

I nearly drop my phone in shock. "W-what? No! I was calling to come clean and apologize!"

He is silent for a long time and then I hear laughter. Is he laughing?

"What is so funny?" I yell. I'm trying to have a serious conversation with my boyfriend, and he is laughing.

"Not funny ha-ha, more so sad funny." His laughter dies away before speaking again. "I mean, what have you been doing? You and I never have sex anymore. Not that we had much to begin with for whatever reason." My cheeks flush at his remark. We had never really been super intimate due to my disorder. Brody has an unfortunate tendency to use people's "flaws" as a way to step over them and I always feared that he would one day do so with me.

Still, I didn't expect my aversion to be thrown back at me like this. "What are you saying?" I ask, a knot forming in my stomach. "Have you been cheating on me?"

"What?" Brody laughs again. "Jai, we would have to be exclusive for it to be considered cheating." My phone drops from my hand. I don't bother to pick it up.

We would have to be exclusive for it to be considered cheating.

Brody has been sleeping with other people this entire time.

"ARE you going to tell me what's up?" Royce asks as we pull into the parking lot of *Nuts About Dough* - the gourmet donut shop I binged on yesterday and fully plan to repeat today. Royce is another content creator. She is all about drama, tea, gossip and that is what her social media consists of ninety five percent of the time. The other five percent is a mix of skimpy clothes, make up and food that she pretends to eat.

"I am just in need of some shame eating." I shrug as we get out of her Benz. Royce is the quintessential SoCal girl. Tall, super thin, large - bought - breasts. Her hair is...well I actually don't know what her hair looks like because she wears a poker straight, white wig that reaches to her ass.

She pulls down her large designer shades and looks at the sign above the small shop. "Nuts About Dough." She repeats and then looks over to me. "You had better have a good reason to pull me out of my penthouse and drive you down to a shop where I guarantee I will gain two pounds simply by breathing the carb-filled air." Her voice is short and hushed as she and I walk in.

Actually, I didn't have a good reason. There was zero chance in hell I would tell Royce anything that is going on in my life. I have more followers than her, meaning she would love to have dirt on me to boost herself. But I didn't want to be alone. Brody called me back several times last night, but I never answered. What Brody confessed to, it just threw me. It's not that I'm heartbroken. He and I were not in love, but for him to just go out there and screw other people.... And then not tell me! Oh my god, I am going to have to get tested just to make sure.

I walk up to the counter and smile at the girl from yesterday.

"I told you they were addictive!" She laughs lightly. I look at her name tag, *Stevie*.

"They really were delicious!" I can't help but perk up at her smiling face. "Can we actually get some donuts and I want an ice decaf latte with a pump of cinnamon and vanilla and some oat milk for here?"

"Oh," Royce looks up from her phone and shakes her index finger. "I have a spin class in thirty, no way am I putting that poison and coffee in me." I flinch and give Stevie an apologetic look. The girl seems unfazed by the remark as she hands me a number card.

"Go get your seats. I'll bring your coffee out in a minute." Stevie turns to head into the back while Royce and I sit at a small cafe table.

"Alright," Royce sighs as she puts her phone down and stares directly at me. At least that is what I assume she is doing; I can't tell because her sunglasses are still over her eyes. "I'm giving you five minutes Jai. I am serious about the class."

I wring my hands together under the table as I chew on my cheek. "Royce, we've been friends for six years. I just thought that we could get some coffee. I haven't been great since my dad died."

Royce removes her sunglasses and gives me a blank stare. "We all have problems Jai but it's not like you are a child losing their parents, you'll be fine. Have the doctor prescribe you some benzos and you'll be good as new." She waves her hand dismissively at me as she speaks. "I mean, sure we've been following each other for years, but friends? You know there are no real friends here. Everyone is faking it to make it. It's all about the numbers. Which by the way... yours are going down. Your engagement is nonexistent and besides that amateur selfie yesterday, you haven't done anything with your accounts in a week! Which, need I remind you, is like a year in our world. You completely missed out on three trends!"

"I've been busy at the shop." I say stiffly, feeling some-what defensive. Royce scoffs and rolls her eyes.

"Oh yes, the little tattoo shop with those oversized apes, Brody mentioned something about them at the meet up."

"They are not apes." I say through gritted teeth. "They have names, they are amazing artists, and–"

"Yes, yes don't get your thong twisted. My god, they are just a bunch of criminals." Stevie sets my coffee and drink down and I notice Royce staring at the girl with a look of judgment.

"Go to your class Royce, this was a bad idea." I take a sip of my coffee while watching her stand.

"Yes, next time, make it a club. A donut shop is just so... sad. Also, your hair is looking a little frizzy." Royce leaves and my face falls into my hands.

Millions of followers and the moment I need coffee with a friend, I have no one.

I hear Royce's vacant chair move and I look up to see Stevie.

"Can I sit for a minute?" She asks. I smile and nod as she sits her own coffee and donut down. "I'm Stevie by the way." She points to her name tag. I nod as I swallow my coffee.

"Janie." I state as I break a piece of my donut off. "I'm sorry about my acquaintance earlier." Stevie waves her hand.

"It's alright, trust me I've had worse. I have green hair, face piercings, tattoos, and I work in a donut shop at *this* size, in southern California. Your barbie friend couldn't hurt me if she tried." I laugh lightly and look over her, though it's hard to tell her shape under the bulky baker's uniform she wears.

"Do you own the shop?" I ask while leaning back in my seat. Stevie shakes her head.

"It's my mom's. She's in the back with my grandmother. The old woman hates dealing with the crowd that comes in after ten, so I take care of the front for her."

"Are you planning on taking it over? I know it can be hard working with family." Not that I ever actually worked. It was more so, I was stuck at the shop while Dad worked.

"Oh god, I hope not." Stevie laughs lightly. "I'm completely happy at the size I am but, if I work here more than part time, I will end up needing a crane to move me." I snort a laugh into my drink. She was so easy to talk to, it was really nice.

"So, what do you hope to do?" Stevie shrugs at my question. "I might go to IT school. I was a piercer in my home town in Louisiana before I... well before I moved back here. I enjoyed my job, but that kind of atmosphere can be toxic." I watch her eyes go distant, and while I want to pry deeper, I know that it's none of my business so instead I grin at her brightly.

"IT is where all the hot nerds are anyway." I tease and watch as she visibly relaxes. It's nice talking to someone about nothing too important. I never had this kind of friendship. Most wanted my follower count and nothing more. Stevie was fun, and at the end of our conversation, we exchange phone numbers so that we can stay in touch, and I leave the donut shop feeling like I made my first friend.

Chapter Eight

FOX

"SO," Ash sits on my table and looks at me with his dark eyes. He has the same stupid grin on his face At gets before saying something to piss me off. "Did you actually get Janie to run away?"

I sigh, she hasn't been at work for four days now. No calls, texts, nothing. I thought about going by her place, but I don't know where she lives. The only thing keeping me from obsessively worrying about her is that Derek had received a response from her the other day when he texted her that he was running low on one of his inks. I mean, all she sent was thumbs up emoji, but still...proof of life and all.

"No Ash," I grumble, feeling uncomfortable over the whole ordeal. "She just needed to take some time off. I think she had some social media internet thing." That's a lie, but Ash seems to accept it as he hops off the table and stretches.

"I miss her." He sighs longingly and I have to fight the pang of annoyance I feel over it. "I mean, she's really funny and a complete ball buster." Atlas and even Derek nod in agreement.

"Plus, she has that a–"

I slam the sketch pad I had been using down on my station and give Ash a warning look. "Careful." I growl out as I glare towards Ash who holds his hands up in defense.

"What Fox?" He laughs lightly. "You can hate her all you want but you know I'm right."

"That's Tony's daughter." I state in irritation even though my stomach twists with a type of guilt I've become all too familiar with since the incident. "Show some respect."

Ash bows at the waist towards me. "But of course, I am nothing if not a gentleman."

Derek scoffs. "Yeah?" His deep, gruff voice laughs. "Who brought you to work today?" Ash tapped a finger to his scruffy chin while staring up at the ceiling.

"Lindsey...Lucy...Something with an L." Ash shrugs and Atlas laughs loudly.

"You said her name was Anna." Atlas shakes his head and Ash snaps his fingers.

"That's right! Anna! Dude, now there is an ass to talk about."

Rolling my eyes and not wanting to hear this conversation – as it's the same one I hear most days – I stand and head to Tony's office, shutting the door behind me.

I need to apologize to Janie, I know I do. But I don't even know how to go about doing so. I took advantage of her, I manhandled her. Fuck I'm old enough to be her father...*her* father was my mentor and best friend. How on Earth did I let that happen?

I run my hands through my hair and squeeze my neck

before I hear the bell on the front door chime. Walking out, I see the men are still debating the best ass shapes.

"No, allow me." I grumble as I walk to the front and give the woman a small smile. She's cute, with turquoise hair, curvy, and a nice set of dimple piercings.

"Can I help you?" I ask as I notice she's carrying a box. She smiles brightly although her body language makes her seem like she is nervous.

"I-is Janie here?" She asks, tucking her chin length hair behind her ear.

"No ma'am—"

"Stevie...please, I'm not old enough for ma'am yet." I nod.

"Stevie, no Janie is off today. Is there something I can help you with." A frown forms on her face as her dark brows furrow.

"I just talked to her an hour ago. She asked me to deliver some donuts to her work. I guess I assumed she would be here." My expression softens and I feel the guilt in my gut return.

She got us donuts...again.

I hear commotion behind me and suddenly At and Ash are flanking me.

"Oh my God." Ash breathes. "I've died and gone to heaven. There is a beautiful woman in our shop holding a box of donuts."

Stevie shifts uncomfortably and averts her gaze. I elbow Ash in the ribs. "Try to control your dick." I hiss as I walk up to take the donuts and relieve the poor girl.

"Thank you, Stevie," I smile softly as I open the door for her to walk out. "I appreciate you delivering these. You have an amazing day." Stevie gives me a short wave before walking away and I turn to glare back at Ash.

"Just for that, you get no donuts." I state.

WALKING from my bathroom to my bedroom, I listen as *The Office* blasts in the background. I grab my pajama shorts and slip them on before looking in the mirror next to my closet.

"Jesus I am going to need the gym if she doesn't stop with the donuts." I mutter as I grab my cell phone and fall into my bed. I surf through the emails I have. Mostly from the website, people wanting appointments, consults. It's all jumbled in there. Maybe her streamlining things would be nice, not that I am willing to tell her that.

I find myself on Instagram and I chew on the inside of my cheek as I stare at the search bar. *What was her online name?*

I type in "J-A-" and the suggestions pop up, showing Janie's face. Hair in a tight ponytail and she has on bright face paint to match the candy themed background. I tap on her page and scroll through the photos. All staged, photo-shopped and fake. Most of them had her with straight hair and her freckles were missing. It's quite alarming to see her without them.

I scroll to the top to see the two newest photos and I can feel the smile tugging at my lips. One is from the day of *the incident* - she's in front of the donut shop. No makeup, no photoshop. I look at the comments and I feel my blood heating up. Who the fuck are these people? I thought people were on here talking about how amazing she is.

"POV - You think you are important enough that people
care that you are at a donut shop."
"I'd like to taste her glazed donut."
"Eat shit and die."
"You think the carpet matches the drapes?"
"So I need to stalk that shop and I'll get to meet her?"
"GOOD GOD is this a freckle filter!? If so it's gone
WRONG! You look DIRTY!"

I notice my hand is tingling and it's then I realize how tightly I am holding the phone. I scroll up to the photo taken three hours ago. Janie is sitting with her chin resting on her palm while staring out a window. The photo is black and white, and she has her curly hair and freckles showing. I read what she had written in the caption.

"Sometimes that 'Happy Glow' is just a filter."

The comments are similar to her other pictures. They hate her hair, her freckles, she's attention seeking. Why does she do this? If this is commonplace, why would she put herself through that kind of mental torture. I consider myself a well-rounded man, I can handle *hate* but even I would feel beatdown after reading these.

"No wonder she hides her tremors." I mutter, I can only imagine what they would say about her disorder over the internet. It angers me to my very core that she could very well be sitting at her place, alone, reading these comments.

No, she's probably out with Brody.

I exit out of her profile page when a heart pops up.

Fuck, I liked her photo. I quickly tap it again, not wanting her to know that I am looking at her profile. Shit...

will it still show up and then she will see I unliked it? Should I like it again?

As I go over the dilemma in my head, my phone vibrates, scaring the shit out of me. I look at the unread message.

> Torch: Derek said we are out of green ink.
> Do you need any others?

Wow...what an absolutely boring text. And since when does she ask me if I need anything?

> Me: I would ask for black, but you'll just get me the shit ink again.

I smirk as I watch the three bubbles bouncing as I await her response. But her response isn't a snarky comeback. No, it's a screenshot of the ink...my preferred ink.

> Torch: This one right?

> Me: Are you alright Torch? I don't know how to handle you actually behaving.

> Torch: Yeah well, I'm just trying to keep everything neat and professional. So is this what you want?

The gut twist is back. She's acting like this because of what I did. I go to text out an apology, but...is that shitty and cowardly? Shouldn't I apologize in person, like a man?

> Me: Yes, you got it.

> Me: When are you coming back to work?

> Torch: Missing me already *winky face*

I chuckle at her smart attitude sneaking through.

> Me: Yeah, about as much as I miss my proctologist.

> Torch: Now Papa Fox, please make sure you are getting your prostate checked. Men at your age need to take your prostate health seriously.

This fucking brat.

> Me: Neat and professional huh?

Janie's text bubbles appeared, disappeared over and over before a simple and final text came through.

> Torch: I'll be back this weekend. Night.

Fuck.

What in the fuck am I going to say to her to fix this?

Chapter Nine

JANIE

I TAKE A STEADYING breath as I stare at the back door of Hel's. After the humiliation of what transpired between Fox and I, it seemed to be in everyone's best interest if I took the week off. I would've taken today off since I am going out with Brody tonight, but I need to be here to sign for packages that requires my signature only.

Part of me feels like going out with Brody will be regrettable, as most of my outings for my birthday are. Yes, today is my twenty-sixth birthday. And after a disgusting amount of groveling that included three videos of him sobbing, I finally called Brody back so we could talk.

"I DIDN'T KNOW JAI!" *Brody sighs as he takes a hit from his vape. I stare at him in the foyer of his stupid creator pad. I hate being here because I always worry if I'm being filmed.*

"Didn't know what Brody? That as a boyfriend, I expected you to be faithful?" Running my hands through my hair I scowl up at him and watch as tears well in his eyes. What is he doing? Brody drops to his knees and wraps himself around my waist. Instinctively I shove him off and step back, not wanting him to feel my tremors that are amping up today.

"Jai," His voice cracks. "Please. I'm a terrible person. I don't deserve you. But please...you have such a big heart, can you please find it in you to give me one more chance? I promise, I– I'll take you out for your birthday! We can go to a nice restaurant and talk. Please? I care about you. We can't just end everything like this. We owe it to ourselves to try and talk it out."

I don't want to. I don't want to talk it out. I don't want to go to a restaurant. And why is he crying? I shake my head in defeat and let out a sigh.

"No social media? No cameras?" I ask as he nods frantically. "Yes! Anything you want!"

USUALLY, I spend my birthdays alone in my apartment. I take a bath in my boring tub; I put on a face mask and watch TV while I drink myself to sleep. It's not the most glamorous way to spend my day but it beats getting stood up like I've been before. Today is different though. I'm going to try to go to a birthday dinner with Brody. I don't know how I feel about it. I've found out over the last week that, during our relationship, he's been with dozens of women. Though dozens is probably conservative. Part of me feels like I should just move on. We were never *close*. We aren't in love, and I don't even feel comfortable enough around him to tell him about my condition, or anything about my life that doesn't revolve around social media.

But, good or bad, Brody has been a part of my life for over a year. And, good or bad, there is something to be said about having that sense of familiarity... right?

So, for the sake of familiarity, and due to the immense amount of guilt I have because of the incident with Fox, I am going to give this another try. Who knows? Maybe this will be a turning point for us.

Grabbing my purse and my backpack with my makeup, hair supplies and my outfit for the night, I take one last deep breath and head for the door of Hel's Ink.

AFTER SETTING ALL my stuff in my dad's old office, I walk through the hallway and into the tattooing area. The familiar aroma of the disinfectants, green soap and ink fill my nose, but unlike on my first day, I'm not filled with sadness. Instead, it's a comfort, like when you return home and your mom is making you your favorite cookies — at least, I think that's what a mom would do.

My eyes scan over the guys. Ash and Derek are going over a sketch of a back piece that Ash apparently has coming up. Atlas is nowhere to be found and Fox has his back to me as he tattoos a very curvy blonde who evidently has no pants on. I am suddenly full of a feeling that I'm uncomfortable with. My stomach twists in a way that makes me both angry and nauseated.

"Hey!" Atlas' voice from behind me causes me to jump.

"You finally came back!" He grins as he walks from the direction of the supply closet.

"Yeah, I was under the weather." I say, not taking my eyes off the woman. What is she saying to make Fox laugh so hard? How can she be that comfortable talking to him in her underwear? There is zero chance she is *that* funny. And where is the pad to cover her exposed areas?"

"Fox said you had business to take care of," Atlas states in confusion, bringing my attention back to him.

"Yeah, and then I caught a cold." I say defensively as I glance back over to Fox.

"So, who's the blonde?" I say before I can stop myself. Atlas chuckles as a devious grin forms over his face.

"What's it to ya, Red?" He gives me a knowing look that I do not appreciate. I put my hand on his face and shove him away before walking up to Fox. I'll just say a quick hello and then go to the front counter.

As I walk up, the blonde and I make eye contact. She stares me up and down, and I notice her features harden. Why is she acting so standoffish? Wait, why am I?

"Good morning, Fox." I say as I start to pass.

"Hey Torch." He says, his eyes not leaving the girl's thigh. He's wearing his adorable glasses again and I hate what it's doing to my body.

"You're new. I haven't seen you before." The blonde gives me a fake smile before I can walk away.

"Oh no!" I laugh and tuck a strand of my currently straight hair behind my ear. It took hours to straighten, but Brody hates my curly hair, saying it always gives off a lazy vibe.

"I'm Janie Pierce. My father was Tony Pierce, the owner and founder of the shop." Did I need to say all of that in my introduction? No. But for some reason I feel as though I need to make sure she knows that this is my arena, and these are my guys.

My guys? God damn it.

The blonde's fake smile turns genuine, and I'm taken aback by the swift change, "Oh hey! I'm Lauren. Everyone calls me Ren. I'm a regular around here. Fox has been my guy for years!"

HER guy?

No...Janie stop. Fox is allowed to be someone's *guy*. Brody...remember Br–

"She's my attorney – the fuck happened to your hair?" I wince at Fox's abrupt question while Lauren swats his arm in a scolding manner. Pretty ballsy considering he's holding a tattoo machine.

"I'm going out with Brody tonight...for my birthday. He likes my hair straight." My voice betrays me as the words come out smaller than I mean for them too. Fox's intense gaze sends my nerve endings into overdrive, and I feel the almost completely faded hickey on my breast tingle as memories of him – no, stop it.

"Oh, happy birthday!" Lauren grins. She seems lovely, and her eyes remind me of rich, warm chocolate. Actually, that is her entire presence. I notice her eyes flick from me to Atlas, who is singing - very poorly - to *Piece of Me* by Britney Spears.

I watch as her cheeks turn a crimson color, and I can't help but smile. Does she have a thing for the shop idiot? I peer over at Fox's work; as always, it's perfect. The large, colorful flowers are perfectly placed down her hip and thigh.

"Your tattoo is beautiful." Lauren beams at me.

"Thank you! Fox is the only guy I trust to tattoo me."

"Why don't you continue to break my heart, Ren!" Atlas

calls from his station, where he is setting up for his appointment. Lauren rolls her eyes, but her still pink cheeks give her away.

"Well, I won't interrupt you anymore," I say softly before heading to the front of the shop. I turn back, and my eyes lock with Fox's. We stare at each other for what feels like the longest second of my life before he breaks contact and smiles back at Lauren.

LOOKING myself over in the mirror in my dad's old office, I finish getting ready for Brody to pick me up for dinner. I'm wearing a short champagne-colored wrap cami sequin dress with black wrap-up heels. My makeup is flawless; not a freckle can be seen with the amount of concealer and foundation I have on. Eyebrows are filled in and perfectly arched. My lips look swollen and kissable in the dark nude lipstick, and my eyes are bright in contrast against the dark smoky effect of my eyeshadow and frosted highlights.

Taking a breath, I spin and look at my ass popping in the dress. I look like I have the best filter on, but still, as I take selfies and small videos to upload later, I make sure to add the appropriate filters. The amount of hate I've been receiving over my last two uploads where I hadn't added the filters has really hurt my mental health and I don't have it in me to deal with another round of it. Last night while scrolling through a content creator tip site, one of the suggestions was a social media break. I had to laugh at that notion. People who take those breaks either are not big enough that it will matter or are too big that they can get away with it. I'm very large, but due to me branding myself as a *trend-fluencer,* if I disappear for more than a couple days, I lose sponsor prospects, trends, trendy hashtags, or drama to put my opinion on. The last thing you want as an influencer is to show up late with opinions that are no longer relevant.

My sharp heels click against the tile with every step I make down the hall to head to the front of the shop. I see Fox standing with Atlas and Lauren, drinking from a water bottle and joking about something I can't hear.

"Is Brody here?" I ask as I walk up to them.

Fox turns to look at me, and I watch his jaw fall towards the floor, along with his water bottle. I can't help the ego boost I get from that.

"Fuck." He hisses as he clumsily reaches for some paper towels and bends over to soak up the water on the floor. I wince as he bumps his head on the tray on his way down. His cheeks start to go pink as he continues to move his gaze back and forth between me and the spilled water.

"Damn girl!" Atlas whistles looking me up and down. "He ain't here, but if I had a girl looking like you, I wouldn't be letting her wait around." I roll my eyes at his comment but can't help but notice Lauren shifting uncomfortably behind him. I watch as her arms wrap around her abdomen as if she is self-conscious. Instantly I feel guilty for making another woman feel bad about herself, I never want to do that to another woman because I know what it's like. That's how all the women in my world are.

I walk over to Lauren and motion for her to follow me out to the front room. I sit on the black leather chairs in the waiting room and cross my legs.

"How long have you been coming here?" I ask her after sending a text to Brody, asking for an ETA.

"Oh, five years probably, I got my first tattoo from Fox after finishing my first year in law school." Her bow-shaped lips form a small smile as she rotates her leg to show the tattoo on her calf. It's a black and grey portrait of Lady Justice, holding the scales and tears falling from under her blindfold.

"My god she is stunning," I whisper as I stare over the piece in awe, as always, by Fox's work.

"So, Fox wasn't kidding?" I ask as I glance back up to look out the window. *Where is Brody?*

Lauren laughs lightly. "He calls me their attorney because the guys hate Frank. But no, I just give them advice. But I'm not dumb enough to actually be their attorney. Those four men would put me in an early grave trying to handle them all." She jokes and I give her a small chuckle. As if she can sense my distraction, she cocks her head and gives me a sympathetic look. "When is your date supposed to be here?"

Looking down at my phone, I sigh before giving her a small smile. "About thirty minutes ago...he would've been considered *fashionably late*."

I see her wince, and I shrug trying to put on my *best face*. "Not the first time I've been stood up on my birthday. I'll give him a few more minutes and then just head home." My head is screaming at me for being so stupid as to think Brody would actually come. He begged me for another chance, why? So, he could make me look like an idiot, well good job. I feel my tremors kicking up. I need to get out of here. I don't want to be seen with pity, I can't.

"What?" Lauren whines out while shaking her head side to side. "No! Absolutely not! You look so pretty! You cannot waste that outfit. If your boyfriend is too dumb to realize what he's missing, we will get the guys to take you out."

My eyes widen as it's my turn to shake my head, probably a little more frantically than she. "Oh no! I mean, that's sweet, but the guys and I don't really get along that well –" I stop talking as I hear a loud *"MOTHER FUCKER"* followed by Fox storming up from the backroom. He looks livid with his darkening eyes and tense jaw.

"What's wrong?" I ask nervously, half preparing to have to jump on the defense in case the anger is directed at me. I watch as Atlas comes out with Ash. What is going on?

"Janie," Ash starts while rubbing his neck nervously. "Is your boyfriend *the* Brody? The social media influencer?" I nod slowly, dread creeping up my body. Has he been in an accident?

Ash holds out his phone. I can't grab it as my hands are shaking too hard. I look at the live video on his screen, and instantly I begin to deflate. In the video, Brody is getting a lap dance from Royce.

I take a deep breath and give them all a smile even though I am mortified. How can I play it off like I don't care when I am dressed like this?

"Well," I force out a laugh that sounds more like a breathy sob. "It looks like he got the party started already." My voice cracks, and so does any confidence I had with it. How could he humiliate me like this? My birthday, Brody has become just another person, another man, to publicly embarrass me on my birthday. The entire internet is getting to see that I cannot keep my man satisfied. Oh god, the selfie I took with the caption "Birthday Date with Bae" I tagged him...I am so stupid!

"I guess I should get going." I state as I begin to walk to

the back room when a strong hand grabs my trembling wrist. As I am about to pull away, I look to see it's Fox and I let him continue to hold me there.

"We will take you out." Fox's definitive tone leaves no room for debate, not that it stops me from trying.

"No, really...I am fine, just going –"

"Oh, come on!" Lauren pleads. "I know I could use a couple of drinks after my week, and since these three are quite the gentlemen," I watch as she gives them all warning glances. "I'm sure they will be willing to treat us to a night of partying." I look from the guys to Lauren and back before sighing in defeat and nodding my head. I really could use a drink.

"Okay, let's go."

"ONE, TWO, THREE! DRINK!"

Myself, Ren, Atlas, and Ash down another shot as Fox watches. Fox had half a beer when we got to the club a couple of hours ago, but I guess he has since decided to be the sober friend tonight. I, on the other hand, am three sheets to the wind. Brody's actions are bothering me more than I am willing to admit and all I want to do is drink this embarrassment away.

"Ren!" I force myself to remember her preferred name, *Lauren* is *too boring* apparently. "Take a selfie with me!" I squish my face against hers as I take several photos of us.

"Are you trying to make Brody jealous?" She asks and takes another shot. I give her a small wink.

"Wanna make him really jealous?" She grabs my phone

and hands it to Atlas who is standing on the other side of the table. She curls her finger, motioning for me to come closer.

"Are you recording Atlas?" Though thoroughly confused, Atlas nods while staring at my phone screen. Ren grabs either side of my face and pulls me in for a sweet kiss.

"Oh my god," I barely hear Atlas say. "This is the greatest day of my fucking life!" He cheers.

I break the kiss to see Atlas and Ash with the dumbest grins on their faces while Fox stands there looking.... very annoyed.

"That'll get him going!" Ren beams and I smile at her before hearing Fox scoff.

"Yeah, make sure you get those precious likes. God, forbid you talk to him instead of fighting over the internet." His words sting more than I am willing to admit currently. I shake off the feelings, as I take another shot before deciding I need to go to dance.

"Foxy!" I yell as I stumble to him. He catches me with his massive hand firmly on my stomach. I feel warmth spread over me as he guides me to sit on his stool. Even drunk I can tell that Fox is over being here. Hell, he said so twenty minutes into our arrival. But no matter what we said, his stubborn ass wouldn't just go home.

"Foxy, can I have that!" I point to the bun on the back of his head. He touches his hair and looks at me, brows furrowing in confusion.

"You want my hair?" I let out a snort that I cannot imagine in any scenario one would find attractive before shaking my head.

"I want to dance! But my hair is getting messy!" Fox rolls his eyes as he reaches into his pocket and pulls out a black hair tie. I try to grab it, but my depth perception is off.

Shaking his head in disapproval, he walks behind me. I feel his fingers combing through my hair, and goosebumps appear over my arms. The feeling of him pulling the hair up off my neck and sliding his hand up the base of my neck to smooth it...did I just moan out loud? I look around at the group who don't seem to notice, thank God.

"I don't think you need to be on the dance floor right now, Torch." I feel his hot breath as he whispers in my ear and... fuck he just gave me a lady boner, the prick.

"I wanna dance!" I pout as he finishes my bun, and I stand and look at him.

"Dance with me?" I pout, and he laughs before shaking his head.

"Not even if there was a meteor heading straight for us and the only way to save all of mankind was to dance."

I stare at him in silence for a long moment before shaking my head. "Okay, a simple no would have sufficed."

I walk away from our table to the semi-full dance floor. There are a lot of people, but everyone has room to move. When I turn around, I see Ren is following me out there, her blonde hair sticking to her face from the sheen of sweat she has over her from dancing earlier. We start dancing together, and it takes only a moment for a man to walk up to us, his eyes set on me.

"How about we dance?" His breath smells of tequila and cigars. I glance up at him, his black hair slicked back and tan skin glowing in the club lights. He's good-looking in a wannabe Hollywood actor type of way. I watch as his dark eyes look over every inch of my body. I shudder, feeling naked suddenly.

"No thanks!" Giving him a timid smile, I motion my head towards Ren who is glaring intently at the man. "I'm with her!" As I turn to go back to dancing with Ren, Hollywood grips my arm tightly and jerks me back around to face him.

"Hey!" I gasp and try to rip my arm free, but his bruising grip tightens further. I watch as Ren shoves his chest to try and get him to let me go but he is well built and barely moves.

"Get the fuck out of here blondie, I ain't a chubby chaser." He sneers before looking back at me. I glare at him before swinging my hand to slap his face, he catches my wrist in his other hand.

"You don't say no to me you –" The man stops his threat and stares behind me, and I watch the color drain from his face and his eyes go wide. I look behind me to see Fox – eyes glaring, nostrils flaring, lip curling. His fists clench and unclench causing the muscles in his tattoo-covered forearms to flex in a very delicious way. I pull my gaze from him to see Atlas and Ash are on either side of Fox, giving similar threatening looks.

Fox eyes Hollywood's hand, still squeezing the holy hell out of my arm. Before I can blink, Fox is at Hollywood's side, digging his fingers into the man's hand and twisting his wrist to get him to release me. The guy falls to his knees as Fox continues to twist until his wrist makes a sickening *pop* and he lets out a loud cry.

Fox grabs the crying man by his shirt and holds him up, so they are at eye level.

"Who in the fuck are you to lay a finger on her? Touch her again, and I'll break your fucking face."

"H-Hey man I'm sorry!" The man cries. "P-Please! I didn't know she was taken!"

Liar. I said I was with Ren.

Fox grabs the man roughly by the back of the head. "Apologize." He growls out. The man starts apologizing to

Fox again and Fox rolls his eyes before gripping the man by the throat. "Not to me you fucking moron. Apologize to them. Now." Fox motions his head towards Ren and me.

Hollywood nervously looks over at us and with his pleading eyes and wobbly lip he begins to speak.

"Ladies, I am so sorry." He manages to get out between his shaking sobs. I put a hand on Fox's bulging bicep. How the seams of his black flannel shirt haven't ripped is a fucking miracle.

Groaning as a wave of nausea hits me and the room starts spinning. "Fox, I don't feel good." I whimper while silently pleading with him to let the guy go.

For a moment, Fox looks as though he might choose to kill the guy first. But instead, he drops the man, roughly, and guides me up the steps.

We walk out of the club, and as the cool breeze hits my overheated body, I feel a stronger wave of nausea come over me.

"I'm going to be sick." I stagger into the alley as the contents of my stomach come up. I feel a firm hand around my hip and waist while another holds the hair that has spilled from my bun out of my face.

I know without looking that it is Fox. Even vomiting in the dark and drunk, the feel of his hands are becoming ingrained in my soul.

"It's okay." He says softly, running his thumb over my hip, trying to soothe me as I continue to hang over his forearm and vomit harder than I ever remember doing so before.

What a fantastic birthday this has shaped up to be.

Chapter Ten

FOX

I STARE at the black coffee in front of me while Liza continues to sob, making a scene in the *Nuts About Dough* Cafe. I wish like hell I was at my house right now, but I had completely forgotten I was to meet Liza here this morning when I had offered to take Janie and Ren out last night.

My head is throbbing. Last night with the loud noises, the stress of that fucking bastard touching Janie and then carrying her ass up to my house with Atlas, Ash, and Ren, I didn't get any sleep. Especially, since most of the night Janie and Atlas were bonding over the toilet, taking turns puking and missing.

"I just," Liza blows her nose into her tissue. "I don't understand! My boys aren't working at the shop, and the insurance company refuses to release his life insurance to me! I was basically his wife!"

I can't help but snort as I sip the coffee. Tony would've sooner married Derek than Liza.

"Liza, I don't know what to tell you," I state, looking into her red-rimmed yet...oddly dry eyes. "If you're not the beneficiary, I guess it's Janie, but she hasn't mentioned it to me, and it's not my business to ask. My legal matters with Tony's death don't go any further than Hel's."

"Well, what about my boys! They were promised places at that shop after the apprenticeship." Liza's hands are shaking, and my thoughts go to Janie, what could I get her for her hangover? She can't have caffeine, but she would still appreciate her usual iced decaf.

"Your sons had their shot at Hel's, Liza. We both know that they were high while there." Liza scoffs, and I flag down a familiar waitress.

"Fox, right?" The turquoise-haired woman gives me a kind smile as she stands next to our table.

"Good memory, Stevie, was it?" I give her a polite smile as she nods.

"You got it! What can I do for you guys?" Liza waves her hand dismissively, but I hold Stevie's attention.

"Can you get me two large black iced coffees and then an ice decaf latte with a pump of vanilla, oat milk... Oh! And a pump of cinnamon please?" Both Liza and Stevie stare at me with a skeptical look. I shift uncomfortably, trying to act like it's no big deal. "What? I like something a little different after my morning cup."

"That's Janie's order." Stevie chuckles softly, shaking her head. "Do you want any food?" I think for a minute.

"Yesterday was her birthday, it was kind of a crappy day, and she is probably not feeling the best this morning." Stevie taps her chin with her pen as she thinks.

"I'll box you up something." She smiles. "You feeding the guys too? Or just Janie?" Her suggestive grin and playful wink cause me to look away and rub the back of my neck.

I clear my throat and give her a crooked half smile. "Uh...the guys too."

Liza coughs and I look back towards her, annoyance filling me once more.

"So, Liza, you sent the text stating you have some things of Tony's?" That is the whole reason I agreed to this meeting, and I have yet to see anything, minus her sobs. Liza shakes her head, looking away.

"No," She says softly. "I just...I wanted to see you Fox. You remind me so much of Tony, and I've been so lonely."

"Stop." I state firmly while reaching in my wallet, pulling out a couple of bills to tip Stevie. "I am not going to even entertain that statement. Now, if there is nothing else, I need to grab my order and head out."

Liza grabs my forearm as I go to leave, and a cold chill runs through me. "That wretched girl is going to destroy that shop." Her voice is a harsh whisper. I instantly stiffen and look down at her, my eyes narrowing.

"You know absolutely nothing about Janie, or that shop, so it may be in your best interest to keep both out of your mouth." I snap, ripping my arm from her hand before taking my leave.

AS I LEAN against the counter in my modern kitchen, I stare at the two men in front of me. Both are hugging their coffees and lying on the cool granite countertop. Ren, the queen of avoiding hangovers, has already left, saying she got called into work. She and Janie shared my bed last night as Ash, Atlas and I were all sprawled out in the living room.

One time, a woman I brought back here said that my house was "cozy." I took it as a compliment, but I believe she meant it as *"too small."* It is just me here, I rarely have visitors, and I am not home that often, so a large house seems wasteful and more work than I can handle. So, about five years ago I bought this two-bedroom, two-bathroom bungalow.

The kitchen and bathrooms have all been updated, but the rest of the home looks similar to a teenager's bedroom. Well, a very clean teenager. I keep the house as immaculate as I keep the shop. That being said, like the shop, the walls are covered in different sketches, paintings, flash arts, awards, and photos from the last two decades of my career. Most wouldn't think so, but I'm a sentimentalist. I enjoy saving items that have meaning to me and displaying them.

"I am dying." Atlas says slowly as he raises his head, only to find it to be too much effort and laying back on the counter.

"Yeah, well, you two are fucking idiots. You both know better than to take on Ren." I have no idea what happened to that girl, but she has an alcohol tolerance unlike anything I've ever seen. She could have all three of us stand in a line and take turns with shots. She'd beat all of us and still be able to carry on.

"Listen," Atlas tries to add some authoritative tone to his voice, but it seems to only hurt his head more as he winces and continues speaking in a more hushed tone. "My manhood was on the table. What would you do?"

"Not be so insecure that a woman beating me at shots would directly impact my manhood." I say flatly, earning two sets of eye rolls.

"Yeah yeah, 'Papa Fox' is always secure with himself." Ash groans as he stands up.

"Come on Atlas, let's get back to the apartment." Atlas

and Ash share an expensive apartment downtown near the shop. I don't know how those two work together all day and then share the same living area, but they seem to make it work.

We say our good-byes, and once I shut the door, I glance toward my bedroom. Janie still hasn't walked out. I walk down the hall to my bedroom and prepare to knock on the door when I hear a sniffle.

Fuck is she crying?

I rub the back of my neck before lightly tapping on the door and opening it a crack. The room is still dark, thanks to my blackout shades.

"You okay?" I ask as I peer in, the light from the hallway casting a warm glow over her. It's then that I notice she is sitting in my bed with my duvet covering her bare chest.

"No." She chokes out between sobs as she bows her head. I walk over and sit on the edge of the bed.

"What's wrong? The hangover?" She laughs weakly. I notice her tremors and briefly wonder if she has her medication in her purse.

"No, it's just...I got a call that I have to pick up Dad's ashes today. I've waited as long as they will give me, and I was hoping not to have to go alone, but Brody ghosted me for lap dances yesterday, so I'm guessing that we are done. I just don't know what to do because I have to order an urn and what if I choose the wrong one? I can't choose a fucking couch, but I'm supposed to pick the container that will hold my dad forever? And then where do I put it?"

I place my hands on her shaking ones and squeeze them.

"Breathe," I say softly. I feel her hands grip mine and I have the urge to pull her against me and make her pain go away.

"Can we call a temporary truce?" She whispers so weakly. I blink down at her and cock my head to one side.

"And why would we do that?" I ask, trying to joke with her. I watch as she takes a deep breath.

"I don't have any real friends that I can trust to see me like this." She gestures to her tear-stained, tremoring face.

"You're the only one who knows about my condition, the only one who has seen me cry. And you were the only other person as close to Dad as I was. Please? I don't want to do this alone." The last part comes out as a choked sob, and her head drops down, causing the still straight but completely snarled hair to act as a curtain for her face. When curly, Janie's hair is long, down to the middle of her back, but straight; it goes to her ass.

"Of course," I say with a small smile. "I would be happy to put up a truce for the weekend and take you. I don't have any clients today, so I'm sure the guys can handle the shop. How about you get up, take a shower, and I'll run you to your place so you can get dressed, and then we can head there." The small smile that appears on her face melts me. Janie is a "smiley" type of girl, but most were just fake, polite smiles. Rarely does one get to see a genuine smile where her cheeks go wide, her nose scrunches just a little, and those fucking dimples...fuck, I just want to –

"Okay," I take a deep breath as I remove my hands from her warm, very soft skin. "I'll let you shower. If you want to borrow one, my closet has some T-shirts in there." I need to get the fuck out of this room. I adjust my half-hard dick, thankful for the mostly dark room.

"I'll be in the living room when you are done. Take your time."

Chapter Eleven

JANIE

I SIGH, probably louder than I intend as we stop at a red light. Fox and I have just left my apartment and are heading to pick up Dad's ashes. Having to show Fox my apartment was probably in the top ten most uncomfortable things I've done. It became evident within five minutes of being there that he hated it, which seems a little over dramatic considering it's a decent place and looks brand new.

"Exactly!" I remember him shaking his head, looking around the living room in astonishment. *"For someone who has such a loud personality, it's amazing that your home is so empty."*

He will never know how deeply those words cut into me. He managed to sum me up perfectly – bright on the outside and seemingly empty on the inside. Deciding I need a distraction, I look over Brody's Instagram because, well, apparently, I am a masochist and enjoy feeling like shit about myself. I scroll through the newest photos before looking at his tagged photos. Frowning, I stare at what appears to be a web news photo. The picture is of Brody and me taken about three months ago at the beach. His lean arms are wrapped around my bare waist as we stand in the water, posing for the camera with the sun setting behind us. The photo was used to tell people about a product we were endorsing — *BreatheLove* – a device that looks like an inhaler. When you are anxious, you inhale the aromather-apy, and it's supposed to make you feel better. It never worked for me, but the paycheck was terrific, so I took it.

But the photo I am currently staring at was not for that endorsement, it has been edited to look like the image has been ripped in half, and the text says: **Ice Queen Jai breaks Heartthrob Brody's Heart.**

"You've got to be fucking kidding me." I growl as I touch the photo and open the link.

"What's wrong?" I barely hear Fox ask and I grunt as a response while I read over the article.

Social Media Star Jai Has Dumped Heartthrob Brody For Booze, Boys, And Brawls

Private sources say that the star, Jai, was spotted at a high-end club downtown last night drinking and dancing with other men. This, of course, goes against her "90 Days of Sobriety" campaign that she started just forty-five days ago.

Jai has recently taken a step back from social media with no explanation to her fans. Many have rumored that she may be pregnant and unsure how to explain this to her fans due to her vow not to have children in her twenties. Others have rumored the absence is due to plans for rehab. This reporter has spoken with a distraught Brody, who had put a birthday party together for her that she never attended.

"She and I have been going through a rough patch," An exhausted Brody sighs as he sits in his home, eyes red from tears. *"I think she is having an issue settling down. Monogamy has been a struggle for her, and I think maybe it's something that cannot be worked out between us. I am broken, a lost soul, and I've lost my best friend, my other half. I don't know what to do next."*
Jai could not be reached for comment.

"What's wrong?" Fox asks again with more force than before. I look up from my screen to the road and back down again. This...this can't be real.

I do a web search of my name and Brody's. Shit, it's true. Tons of media sites are posting it. Screenshots of Brody and Royce are everywhere with the captions: **Trying to move past it with friends.**

There are photos of me at the club, of that guy grabbing me and Fox and the guys defending Ren and me. But with it right next to the photo of me kissing Ren...it looks like I was looking for trouble. Like I'm some loose party girl. I feel the burning in my nose and my vision becomes watery.

"Brody," His name comes out like a choked sob. I feel my bottom lip begin to tremble and I try to take a steadying breath. "He got a reporter to slam me online. They made me out to be some selfish drunk party girl while he is the doting boyfriend that I stomped all over." I say softly, staring straight ahead as reality hits me like a bucket of ice water.

Brody just canceled me.

FOX OPENS the passenger door to his black pickup truck and I'm only mildly aware of his large hands on my lower back and side as he helps me in. I feel numb, and there is zero chance I could recap what has happened over the last two hours. My phone hasn't stopped going off. There are rapid dings, vibrations and phone calls every couple of minutes. And on top of that, we went to pick Dad's ashes up, and they wanted me to select his urn. It was too much and at some point, I completely shut down. And when I shut down, Fox took over. He silenced my phone before stuffing it into his jeans pocket. He talked to the people and, I guess, chose the urn. Now he is helping me into his truck because between my short stature, his high truck, and the fact that I'm zoned out, shaking, and have a death grip on the small brown box that says - **HUMAN REMAINS - PIERCE, TONY** - I am completely useless.

The ride is silent as he drives us back to my apartment. My brain is short-circuiting. I'm thinking a thousand thoughts and no thoughts at the same time. All the while, I cannot let go of Dad.

Six pounds.

That is what my larger-than-life father has been reduced to. His bright blue eyes, and booming laugh. His intimidating frame but teddy bear heart. His light, his love, his protection...it's been condensed to this small box that weighs six pounds.

I shake harder as memories start taking over my overwhelming "not thinking" thoughts. The bedtime stories, the coloring sessions, the pizza, and movies. The tattoo he had on top of his hand that I did at nine. My name with a winky face over the "i." That tattoo is gone now. And with it, my greatest protector. Despite our differences at the end, I knew Dad was always in my corner. And if I ever needed help, he was there.

But now, here I am. I'm alone and scared. I need help and he's not here. I'm alone... holy shit. I'm actually alone.

"JANIE!" Fox's booming voice and firm hands on my arms snap me back into reality. I look around—we are in his driveway.

"What?" My chest hurts, and I'm panting. I touch my face, noticing it's wet from tears that I didn't know I had been crying. Fox is standing at the passenger side of the truck. His eyes darting back and forth, and his face looks panicked. His brows knitted together so tight there is only a deep line separating them.

"You've been sobbing and shaking for ten minutes without responding to me." His warm hand cups my cheek, and it feels like someone has wrapped me in one of those anxiety blankets. That one gesture makes me feel safe, even if it's false.

"W-why are we at your house?" I ask softly as he helps me out of the truck.

"Well, besides the fact that I'm not leaving you alone in this condition." He states, gesturing to me. "Did you not see the front of your apartment?"

I blink and try to think. I don't even remember driving away from the crematorium. I shake my head slowly, and he lets out a sigh, rubbing the back of his neck.

"Janie, there was a mob of people trying to get into your building. How do your followers know where you live? I thought all of that was private."

My head starts spinning, and my legs start to tremble. It's too much. It's all too much. There is a loud ringing in my ears, and I feel myself beginning to fall, but Fox's strong arms catch me, and lift me up. I rest my head against his firm chest and listen to his heartbeat as he begins to walk. The warmth and safety I feel at this moment are enough to make me want to fall asleep. I'm almost embarrassed to admit that I dread him letting me go. Walking inside, Fox sits me on his oversized brown couch before kneeling in front of me.

"How about I take this box and –"

"No." I interrupt, my tone sharper than I intend. "No," I repeat softer, almost as a plea while I grip the box tighter. "I...I'm not ready to...to..."

"Shh," He whispers as he runs a thumb over my cheek. I look at him and my walls completely crumble. I know he sees it by the pained look on his own face. I let out the loudest sob as I stare at him.

"I want my dad." I cry out and in an instant, I am buried in his chest, his arms wrapping firmly around me.

"It's okay, baby doll," I feel him pressing his lips to the top of my head. "Let it out, I'll keep you safe." I have no idea how long I cried into Fox's chest. But he never complained. Never moved me away, never shifted. He simply held me and continuously stroked my head and told me I was safe, and I believed him.

I close my eyes and bury myself deep into his soft chest.

He smells so inviting, and I allow it to ground me. Amber-wood and pepper hints fill my nose as I feel him rest his chin on top of my head.

"You're going to be okay, baby doll." His voice is soft, and so far, away, like I'm losing consciousness.

"I'm here. You aren't alone."

Chapter Twelve

FOX

THE NEWS PLAYS on the television at a low volume as Janie snores lightly on top of me, her small hand still clutching Tony's box of ashes. I didn't understand earlier what she meant when she said that her boyfriend... her *ex-boyfriend* had "canceled" her.

I had pulled up to her apartment building, already apprehensive about leaving her alone after how upset and overwhelmed she was during the meeting to pick up Tony's ashes. But when we got to her building and I saw the literal mob of men and women holding signs, several of which said *"Jai the Slut"* filled me with so much blinding rage I very nearly pulled over and beat the shit out of each one of them. I couldn't leave her at her place, there was no way. Somehow, they found her home address, Janie was no longer safe in that apartment. There was zero chance I was allowing her to stay there alone. So, the only logical solution was to bring Janie here.

The whole ride, she was glazed over, crying, shaking, and whispering that she was alone. I've never felt the amount of heartache and helplessness that I did during that ride. And never did I think Janie would be the person I would feel it for. When I got her to the couch, I watched as she completely broke. There was nothing left of the armor that her petite body wore every day, she was broken, vulnerable, raw and scared. And in that moment, I realized it was time to put our petty differences aside. I need to protect her. She's alone in this world, her life has been chewed up and spit out and I didn't have it in me to allow her to go through this on her own.

Once Janie had fallen asleep in my arms, I maneuvered her back onto the couch and intended to get up.

Really, I did.

Well, mostly. Regardless, my intentions did not matter because when I "tried" to move, she started crying and held onto me like Tony's box. So that's what led us to be here. Me, lying on the couch with her tightly tucked into my chest. She's so peaceful when she's sleeping, and I notice her tremors are gone, which gives me some sense of peace. I'm glad to know that at least in her sleep her body can rest.

I look at my phone and sigh. While I admit I'm not up with most of the inner workings of social media, I'm not a complete idiot. One simple web search for *"Jai"* and all the articles appeared. The hateful comments, photos of her and I as I helped her out of the club. Meanwhile, that mother-fucking poor excuse of a human, Brody, looks like the fucking victim.

I don't understand. Where are the photos of him with other women? Fuck what about the video of him getting a lap dance? But everywhere I looked, it turned up empty. It was as though the social media sites **wanted** her to be "canceled", as she put it.

I turn my attention back to the sleeping redhead on my

chest. I brush the wild curls out of her red face. She groans in protest and nuzzles into my neck. I close my eyes and take a slow breath, willing my treacherous cock to stay the fuck down. I notice her loosened grip on Tony's box, and I take the opportunity to grab the box and set it over on my end table. I love Tony but having him on my chest with his daughter while fighting an erection is too much.

Janie whimpers my name in the softest, saddest tone I've ever heard, as her now free hand trails up my neck and into my beard. How far do I let this go before I am no longer a caring person but instead a pervert?

Fucking dick, come on, man! I stare at the prominent bulge painfully pressing against my jeans and fuck, I can't be thinking like this about her! It was bad enough in the shop the other week, but I chalked that up to us both being filled with so much anger we just exploded. It was a mistake. But this would be different, she's fragile, and there is no way I'm taking advantage of her like this.

It's killing me that I am having an increasingly difficult time remembering why I need to continue to look at her as Tony's daughter and not a grown woman.

Fucking hell.

I OPEN my eyes and look around the dark room. I grab my phone and squint to see the time, *ten o'clock.*

Looking down, I see that Janie is no longer in a tight ball, but instead, she has her head under my chin, arms under my armpits, and she's straddling my waist. I notice a wet sensation on my neck and move my hand to feel the small puddle of...oh for fucks sake; the girl is drooling on my neck. I don't know who I am more disgusted with. Her for doing it, or me for kind of finding it adorable.

"Torch." I tap her shoulder. I really need to get up. I need to piss, my old body is stiff, and I'm starving.

"Torch." I say louder as I start moving. She grumbles but wakes up. I feel her whole body stiffen, and her breathing stops.

"Fox?" Her voice is small, I respond with a short *mhm*, and she groans.

"I was hoping that it was all a bad dream." She sits up and maneuvers off of my waist. Funny, I wanted her off, and now that her weight is gone, I need it back. Shaking those ridiculous thoughts out of my head, I stand up and stretch my stiff body out.

"Are you hungry?" I ask as I watch her eyeing her phone. She blinks and looks up at me.

"I'm starving." I nod and pull out my wallet, handing it to her.

"Pizza or Chinese will deliver this late. I don't care which, just get a lot from either." She gives me a slow nod before I head to the bathroom. I need to piss and probably rub one out if she's going to be staying the night.

"I SWEAR TO GOD, Fox, I will throw my shoe at your television if you make me watch the news for one more second." I laugh as I watch Janie take a large spoonful of fried rice and shove it into her mouth.

She has changed into one of my hoodies, and I would be

a fucking liar if I didn't admit that seeing her swimming around in my large clothes didn't do something to me. It was adorable when she ran out in it, squealing in delight that my hoodies were like Snuggies on her. And with her bare legs sitting criss cross the hem is inching up her thighs so very slowly.

My eyes go to the box sitting on my end table, and I can feel Tony's warning gaze burning into me.

Janie is off-limits.

That was the number one rule in Hel's Ink. The moment anyone looked at her for a second too long, Tony would take them out back and put the fear of God in them. I watched many men try to get apprenticeships or shop jobs at Hel's just to try and get in with Janie, especially when she got big online. Tony had strict rules about us not following or watching his daughter's videos or pictures. Of course, he couldn't really enforce that, but the man certainly tried. And I don't know. I guess I just believe in respecting that wish of his. Tony gave me so much that it is the least I could do.

But now, it is becoming increasingly hard to look at this fully grown woman and see her as Tony's kid, which is filling me with a kind of disgusting guilt that I hadn't expected. Though that guilt hasn't stopped the masturbation sessions I've had thinking about her since we made out. Including the *three* since she and I woke up. Three. I am forty-three God damn years old and I had to jerk off three times in the last two and a half hours. Like I said, disgusting guilt.

"Are you even listening?" Her voice catches me off guard, and I see her staring quizzically at me.

"Sorry," I mutter, straightening my posture. "You talk so much it becomes white noise after a while."

"Listen here, old man, I will take you down." I laugh as Janie stands on the couch and points an accusatory finger at me. My eyes betray me as they go from her challenging glare down to her bare, creamy legs. Like the rest of her, her legs were dusted with light freckles, and - God help me - I need to know how each one tastes.

"Fine," I say, needing the subject to change quickly before I have to excuse myself for a fourth time. "What would you like to watch?" I hand her the remote, and as her fingers touch mine, a jolt courses through my body, ending in my dick. Yep, number four is coming. Mother fucker, I should have better control over my –

"Oh, The Office! Score!" I look at her as she starts up the episode before grabbing an egg roll out of the container in my hand and tucking her knees into the hoodie.

"You like The Office?" I am unsure what I'm feeling. Possibly shock? I mean, that's a little dumb to be shocked. The show is popular, and it cannot be that weird that two people like it.

"Yeah," Her mouthful of egg roll squeezes at my chest. God, I need to get laid.

Wait, was that it? Maybe all of this…. whatever I'm feeling for Janie is because I haven't had sex in a while, and she's just a girl that has been in close proximity to me.

I lean back, feeling a lot more relaxed with this new revelation.

"I love watching The Office." She beams. "It's my comfort show. I fall asleep with it playing on my laptop most nights."

Fuck.

"R-really?" I say skeptically as my body goes rigid when she leans over me to pluck a dumpling from the container.

"Oh yeah," She says while eyeing each dumpling. God

damn she smells good. This is wrong...This is wrong... Grandma in a nightie. Saggy tits, toilet paper stuck to the ass, PLEASE make this boner go down.

"I'm not as big of a fan when Michael Scott leaves," She pops the worthy dumpling into her mouth. "I mean, I'll watch them, but I don't binge them as much." She stops talking and stares at me. "What is it?"

I open my mouth to speak, but I can't. Instead, I reach my hand up to her face and run my thumb over her bottom lip. She inhales sharply, snapping me out of my lust-filled stupor.

"You had a ummm..." I quickly rubbed her lip again to act as though I was removing a crumb. I watch her neck and cheeks pink up and she turns away from me to watch the show.

Smooth Fox. Fucking smooth.

Chapter Thirteen

JANIE

"I'M FINE!" Fox grumbles as he manages some kind of impressive cough sneeze hybrid. I roll my eyes as I watch him grab *another* blanket and wrap it around himself. He kept me up most of the night last night because I could hear him coughing, sneezing, puking and whining. Seriously, for a big strong lumberjack man, he's kind of a wimp when he has a cold.

"Fox, you are sick." I pinch the bridge of my nose in frustration. "I've already texted the guys and Atlas says that, while he is not concerned about your plague because his mom used to make him get sick with his siblings, Derek has threatened to hide your machines if you try to come in. And to let you know that yes, that includes Vanessa."

He groans as his massive, shivering body falls onto his couch, still in his cocoon.

"Listen," I think he is trying to sound authoritative, but the floral quilt and the muffling of his voice due to the couch cushion is making it very hard to take him seriously. "I am going to stay home today because I feel like I deserve a day off. But that doesn't mean I'm too sick and also, I am putting At in charge so don't think about going in there and trying to take over. And you tell Derek that I know the exact position Vanessa was left in and if she is touched in anyway, I will come over there and ram my tongue down his throat."

God he's such an idiot.

I shake my head as I sit next to his head deciding we would circle back to that later. "So, you'd put Atlas in charge over me?" Sitting this close I notice his body shaking and I am starting to wonder if he has a high fever.

"Yes." He says into the cushion.

"Why?" I ask only half interested in his response as I stand to go to the kitchen. I need to see what he has in terms of medication.

"I trust his judgment." I hear him say and I bark out a laugh as I look at his empty medicine cabinet. Only the smallest bottle of ibuprofen and it's expired – by four years.

"You trust the judgment of a man who got his butthole tattooed, over me?" I cross my arms over my chest as I stare down at him in shock. Fox perks up, wincing as he does so. He grips the back of his couch and points his finger at me.

"It was the ass cheek, and it was for charity." I give him an incredulous look before realization hits me.

"Oh my god...you have the same tattoo!" His grey face goes even paler, and he curls his accusatory finger back to his chest before covering his head with the blanket.

"I don't want to talk about it." He grumbles and I cannot hide the massive grin on my face.

"Show me."

I hear him attempt a scoff, but he ends up coughing. "I am NOT showing you, my ass."

I roll my eyes and humph. "Fine, I guess I will just leave

you here to die by yourself. I wonder how much I can sell your tattoo guns on eBay for."

"They are machines, you know that you brat!" He growls and flips me off as I leave his house.

I FROWN, pulling back into Fox's driveway. While on my way to Hel's, I had sent Fox a text saying to check his temperature. To which I got zero reply. I figured he was being a dick, or asleep. But I sat at the shop for all of ten minutes and... I don't know, I hated the thought of him being sick alone and then knowing he had nothing to make him feel better. So, I left, much to Derek's pleasure – the fucking germaphobe – and went to the pharmacy. After leaving there I tried to call Fox, and I got nothing, literally, it went straight to voicemail.

So now here I am, in a downpour, trying to carry these bags up the wooden steps that lead to his wrap-around porch and front door. I open the door and instantly hear the sounds of vomiting. I wince at the violent noises and make my way into the kitchen.

"What are you doing here?" His weak, gruff voice says as he walks into the kitchen several minutes later.

"You weren't answering your phone and you have nothing here to help you with your cold, so I went to the pharmacy." I walk up to him and press my hand to his forehead before jerking it back.

"Fox, you're hot!" I watch as he tries to give me a sly grin, but it doesn't deliver. I grab a thermometer and begin to unpack the device and pop it in his mouth. "Go get on the couch." He groans but does as he is told as I grab him some drinks and medicine.

When I walk out, I snatch the thermometer out of his mouth and sigh.

"One hundred and two." I set the thermometer down before taking off his blankets. He whines and then I see he has layers of clothing on.

"Jesus, Fox, are you trying to kill yourself?" I begin to pull his hoodie off and he fights me.

"Stop it, Torch! I'm cold!" He snaps, and I feel bad, his teeth are chattering so hard I fear they may break.

"I know, it's the fever." I say softly as I place a hand on his burning cheek. "Trust me and let me take care of you, okay?" He stops fighting. I'm not sure if it is because he wants to trust me or because he is that exhausted. Either way, I take advantage of it and finish stripping off his multiple layers of shirts and hoodies.

Once he is left in a white undershirt, I grab his blanket and wrap it around him. "Okay, it's noon, so I'll give you this now..." I mumble to myself as I open the cold medicine and hand him two pills and a bottle of water. Once he takes it, I make a note in my phone, so I remember when to give him another dose.

"Alright, are you hungry? I can make you some soup?" Fox shakes his head.

"I'm really not, I am just nauseous." I nod and decide to give the medicine some time to work before forcing food on him.

I go to stand and give the large man the couch to lay on, but Fox grabs my wrist with his scalding hand. I try to ignore the pounding in my heart as I look from his tattooed hand to his hazy, red rimmed eyes.

"Don't." He whispers firmly and I wrinkle my forehead in confusion. "Stay, please."

"I wasn't leaving," Stroking the top of his hand with mine, I give him a small smile. "I was just going to give you the couch, I can hang out on the porch or something and listen to the rain."

"Stay." His voice is firmer this time, and his gaze is fixed on our hands. "Please."

I inhale deeply before nodding and curling up on the end of the couch. I motion for Fox to come to me, which he quickly does, and I guide him down to my lap. I can feel him hesitating at first, but after a brief coughing fit, Fox rests his head on my lap. I pull his blanket over his broad shoulders before I begin running my fingers through his long, sandy blonde hair.

"You smell good." I hear him mumble. I look down and notice his eyes are shut.

"Thanks, I try to hose down every now and then." My joke causes him to give me a weak chuckle.

"I like you, Torch." I feel my heart flip flop at his confession. I look down at him, my mouth agape. What should I say? How does he mean that? How should I take it?

I must ponder this for too long because after a moment I hear his soft snores. I can't help but smile. This giant tattooed, mean asshole is cuddled on my lap under a floral quilt snoring and not wanting to be alone because he doesn't feel good. It makes me wonder how many colds Fox has had where he wanted something like this, and he was forced to deal with it alone.

Unlike Ash and Atlas, Fox never mentions women. I mean, I'm sure he dates, someone that looks like him would have to... right?

Still, in the time I've been here, there hasn't been one girl that stopped by.

I like you Torch.

I sink my teeth into my bottom lip to try to hold back my smile as I continue to run my fingers through his hair.

I think I like you too, Fox.

"ARE you sure you're going to be alright?" I ask hesitantly as I stand in front of the door to leave. Fox rolls his eyes before giving me a look of complete annoyance.

"Torch," His poor voice is so raspy. "I am fully capable of handling myself. Go to work and make sure the guys didn't burn it down." I let out a sigh and grab the keys to his truck.

"Fine, but you better stay up on your medicine! And I want a temperature picture every two hours." I state as I grab my purse and phone.

He gives me half a salute. "Yes mom. Would you also like updates on my urine output?"

I raise a brow, "Color and frequency." Grinning at his one finger wave, I walk out of the house with the umbrella and head towards the truck to go to Hel's.

As I drive through the rain towards the city, I try to ignore the vibrations of my phone alerts. I haven't had my phone on except when I left yesterday to get Fox medicine. It's been nice. It's quiet, being in the dark on what is happening, what others are saying about me. But I know it can't last, eventually I am going to have to face the music.

"Not today though." I whisper to myself as I turn into the parking lot of Hel's Ink. "I'm Janie today, not Jai."

"DEREK," I groan, in exasperation. "It's just a cold! He's doing better today, and I feel fine."

"Back, Janie." He warns while holding up a bottle of disinfectant while he secures his face mask over his nose. "I like you and all, but I will unload this entire can on you without a second thought."

I shake my head and walk over to Atlas, who is currently swiping on Tinder.

"You think she's hot?" He asks while shoving his phone in my face. I look at the petite girl with green eyes and raven hair.

"Her eyes are fake, that hair is a wig, and that photo has been warped." I state handing the phone back to him. He frowns and looks at the picture as if it betrayed him.

"What's this world coming to when you can't trust the hook up sites?" I snort and shake my head as I see the next profile that shows up. I watch Atlas' hand twitch over a photo of Ren. She looks really pretty, though totally not the typical Tinder profile. She is smiling, her long hair in a loose side braid. She has on light make up and is wearing a flowy autumn color maxi dress with little flowers and a neckline that clings to her very blessed chest.

"Oh shit," I muse. "Get it Ren." I watch the muscle in Atlas' sharp jaw tick as he shuts his phone off before standing up.

"So, did you kill Fox?" He asks and I can tell he is trying

hard to move on from what he saw. His hand continues to clench and unclench as he walks back and forth straightening...nothing. What is he doing?

"Uh-" I let out a laugh. "No? He's probably vegetating on the couch... or hurling in the toilet." Atlas smirks as he leans against his station. "Spending quite a lot of private time with the old man, don't you think?"

I raise a skeptical brow. "I suppose." I say slowly. "But I had a rough day and then he got sick. It would've been an asshole move to leave him with a fever."

He gives me a short shrug. "Hey, I ain't saying anything...just that a couple of months ago you would've prayed that this would be the end for him. Now you're rubbing his feet."

"It was his head!" I shoot back before realizing what I've said. I stare at Atlas with wide eyes, his eyes match mine, though where mine - I'm sure - show horror, Atlas looks like a kid on Christmas morning.

"Shut up." I warn and look at the other two, equally shocked men. "All of you! He was sick and I was trying to be... Atlas stop it!" I shove him, though it's no use, he stands like a massive statue grinning that stupid grin.

"Fox and Janie sitting in a tree..." Atlas sings as Ash and Derek snicker.

"You all can kiss the fattest part of my ass. I'm out of here." I grumble as I grab my bag and head out as they all make kissing noises. I know that they are busting chops and I'm not *that* pissed off. More so embarrassed that I let that slip.

"Fox is going to kill me." I mutter.

Chapter Fourteen

FOX

CRACKING OPEN MY EYES, I look around the dimly lit room. I hear *The Office* playing at a low volume on the TV. I move my stiff arms, feeling overly hot and uncomfortable. A small groan sounds from under me and my pillow moves. I look down and see in the shadows that my *pillow* is actually a soft, freckle clad and very bare stomach.

Fucking shit.

I sit up and Janie's small hand falls out of my hair as she continues to sleep. I try to recall today's events that would've led me to nuzzling into her bare abdomen while we slept. I remember feeling alright during the day while she was at work, but the later it got, the crappier I started to feel. I remember after she got back, she made God-awful soup, seriously, how do you make bad soup? Then we watched tv and... I look back at her and groan in frustration as my cock betrays me again. I stand from the couch just as a loud rumble of thunder rattles the house and windows. I look to see the redhead still out cold. Honestly, it's concerning what she can sleep through.

I remove my socks and let my feet feel the cool hardwood floor as I make my way to the sliding glass door. I open it and step outside, enjoying the cool air and the loud rain. If Janie saw me out here, she would probably scream since I'm *so sick*. I smile at that thought, then scold myself for smiling. The last thing I want to do is read too much into this.

I'm sick, she is just being nice.

Really nice.

I try to remember the last time I had someone take care of me, but I am drawing a blank. My mom and sister were not people that took care of you, but instead were ones that needed caring for. Don't get it twisted, my mom and sister, Lacey, were as loving as they could be. But given the fact that we were trapped in a home with an abusive man, and they needed my protection, love was something that was put on the back burner.

I stare at the streetlight and the rain streaming through the light. I hate thinking about them. I hate that I couldn't give them the life they deserved, and I hate that my fucker of a father outlived them both. Thinking about the accident that took my mom and sister is hard. Forgiving the driver that hit them because he was overworked and fell asleep at the wheel is even harder. But the thing that will eat away at me until the day I die is, I had just moved out here to start an apprenticeship with Tony after he had seen my work at a shop back in Washington. I had barely been in my apartment a couple months when it was decided that Mom and Lacey would come down to live with me. I was finally getting my shit together and able to get them away from my father, for good, it would've been tight for a while. We would've struggled, but they would've been safe.

I wince as I feel the sharp pain in my chest and the guilt washes over me like it always does.

"Fox?" Janie's sleepy little voice pulls me out of my thoughts. I can't help but smile slightly as she rubs her sleepy eyes. "How are you feeling?"

"Better." I say softly as she walks up to me, eyes still squinty. She puts her hand on my head, then down my cheek and fuck I feel like I want to melt into her touch.

"Are you crying?" My eyes widen as I feel her wiping the moisture off my face with her thumb.

"What? Torch, come on. I may be sick but I'm not crying." I pull my face out of her grasp and jerk my thumb over my shoulder. "It's raining."

"Yeah, from your eyeballs." She deadpans, not accepting my excuse.

I rub the back of my head. "It's... nothing. Just thinking about my mom and sister." I watch her face soften and inwardly groan.

"Don't do it." I warn and her innocent eyes grow wide.

"Do what?" She huffs.

"I don't..." I make a grunt, uncomfortable with the direction the conversation is going. "I don't talk about them, I don't want to open up, and I don't need your pity or sympathy." Her arms cross over her chest and she shrugs.

"I wasn't going to give you pity or sympathy, trust me. I've given you enough over the last couple of days." Her voice is clipped as she speaks before she turns on her heel to go back inside but I stop her.

"Wait." I wince, feeling bad for snapping. "I'm sorry. You're right. Thank you for being so nice to me. It's been a really long time since anyone has..." My voice trails off and I look down at her as she steps closer.

"Has what?" She asks and I blink several times as I try to find the words. Fuck her smell is intoxicating when she's this close. It is inviting and mysterious, floral but light and it drives me mad that I can't pinpoint the exact smell.

"Has," I sigh and look down at her, deciding just this once to open up a little. Even if it is to Hel's brat. "Has cared for me... or about me." I admit and feel a wave of embarrassment wash over me. Janie doesn't laugh, and she doesn't stare at me in pity. She cocks her head and stands on her tiptoes as she pressed her soft, pillowy lips to my cheek. The moment is so gentle and sweet I start to feel emotional.

Fuck this cold and shit making me weak.

Her small arms wrap around my neck as she holds me to her small frame. I wait for her to speak, but she doesn't. She simply holds me to her as the rain continues to pour around us in the cool night. I stand motionless for several seconds before I snake my arms around hers. I'm sure she can feel the hard hammering of my heartbeat in my chest. The way she is holding me, it's unlike anything I've ever felt. My whole life I've been the strong one, the protector, the one that fixed everything. And when it came to women, there was no hugging or holding. I made sure they felt good and left satisfied, but I made sure they left. This now, with Janie...it is something that I didn't realize I have been craving. And it's scaring the absolute fuck out of me.

Chapter Fifteen

JANIE

THIS CANNOT BE REAL LIFE.

I must've been in a horrible accident where I suffered severe head trauma and am now in a coma, and this is my dreamlike state. That is the only plausible explanation for what I'm witnessing on the back of Fox's porch.

The axe slices through the giant piece of wood like a hot knife through butter. And when the very shirtless, sweaty Fox grunts on the axe's impact to the stump underneath... my thighs one hundred percent squeeze together. Again, cannot be real life.

Fox glances up to spot me and I am welcomed to the view of his powerful, tattoo covered body glistening in the sun from the sweat running down him.

"I'm going to start charging a viewing fee if you keep watching." He calls out with a smirk, and I flip him my middle finger.

"What are you doing?" I ask as I walk down the steps of the porch to get closer to him. Bad move, he's hotter up close. I can see his bulging muscles, hear his labored breathing, see that light trail of hair slipping below his jeans.

"I'm baking a pie." He deadpans. There he goes, ruining my fucking fantasy with reminding me that it is in fact *Fox* that I am staring at like a starving lioness.

"Listen smart ass," I growl as I glare up at him. "I'm trying to figure out why your senior citizen ass is out here chopping wood when the risk for a heart attack dramatically increases for men your age."

I watch as Fox drops the axe into the stump and walks closer to me. He leans down and stares into my eyes and his mouth pulls, forming a playful smirk.

"Torch," He breathes, his voice low and gravelly. "You had better stop being so mean to me before I fall in love with you." He gives me a wink before looking behind me towards the driveway as Atlas' *Tahoe* and Ren's *Rav4* pull up, thank God for their timing because the blush I can feel creeping up my face is almost too much.

Fox heads over to greet everybody as we are doing a small party for Ren getting her first "Real Lawyer" job at a law firm downtown. I wave my hands in front of my face to cool my flaming cheeks down before running over to the group.

"SO," Stevie starts while she and Ren help me set out all the food that's just been delivered. "You just live here, platonically... with Fox?" I raise my gaze to my friend and must suppress the feeling of jealousy that starts to surface.

"Yeah, why?" I ask, probably too harshly. Stevie shakes her head as realization comes over her.

"No no no! I'm not into him." She waves her hands. "I just...I've seen the way he looks at you." She shrugs as she pulls out some bottles of beer to stuff into the cooler of ice.

"How does he look at me?" I ask and Ren snorts.

"The same way you look at him." She mumbles as she elbows me playfully but her face falls and she instantly busies herself as Atlas walks up to us.

"My god, look at these lovely ladies." He beams as he walks towards the cooler. "I've come to offer my...services." He waggles his eyebrows suggestively as he flexes his bicep.

"Sure," Ren says quickly as she moves out of the way. "Take it out back." She mutters before walking back into the kitchen. Once out of earshot, I look hard at Atlas who surprisingly looks as though someone told him Christmas was canceled.

"What did you do?" I groan and he stares at me, offended by my question.

"Red, I swear..." He states while holding his hands up in defense. "I haven't seen her since your birthday, I have no idea. But she's been like this since we all met up at the donut shop."

I give him a skeptical look but nod. "Tell the guys we're grabbing the food and will be right out." I say as I watch him heave the full cooler like it was nothing and walk back outside.

Ren comes back out of the kitchen with plastic cutlery and dishes. "What?" She asks.

"You know whatever Atlas did," I start and notice instantly that she stiffens. "He probably didn't mean it."

Ren shakes her head and starts towards the door. "It's

nothing. He just made a comment that made me think he might've seen my tinder profile." My face falls and I open my mouth but Ash walks in before I can speak.

"Listen," He sighs as he leans against the doorframe. "You have four very large, very hungry men out here. If you don't feed us soon, we will result to fist fighting each other." I sigh and shake my head as we all head out to the table.

"SO HOW IS it going with the Brody thing?" Stevie asks as we all sit around the fire pit after dinner. The sun was setting, and we were all in our own Adirondack chairs, drinking beer and shooting the shit. It's something I've never really had in my life and, up until this moment, I was enjoying it.

Shifting uncomfortably, I let out a breath and look at everyone staring at me. "Yeah, I guess I should update you guys."

"Oh," Stevie shrugs. "You absolutely don't have to do that! I didn't know this was personal, it's constantly being brought up online."

"Yeah, I know," I grip my hands tightly as they begin to shake harder. "Apparently, I cheated on him," My eyes flash to Fox's for a second, but it was enough to tell me he was staring at me too. "And I have an alcohol problem and need to go to rehab. There is also talk that I've been stealing money from my sponsors and not making good on contracts, which is bullshit and I'm having Frank look into it after next week since the shop will be closed."

Fox clears his throat to get my attention. "You aren't going to Vegas with us?"

I shake my head. "No, I need to deal with this, and I was thinking about trying to get to a meet and greet happening around that time, maybe I can get this turned around." I watch as he rolls his eyes and looks back to Ash.

"Bro this convention is going to be awesome!" Ash grins as he sits back. "No babysitters and in Vegas. I'm going to get so much pus–"

"Okay." I state as everyone groans. "Your main objective is to represent the shop, not bury your dick."

"I mean," Atlas shrugs. "Can't we do both? Which reminds me Fox, I need your phone so I can set up your tinder like we talked about." My heart sinks and my eyes shoot straight to Fox who looked mortified.

"Well," I force a smile to hide the fact that I want to cry suddenly. "I hope you all have fun and don't come back with an STD. Now excuse me, I need to pee." I state sending glances at Ren and Stevie who follow me back up to the house. I need away from the guys, away from Fox right now. I don't want to think about him going to the convention and fucking other girls. It hurts too much and I'm not ready to delve into why.

Chapter Sixteen

FOX

AS SOON AS the girls are in the house, I take an unopened can of pop out of the cooler and hurl it at Atlas, hitting him in the knee.

"Mother fuck Fox!" He cries out as he grips his knee. "What in the fuck was that for?"

"Tinder? Really?" I growl, itching to hit him again.

"Yeah Tinder! You said weeks ago you needed help setting it up before Vegas because your old ass couldn't figure it out. I think you broke my femur." He whines and Derek snorts from behind his water bottle.

"Your kneecap is the *patella* you idiot."

Atlas glares at the man before standing up and trying to square off. "Yeah? Well, if you're so smart, what's it called when you get your dick broke in half?"

I close my eyes, preparing for the comeback. Derek lets out a chuckle. "That's called letting your mama ride on top."

"That's it Virginia boy!" Atlas goes to lunge at the chuckling man who hasn't moved from his chair. I get in between and shove Atlas towards the driveway.

"Come on Atlas, walk it off." I state as I walk with him. Once we were no longer within earshot, I turn to my best friend and really look at him for the first time in the last couple of days. He looks tired, on edge, his eyes look blood-shot, and his shoulders are rolling inward. All things that are not normal for him.

"What's going on man?" I ask him as I lean against my truck.

Atlas scoffs and rolls his eyes. "You busted my kneecap and then fucking diva Derek over there made a mom joke. That's against our code. We agreed on no mom jokes."

"First off, I'll talk to him about the mom joke, though you hate your mom so I'm not seeing the–"

Atlas cuts me off. "It's the principle. Bro code man."

I hold my hands up. "Fair enough. Anyway, the kneecap thing barely phased you, you're being a bitch about it. What is going on, you look like shit." I watch as At groans in frustration while running his hand over his jaw.

"Lauren is mad at me, and I don't know why." He mutters quietly.

"Okay, and?" I wait for him to finish but he just looks at me.

"And what?" He asks finally.

I sigh and pinch the bridge of my nose. "AND what if she is?"

He scoffs like I just insulted him. "It's driving me insane!" He yells as he waves his arms around. "I'm adorable, funny, and charming." He counts on his fingers. "There is *zero* reason for her to be mad at me, yet she is, and it is driving me insane! I can't eat, I can't sleep, I can't fuck."

I smirk at my friend and shake my head at his frustration. Atlas must be loved. If you don't love him, it will eat at him until he remedies the situation.

"Did you ask her what you did?" I ask, trying to fake the seriousness that he is expecting in this situation. At has a crush on Ren. Of course, he will never act on said crush because Ren is in a different world than us, especially now with her job at this new firm. We all look like criminals; we are the men that the moms warn their daughters about. So, I've watched how At refuses to sit next to Ren when we hang out. Or how he will not tattoo her. He will flirt with her, shamelessly, but only in public so he can use the excuse that he is like that with everyone. Which is somewhat true, though he doesn't look at anyone the way he looks at her.

"Can you just…" Atlas trails off as the group makes their way over to us, minus Janie. I frown and look towards Stevie and Ren. My question must be evident because Stevie speaks up.

"She got a death threat sent to her DM, her tremors are really bad, I don't think she could stand for long." Apparently, while I was out sick last week, Janie went ahead and told our group about her condition, I was proud of her for opening up to them, and happy that the guys knew better than to give her shit, but a selfish part of me was a little annoyed, because I enjoy knowing things about her no one else does.

"Death threat?" I growl as Stevie's words click in my head. I say goodbye to everyone and take my stairs two and three at a time until I get to the door and walk in. I look around the empty living room, hearing a sniffle in the back of the house, I walk towards my room and open the door. I freeze when I see Janie hugging her knees while sitting in the middle of my bed. This is weird because Janie has a bedroom, with a bed.

"Torch?" My voice causes her to stiffen, she turns her head and brushes her hair out of her face to look at me. My heart sinks at her tear-stained face. "Baby doll..." I whisper and apparently that does her in. She crumples into a ball and starts sobbing. In an instant, I'm on the bed, scooping her into my arms and pressing her head to my chest.

"They know..." She says between sobs.

"Know what baby?" I ask softly as I run my hand over the side of her face.

"A-about the shop...they're going t-to hurt me there." My blood runs cold and I pull her away to look at her sobbing body.

"Who?" I ask, trying to keep the panic from my voice. I need to know who is going to try to hurt her. I'll destroy them before they even get the chance. She shakes her limp head before curling back into my chest.

"I don't know." She whispers. "The DM is from a spam account."

"I'm going to add cameras around the building," I state firmly as I hold her tighter. "And no more walking alone to your car. I know you said you aren't going to Vegas, fine. But I'm going to see if you can stay with Ren while I'm gone to keep you safe." I hear a harsh laugh escape her before she looks up at me.

"Yeah," She sniffles while rolling her teary eyes. "Don't wanna ruin your tinder-thon with the guys."

"Janie —" I groan, and she waves her hand to dismiss me. She tries to move out of my grasp, but I grip her hip to hold her still. Looking up at me, her blue eyes are full of so many emotions it's overwhelming. Fear, sadness, loneliness and maybe lust?

No...that's–

My thoughts go unfinished as she straddles my lap and presses her lips to mine. I don't think, I just react. I grip her perfect ass in one hand as the other runs up to the back of her neck so I can control her better. It becomes evident to me very quickly though; Janie isn't handing over control without a fight.

I groan against her lips as she grinds against my rapidly hardening cock. She grips my jaw roughly and opens my mouth before slipping her tongue inside. Fuck she feels good. She lures my tongue into her mouth and when I enter, she curls her lips around my tongue before sucking it.

"Holy fuck..." I growl feeling my balls tighten at the act. Her hand makes its way in between and I let out a hiss when she grips my bulge through my pants. She continues to do whatever this pornographic witchcraft is to my mouth and before I know it, my pants are unbuttoned and she's working on the zipper.

Panic begins to fill me. Am I taking advantage of her? She's young, scared, emotional. Fuck.

"J-Janie." I moan out between a pant as her small hand slips in between my jeans and boxers. I know by the smirk on her face her fingers found the wet spot from the pre-cum. She grips me again and I roll my head back. I can't do this.

"Janie..." I say again and I hear her growl in frustration.

"Don't start thinking now Fox." She breathes in my neck before licking my flesh and biting down.

I'm going to cum.

"S-stop!" I all but cry out. In an instant, Janie backs off of me with her hands out.

"I'm sorry, I thought you wanted... I'm really sorry." I

see the embarrassment and rejection on her face. Instantly I feel like a shit, I run my hands over my beard as I let out a sigh.

"No, baby doll...It's not that I just..." I scratch my head trying to come up with the right words. "Janie, I don't feel comfortable doing this with you when you are in this state." Her eyebrow raises.

"What state is that?" The hostility isn't lost on me. Fucking hell.

"A lot has happened in the last week, hell in the last few months and..." I watch as realization washes over her and she looks almost ashamed.

"You're right. I'm sorry, I shouldn't have done that, I think that maybe with everything that has happened. I am just feeling lonely. And you are like the only one I trust... That's stupid. God, I feel so embarrassed right now." She goes to move off the bed, but I stop her.

"Janie...Don't be embarrassed. You aren't the only one that was feeling it alright?" I tuck the lock of hair behind her ear and laugh lightly when it springs back, like always. "Trust me, you about made me cum, which would've been mortifying for me to do that in under two minutes."

She rolls her eyes but nods. "Alright well, I should get to bed. Good night, Fox."

"Night Torch."

I LOOK around my bathroom and frown when I don't see any towels. Figuring Janie took them all to her bathroom to inconvenience me, I chuckle to myself and head down the hall. Janie had gone to bed about an hour ago and there is zero chance I am getting any sleep without rubbing one out. So, figuring I'd kill two birds with one stone, I want to shower and jerk off.

I go into her bathroom and sure enough, all of the towels are neatly folded in the closet.

Brat.

I go to grab several when a soft noise stops me. I'm quiet as I try to listen for the noise again.

"Mmmm...that's it." Janie's soft voice moans. It's then I realize what the faint noise I'm hearing is. It's a vibrator.

My cock is *hard* hard. It was already an annoying semi but now it was a solid rod poking right through my boxers.

Because I'm a pervert, I get closer to the wall and listen as Janie inhales sharply, obviously hitting a special spot between her legs.

"Oh..." She pants, "God I'm so fucking wet." She whispers in almost astonishment. Fuck what does it feel like? What does she taste like? I stifle a groan as I tug at my painfully hard erection. God, she's turning me into a mad man. She is all either of my heads think about, and now, they are working together. My mind envisions her laying on her bed, completely naked, legs spread wide as her vibrator dances over her swollen clit.

I stroke faster to match her faster breathing. Is she playing with her soft tits? God, I want to lick and suck those pebbles while I drive as far into her as her body will allow. I feel my balls pull and my cock pulsates as I am about to fall over the edge. I brace my arm on the sink and prepare to imagine her cumming when her voice sends me over.

"I'm cumming," She lets out a hushed cry. "Oh god! Oh Fox!"

My mouth goes slack as my brain shorts out and I cum

all over my hand as she continues to moan my name over and over while she comes back down.

This is definitely a problem.

Chapter Seventeen

JANIE

I RUB my throbbing temples as I look at the front of Hel's Ink. The window has ***"Jai the Slut"*** crudely painted across it in red.

"They could've at least worked on the calligraphy." Atlas mutters as he and Fox stand on either side of me.

"Or paint it in print, I mean shit." Fox sighs.

"I'll give them points for proper spelling." Atlas jokes and I can feel him looking at me. "As I know how important spelling is." Turning around, I place my fists on my hips and glare at the two men.

"I am *so* happy that you two find this so amusing." I snap.

I don't know how much more I have in me. I am officially canceled on social media. I've lost all my sponsors, and people are connecting the shop with me and have been coming in to harass me, send me death threats or vandalize the place.

Fox shrugs as he puts his hands in his pockets. "Torch, it's alright. It'll take us ten minutes to scrape it off the window. Derek is looking at the security camera, so we will find out who did it." He goes to touch my arm, but I move away.

"You just don't get it." I snap again as I shove past them and walk into the shop, slamming the door behind me.

"Hey, Janie," Derek's deep, oddly calming voice surprises me.

"Oh hey, what's up, Derek?" He motions for me to come over to his station. I look at the screen of the laptop he's on.

"Is this your ex?" I look over his shoulder, and my heart sinks. I feel my entire body deflate as I watch the security camera feed of Brody spray painting the shop's window.

"Yeah." My voice sounds small and dry as I stand up. "That's Brody."

"H-hey don't freak out, it'll be alright." I look at the absolute panic on the man's face as he stares at me like I'm a bomb. It's honestly adorable. Derek comes off as a cold person, an absolute grump. But it's pretty cute when he gets all uncomfortable like this. It's sad though, the fact that he chooses not to get close to people because he doesn't know how to handle people like this. At least that is the conclusion I've come to in the months I've been in contact with him daily.

I give him a reassuring smile and I pat his firm shoulder. "Don't worry," I laugh. "I won't cry in front of you." I laugh harder as he visibly relaxes. "Derek Rowe! You need some serious therapy if my crying got you that tense."

He gives me a light laugh but something in his eyes looks almost pained. "Yeah, did that. Doesn't help. Find it best just to steer clear of females with their tears and shit." I shake my head and decide to let him go back to looking at the cameras while I head to the front counter.

What am I going to do? I've spent my life turning myself into a brand, and now because of Brody, I'm tainted goods.

Unmarketable. No one will endorse me now. To say that I'm terrified is an understatement. But the fear isn't wholly over being canceled. In fact, a lot of my stress is due to the fact that I am not as stressed as I feel I should be after losing my life.

I've been in hell since Dad passed. But I entered the seventh circle of said hell on my birthday and I've been stuck in a nest of anxiety since. Well, except when I am at Fox's. When I am there, he makes me turn my phone off and leave it on the table by the door. And those evenings, I spend doing anything I want. Sometimes we hang out and watch The Office. Other times he's working on a tattoo, or I walk or practice yoga. Not to mention the fights over showers, me showing him how to play Gin, him teaching me how to cook something that didn't come with a seasoning packet included.

And then there was the discovery of how Fox is built the way he is. It's been a long running joke that because of the flannel and his physique, he resembled the paper towel lumberjack. Albeit a heavily tattooed, much hotter version, but still.

Memories of the other night during the party came into my mind. Finding the man, shirtless, swinging a fucking axe like it weighs nothing. Muscles bulging, sweat dripping, and the noises he made... shit.

I thought about that night and attacking him. I was so embarrassed, though not embarrassed enough to not need a release. Like the pervert I am, I went to my room, pulled out my vibrator and I didn't stop until I began to fear he would hear me screaming his name through the pillow.

Running my hands through my hair I glance up at the window as I watch Fox removing his shirt, so it doesn't get stained while he climbs the ladder with a bucket and sponge. I try not to stare, I really do. But watch his tanned, tattooed body move and twist...

"Hey good looking!" I hear a female voice outside and instantly I stand and walk towards the window. Peering out, I see a tall thin brunette with a couple girls flanking her. The brunette is stunning in her black lace skirt that stops mid-thigh and her white crochet top that I'm guessing is supposed to mimic a bikini top.

I watch as Fox finishes washing the window before walking down the ladder. He smiles at the women, and I feel my blood heat instantly.

"Good afternoon, ladies," he says, still with that smile. Why is he smiling at them? Fox doesn't smile at strangers, or hardly anyone. "Watch your step on the sidewalk. Don't want to get those nice shoes dirty."

The brunette giggles. Giggles? He said *nothing* funny. I watch as she puts her long, slender arms behind her back to press out her chest and... that's it.

I walk out the front of the shop and directly in between the brunette and Fox. The woman actually flinches when I look at her.

"You ladies looking for a tattoo?" The amount of hostility in my voice is thankfully not lost on them. Unfortunately, though, the brunette didn't seem to want to back off.

"No," She crosses her arms over her chest, seemingly annoyed. Same girl, same. "Though I might be looking for an evening with a tattooed man." She winks at Fox who instantly shifts uncomfortably.

I glare back at her, "Well there's a biker bar two streets over, they open at four." I watch as she eyes me up and down before huffing a laugh. I know that scan. She's decided I am not a threat to her.

"Why go to a biker bar when I found this one right here. I'm Lily." The way she emphasizes the "L's" in her name grates at me. I go to speak but Fox beats me to it.

"Lily," Oh I don't like her name on his mouth. Not. One. Bit. "While I am very flattered,"

"He's not interested." I growl as I grab his arm and drag him towards the building. He must agree with me because there is no way I would be able to drag him, yet he is following me.

As we reach the door *Lily* scoffs. "Then get the hell off of Tinder if you got someone you pig."

I freeze halfway through the door as I hear Fox mutter a "*fuck*" under his breath. Well, don't I feel like a fucking idiot. I turn to look up at the man towering over me, giving him a slow nod, I turn and walk in the shop before slamming the door in his face.

MOST OF THE afternoon has been spent with Fox and I desperately trying to avoid one another. Thankfully it isn't too hard as he's been working on an appointment for the last three hours. I remember the party and Atlas talking about wanting to put Tinder on his phone, but for whatever reason, I just thought Fox decided against it.

So he was on the app, active and *Lily* saw him and that he was close. And I went out there looking like a goddamn psychotic girlfriend. God I'm an idiot.

Sighing to myself, I decide that I need to focus my attention on something else... *someone* else.

My eyes narrow as I pull out my phone. I scroll through

the hundreds of unanswered texts until I find Brody's name, and I quickly tap out a message, this time refusing to speak to him in that bullshit chat speak.

> Me: I know what you did. Next time wear a hat to cover your purple hair.

It surprises me to see that he chooses to drop the chat speak as well.

> Brody: No idea what you are talking about Jai. I'm really worried about you. I know we are having issues but I still care and want you to get the help you need.

> Me: Wow. Are you planning on uploading these texts to make you look more like the victim? You won okay? You canceled me, enjoy the fame you got by riding me into the ground.

> Brody: It was never about the fame Jai. It was about us. I just cared more about this relationship I guess. That isn't your fault.

> Me: You know what's funny? Never would I, or will I, run you through the mud the way you've done to me. We both know that the internet might hate me, but that's only because I haven't fought back. My following is bigger than yours will EVER be Brody. Hell, I've lost more followers than you've ever had and I still have multiple times your amount. All it would take is one photo and you would be destroyed. Keep that in mind the next time your dumbass decides to spray paint my father's building.

I watch as the dots appear and then disappear, never coming back. Sighing, I put my phone down so I can start inventorying the merchandise. I need to distract myself. Everything is becoming too complicated.

"YOU KNOW we are closed next week, right?" Fox asks as I put the mop away. It's closing time, and we are the only two left in the shop, not that it should matter. He and I have been alone together a lot recently. Still, after this afternoon and us not speaking at all, it just feels weird.

"Yeah," I say as I stretch my arms over my head. "I remember the convention. I'm supposed to go to a meet and greet, but other than that, I'll probably spend my time ordering inventory for here and getting my stuff organized back at my apartment."

"You're going back to your place?" The sharp tone in his deep voice does nothing to hide his obvious irritation. I stare at his now rigid posture and give him a half-shrug.

"Yeah, I mean you won't be at your house, and I am sure you are ready to have your place back to yourself." I try to fake a laugh but it comes out weird. I don't want to go back there. It's lonely, empty and I probably still have people waiting to harass me.

"Stay as long as you need to. You don't bother me...there anyway." He mutters as he becomes overly focused on lining up the labels on his ink bottles. My heart begins to flip flop in my chest, and I go to tell him that he better not be so nice to me, or I might never leave. Until I hear a familiar notification chime, and my whole body deflates.

"Ah, another Tinder hit." I try to make it sound like a joke, but it comes out more like a bitter comment.

Fox rubs his forehead as his eyes look away and...is he blushing? He snatches his phone off of his workstation and turns it on silent mode.

"No! Well...yeah it was. But I didn't download it...At did yesterday." Was that supposed to make it okay?

Wait...why wasn't it okay? He's single. The churning in my stomach tells me exactly why it wasn't okay with me. Somehow, the man I hated to my very core, found a way to twist my hatred into something else. Something warm and nice but also confusing and uncomfortable.

"Well," I force a small smile his way even though I want to fucking die inside. Why does this have to bother me as much as it does?

Maybe because a couple of weeks ago, he kissed me in a way that I had never experienced, and then we did it again in his bed. Maybe it's the debates over dinners, the fighting over who gets the bigger shower first, even though I obviously could use the smaller one. Maybe it's because I wake up in the mornings, dreading the day, but he always makes sure to grab me a coffee and sometimes a donut to start my morning even if he's not there.

Maybe it's that intoxicating smell of his that has made me steal his clothes so I can be consumed by it. Or maybe it's the way his hazel eyes stare at me in a way that makes me feel warm and safe. Maybe it's all those things, or perhaps it's none of them.

"Well, what?" Fox says as he crosses his thick, veiny arms over his immaculately sculpted chest.

Damn it Janie! Stop Thinking about his body!

"Well, I will get my stuff out of there tonight, so you don't have to worry about where to take your company."

Fox shifts uncomfortably as he looks my way.

"Torch." His voice is strained and pleading, as if he doesn't want to talk about Tinder. I hold my hands up.

"Dude, it's cool. I hope you have fun and make good choices." Fox groans loudly as he smacks his face.

"First off, never call me 'dude' again. I'm not your dude." He warns. "Second, I am seventeen years older than you, Torch. This is a weird conversation for us to have." Why that strikes a chord with me, I don't know. But I sure as shit have things to say on the age difference.

"Oh, is it? Because it didn't seem to bother you when you left a hickey on my tit." Fox goes slack-jaw as he stares at me, eyes wide. I walk over to him and pull down the collar of his shirt to reveal the fading hickey at the base of his neck. "Didn't seem to bother you then either."

"Janie, that time in here, it was a mistake, and I am sorry. And I should've never taken advantage of you then, or at my house."

It was my turn for my jaw to drop. "A...mistake?" I blink and suddenly feel self-conscious. I look at the white floor for a long moment and try to organize my chaotic thoughts. Wow Janie, rejected by the guy a couple times now, when are you going to take the hint that he doesn't want you?

I flinch inwardly at the realization as I rub my shaking hands together nervously. I don't do well with rejection or embarrassment. I just want to run and hide. But I live with him. I work with him. God this is such a mess...

Finally, I look up at him and nod. "Listen, I was thinking that..." I try to swallow the hard lump in my throat. "I think I will step back from this whole shop owner thing after my meet and greet. Hopefully, I can find someone there willing to work with me and I can get back on track."

"What?" Fox's brows furrow together as his lips form a deep frown. "Janie, why would you do that? After everything that happened to you online over the last couple of weeks."

I shrug and stare out at the showroom. "That drama is way easier to deal with than this place." *Than you.* I chew on my bottom lip nervously as I look up at his dark, angry expression. Usually I live for his anger and annoyance to be directed at me. But not now.

"And what does that mean?" Fox's demeanor hardens as he stands in front of me, almost defensive.

I take a breath, preparing to say the lie that I had planned out months ago if Fox ever thought to question why I wanted out of here. Honestly, I never thought I would have to use it. "Fox, we both know I hate this place." I really hope that sounds believable to him. "I'm of little to no use here anyway. I would just rather get the money and move on." I hate how badly those lies taste, but there is some truth in my statement. I am of very little use here. So regardless of how much Hel's Ink is starting to feel like something special again, I could never keep it afloat alone. And Fox and I could never run it together.

Fox shakes his head, as if disappointed. "It amazes me," He laughs dryly. "That you, being as attached to that box of ashes as you are, are willing to give up the place that your dad created from nothing." My heart begins to pound in my chest as he hits me with his harsh words and icy stare. "You know what I was given from my father? Cigarette burns and broken bones. A voice in my head constantly reminding me of what a piece of shit I am. That everything and everyone I let near me will be worse off just by knowing me." His voice cracks and he forces himself to clear his throat before glaring at me again. "Tony did nothing but talk about how fucking amazing you were. Every god damn day. He was so fucking proud of you, and my fucking god, if you were coming in or calling him, it was as though he had won the fucking lottery. He worked himself to death to give you a well-oiled money-making machine that would take care of you. I busted my ass, fuck all of us here did! Just to get the occasional head nod from that man. Your dad just gave this to you...and you're willing to throw it away?"

My eyes are tightly closed as he continues to shout at me. I can't stop shaking, if I open my eyes, the tears will fall. I hate this man in front of me right now.

"Stop it." I am barely able to get the whisper out. Fox doesn't listen as he continues to tell me all the wrongs I've done.

"When he first died, and you said you'd give it to me, I figured you were just stupid, and Tony was one of *those* dads that would take care of their dumbass useless kids forever. But damn it Janie, that's not the case! Over the last couple of months, I've learned just how fucking smart you are. So, for you to just say you want to walk away from this, from him, all I can think is that you must just be a selfish fucking brat."

The loud crack of skin hitting skin echos in the shop before I even register that I've slapped Fox across the face. My bottom lip quivers, and my vision blurs as I look at him.

"This place is not a gift." I say through a shaky breath. "It's a curse. You're right, it is a machine. A machine that you can never stop feeding. It was my father's mistress, his favorite child, his fucking God. Everything revolved around this fucking shop while I got locked in the fucking back room like a damn prisoner!"

I can tell by his movements Fox is gearing up to fire back, but I continue to talk. I have had enough of this "Spoiled Janie" crap that everyone seems to see with me.

"And you know what the worst part about it all is? I

wanted this." I look up at the ceiling and squeeze my eyes shut before looking back at him.

"I wanted to be the next generation of Pierce tattoo artists. I worked...I worked so fucking hard. But these..." I hold my trembling hands up. "You can't be a tattoo artist if you can't tattoo a fucking straight-line Fox!" I shout as I slam my fist on Ash's tattoo table, the tears start to freely fall now as I run my hands through my hair as I think about the heartbreak, I've endured over not being able to tattoo. The disappointment in Dad's eyes when he saw my trembling hands and he knew I would end up like my mother, making it impossible for me to sketch anymore. It still pains me to think about.

"When I finally accepted that I would not be an artist, I asked Dad if I could do the business side. Advertising, designs, media. I would go to college to learn financing, I was gaining traction on social media, and I thought I could do the same here. He told me that he didn't want me here." My voice hitches as I say it.

He didn't want me here.

Fox doesn't want me here.

"It wasn't a good place for me to just be hanging out," I continue as I wipe my wet cheeks on my shirt sleeve. "He told me to just not worry about it. That he would make sure I was taken care of. My tremors started and...I don't know, I guess he was scared they would get as bad as my mother's were and he didn't want me to have to worry about obstacles." Regardless of how I felt. I let out a long breath feeling suddenly exhausted, but as soon as my gaze finds Fox's glaring one, I feel the adrenaline once more.

"I wanted this place more than you will ever know, Fox. I wanted nothing more than to feed this fucking machine. So don't you dare call me selfish. You may have worked here and donated your sweat. But I gave my entire fucking childhood, my relationship with my father and his fucking life." The silence between us is painfully long. Finally, Fox lets out a loud sigh before taking his hair tie out of his bun so he can run his hands through his hair.

"How did we get here?" He asks, looking around before chuckling. "I mean, we went from someone liking me on Tinder to –"

"Swiping." I correct him.

He arches a brow. "I am not calling it "swiping" that is dumb and lacks any emotion."

I can't help but laugh loudly. "You're joking, right? Tinder is made for that exact reason. It's a hook-up app."

"I know what it is, Janie." He snaps, cheeks red. "I have had my share of one-night stands, which is what it is for, but it was for Nevada, not here."

"What's the difference between there and here? A hook-up is a hook-up." I scoff and I plant my fists on my hips.

"Jesus fucking Christ." He growls as he runs his hands over his bearded jaw. "You're fucking here!" My eyes widen as I open my mouth to speak, but nothing comes out.

"Don't." He states after rubbing his hand over his forehead now. "Don't read into that. I'm not going to go any further than that just...I can't have a one-night stand and then look at you. And I am not kicking you out of the house to fuck someone else."

Not going any further?
Someone else?

"You are throwing out so many signals I don't know what I'm supposed to say or do." I say softly as I twist my fingers together nervously. Fox rolls his eyes and lets out a dry laugh.

"Welcome to my hell. Don't worry, as I said. We aren't going any further, so let's drop it."

"Wait!" I grab his forearm as he starts to walk away. I feel the muscles and tendons moving as I grip him tightly.

"Why?" I manage to weakly get out.

"Why what?" He sounds like this conversation is exhausting him, but that is just too damn bad. He started this.

"Why is this not going further? Is it because you're not attracted to me?"

"No." He says shortly, still not looking at me.

"Is it my personality?" I try again.

"No, Janie..." He whines, while lifting his head to the ceiling in frustration.

"Is it my...tremors?" That catches him by surprise. Fox whips around, eyes blazing as he looks down at me.

"That was never even a thought in my head, and you better not have it in yours." His voice is low and comes out almost like a warning.

"Then what's so wrong with me?" I don't know why it matters what it is about me that makes me not an option in his eyes. We've never shown any interest in one another – well, mostly never. But since that first kiss, hell maybe even before that...I can't stop thinking about him.

"Because you are off-limits. I broke that once; I will not do it again."

"Off-limits?" Realization hits me. I remember hearing that. My dad used to say it to every new hire at the shop.

I narrow my eyes as I glare at him. "I'm a grown woman, Fox."

"Janie, you were fifteen when I met you. You were a kid. It's just...it's weird and wrong, and your dad would haunt me if I pursued anything and— AH! Just stop! This conversation is over. I'm leaving for Nevada with the guys tomorrow night. I got you a copy of my –"

"I don't need them." I snap as I reach behind the counter and grab my purse, embarrassment and rejection filling me up completely. That's it, that is the final drop. My bucket cannot hold anymore. I will not continue to allow myself to be turned down by this man.

Fox huffs as he stands in front of me to block me from leaving. "Don't act like a –"

"Say child, and I swear to God, Fox!" I yell as I stand toe to toe with him while craning my neck to look about at his stupid face.

"What, Janie? Are you going to smack me with those tiny hands again?" He taunts with a "try me" smirk on his face.

"I fucking hate you." I spit as I shove his chest. Like the fucking tree trunk, he is, he doesn't budge. He chuckles, which pisses me off more, and I push him again. This time he grabs my wrists to stop me.

"I hate you more, trust me." He growls and shoves my wrists away.

We stare at each other, gazes burning, breaths quickening. I blink and his lips are on mine, my tongue is forcing its way into his hot mouth, he is gripping my sweater between his large hands, and as if it were tissue, he rips it apart. I grab his bottom lip between my teeth and bite down. He lets out a loud growl, and I taste the copper on my tongue. I pull his shirt over his head and take a second to admire his tattooed neck and torso before going back to his mouth. I feel him grab me under my ass and lift me onto Atlas' table before his hands go to my jeans.

I gasp when he rips them down my legs and throws them over his shoulder. There is no tenderness, no patience. It is as if we both have something to prove to the other.

I sit up to remove his pants but am met with his hand on my throat. He gently pushes me back down, and I listen as I hear his jeans fall to the floor.

"Fox, this table can support us both, right?" I pant as his one hand stays on my throat while the other reaches behind me and unclasps my bra with an ease that even I haven't achieved. I feel him squeeze gently on my throat, and it's like someone turned my arousal to max volume.

"Not one more fucking word unless it's stop, got it?" He says through gritted teeth next to my ear. I nod rapidly as I look at him. His eyes are wild and dark, his pupils massive. He's filled with lust, rage, and grief – I know this because I am too.

His hand moves over my stomach and down to my panties, which I am sure are soaked clean through. He takes them off in one fluid motion, leaving me completely bare on the table.

His hand leaves my throat, and I bite back a whimper in protest. I watch as he grabs Atlas' chair and sits in it before wheeling it to the end by my feet.

I know he said not another word, but I need to ask like, six questions, seven tops. As if reading my thoughts and denying me permission to ask questions, Fox grips my hips and roughly pulls me down to the end of Atlas' table. My legs go up over his broad shoulders, and before I have time to think, this fucking man slips his tongue right between the lips of my wet aching pussy.

Am I a virgin? No. Am I experienced? Nope, not even close. With my disorder, I don't allow others to get that close to me. I've had sex with two guys and given a few hand jobs. I'm not exactly experienced, and no one has ever given me oral, and oh my god.

I cry out and arch my back as he rolls his tongue around my swollen clit. His firm and I do mean firm grip on my hips make it impossible for me to escape. I moan loudly as my hands find their way into his loose hair. I grip tightly, earning an honest to God primal growl that sends a wave of pleasure through me. I feel his fingertip run up and down my entrance. His teasing drives me insane, but I dare not speak for fear of breaking whatever this is. He inserts one finger, one fucking finger inside me, and I feel full. I whimper and shift around him. I feel his mouth move away from my clit, and this time I'm the one to growl as I push him back. I'm too close. He cannot stop now. I will murder him right here if he stops.

Thankfully he takes the hint and continues licking and sucking and teasing, all while slipping a second finger in and curling his fingers against a spot no human has ever touched. I had a g-spot vibrator that hit that area years ago, and it has nothing on this man's gifted hand.

My pants and whines increase as I feel the pressure building. I cannot control my shaking legs or hands, but it doesn't faze him. As my lower half arches off the table, Fox's hand splays out over my tensing stomach to hold me down.

I feel the pressure reach its breaking point, and I cry out as I cum against his face. I grip his hair tightly while I ride out the waves of pleasure. Fox stays put, lapping up my desire while the hand on my stomach gently moves to almost pet me. His thumb runs back and forth over my navel so softly, it's ironically almost too intimate.

Once I come down from riding out my orgasm, Fox licks

me clean before, finishing out with sweet kisses against my center and down my thighs.

It is the best orgasm I've ever experienced, but I want more. I *need* more. Apparently, Fox is a mind reader at this point because he stands and leans over my panting body before devouring my lips. I moan as the taste of my orgasm enters my mouth. I gasp as he leans over me. It's now that I realize his dick is free from his boxers. I look down and...oh, you have to be joking. I had felt him before, but never in my wildest dreams did I envision that he would be this big.

Fox is massive, thick and long, hard as a rod with the slightest upward curve. I stare at the thick veins starting at his base and leading to his tight shiny looking tip.

I look up at him, mouth open, and he gives me a shy grin. "Yeah, I'm not sure we should continue. I'm not sure it'll fit."

Most guys say this, and you insert an eye roll. This is a genuine concern with Fox. But it's not a concern I can think about at this point. I'm too deep into this.

"Condom." It's the first word I've said, and he doesn't seem upset about it. I watch as he rifles through Atlas' station; of course, Atlas has condoms in his workstation.

I watch Fox rip the foil packaging off with his teeth before rolling the condom over his impressive length.

"Now," He says while stepping between my legs. "I am going to start slow. You have to tell me more, less, or stop. I'm serious, Janie."

I look into his dark gaze and nod. "Okay," I say weakly. I'm on a post-orgasmic high. I'm filled with anxiety, lust, and fuck can he just let me feel him.

Fox angles himself against my entrance, and the pressure I feel from just the head pushing in makes me cry out.

Fox is true to his word; he is slow and lets me decide

when to take more, all while he kisses my lips and says things that I wish he hadn't because this is quickly leaving the "angry fuck" territory.

"Okay, baby doll, a little more. You're doing great. That's my girl." That should not affect me the way it does. Fox is finally as far in me as possible, and he holds still... completely still. I furrow my brows and move slightly, causing him to gasp and grip my hips.

"S-stop!" He bites out. "Janie...fuck, you can't do that." His voice is shaky as he speaks.

"Do what?" I ask, genuinely confused. Have I been having sex the wrong way my entire life?

"J-Janie, you are...fuck...you are really, really tight." He pants and I see the almost pained expression on his face. "I just – god damn it...I need a second, or I'm going to explode in less than two pumps."

Okay, I get him blowing his load in five seconds would suck; I do. But the kind of power that I feel knowing that I can do that to him...maybe just once.

I rock my hips again, and he lets out a cry. "Janie, God damn it! I'm not kidding!"

I stare at him innocently as I squeeze my walls around his cock. I watch his eyes roll back in his head, and then he thrusts into me. I let out a moan as my fingers grip his shoulders. His thrusts start moving faster and in a rhythm. Each one makes me cry out for more. I toss my head back as he drives deeper inside of me. I allow my legs to fall out to the sides to allow him to go deeper.

"Fuck!" He pants as he thrusts again. "God damn it you feel too good." I let out a small cry of pleasure as he hits a spot that sends a sensation to my belly button. "You make that noise again and it's over for me baby doll."

"So..." I pant as I scrape my nails down his strong,

flexing back. "So close!" I feel his hand slip between our slapping flesh and land on my clit. I scream as the hot pressure begins to build again.

"Say my name." He growls in my ear as his thrusts become more frantic. His cock feels somehow harder inside me.

"What?" I pant, about to go over the edge.

"Say my name when you cum. Look at me and say my name." His hand finds my throat again and he applies just a little pressure. That, mixing with his hand on my clit and his dick...there is no chance of me lasting one more second.

"F-FOX!" I cry out in a near sob as a bone-tingling orgasm reverberates through every part of my body. I stare into his wild eyes as I watch the look of shock, pleasure and desire wash over his features while he stares back at me. I scream louder as another wave hits me.

Fox leans over me and begins kissing and licking my earlobe and neck while his thrusts become more erratic and desperate.

"That's my girl," He breathes against my ear. "You're doing so good, milk my orgasm baby doll. Take it as your own." I wrap my nearly jelly-like legs around him as I thrust up against him. I stare into his eyes and run my hand through his beard.

"Cum for me Fox." I moan lowly, not breaking our eye contact. His eyes go wide as he drives himself deep inside of me as he rides his orgasm out.

"Fuck!" He hisses and thrusts again. "Janie...fuck... baby...FUCK!" He moans loudly between each of his final thrusts. Before collapsing on top of me. His warm, sweat covered body stuck to me in a way that gives me great comfort.

After a minute or so, but definitely not long enough. Fox

removes himself from inside me. Instantly I feel cold and empty. I hate it.

"What now?" I ask as we quickly begin to redress.

Fox looks at me and I see the regret forming on his face. The panic, the fear. Oh god, no...this isn't happening, not again.

"Janie–"

"I meant, are you okay with it being a one-time thing and us moving on?" I ask and want to die when I see the relief fill his eyes.

"Y-yeah, I mean... are you good with that?" He asks and I smile at him, nodding slowly. Of course I am. Because it doesn't matter what I actually want, only what I am supposed to want.

Chapter Eighteen

FOX

I STARE at the thirty something year old man in front of me as he thumbs through my portfolio. "I would love to get tattooed by you!" He lets out a breath before setting the binder down. "I just don't think your pricing is reasonable."

I fight back a laugh. By the looks of the scratcher work that covers nearly every inch of his body, I'm guessing he's never paid more than fifty bucks and a pack of smokes for a tattoo.

"Well," I force a smile that I guarantee doesn't meet my eyes. "I will have to take that under advisement." I lie as he walks away, and my scowl instantly returns while I walk over to the folding chair behind our table and sit down. My fucking body hurts, I'm annoyed, tired and I miss my fucking bed.

We've been in Nevada for three days and while the guys went out, got drunk, gambled and banged any woman they could find, I stayed in my hotel room playing – *The Office* trivia with Janie while trying to get her to talk to me. It hadn't gone well. I know that she lied about being good with a one and done session, but I didn't want to press her on it. I freaked out when the lust fog cleared, and I realized what I had done.

It isn't even that I fucked Tony's daughter, not that I won't continue to use that excuse if ever asked. It's that...I *fucked* Janie, and what I thought would easily be a hit and quit ordeal, is anything but. Her soft skin, her cries, when she screamed my name, and I watched her eyes glaze over and her nipples harden as she came around my cock. Or when she looked me dead in the eyes and told me to cum for her...fuck I'm getting hard again.

Exactly my problem. Janie is the first woman I have been with that I continue to think about after sex. It's annoying and I don't like it at all. I don't like that when I dropped her off at Ren's, I wanted to kiss her goodbye. I hate the fact that the moment the guys and I landed in Vegas, they got their phones ready for hookups while I deleted Tinder. And I loathe the fact that I keep looking at my phone, waiting for her trivia question – since it's all I can get out of her. I shouldn't want Janie Pierce; I shouldn't miss her. This needs to stop, I'm not allowed to miss her.

But even as I tell myself not to, I fucking do miss her. I miss her smell, her sarcasm, her snarky remarks. I miss her flipping her unmanageable curls out of her face a thousand times a day. I miss the way her eyes twinkle with mischief as she and I banter back and forth, and I fucking know she is about to hit me with a smart-ass remark.

"So, what's with the lost puppy vibe, dude?" Atlas interrupts my torturous thoughts as he sits down on the folding chair next to me behind our table and hands me an energy drink. I had stopped drinking them when Janie came to stay with me. I don't know why really, I guess she had just started taking over the shopping and since she couldn't have caffeine, I didn't drink it.

I shrug as I set the unopened can on the table. "Just feeling a little old for all of this chaos, I guess." The statement is half true. None of us knew where we should be or what we were supposed to bring, and Janie and Ren ended up having to overnight us the merchandise that we didn't bring. And while everyone else had all this tech social media shit, they were showing off. The four of us had our printed fucking portfolios like a bunch of idiots. It wasn't boding well for us for day one of three.

Atlas leans back against his chair and stretches his legs "I don't think it has to do with age Fox." while gesturing to the old-timers around us. "I think it has to do with not being willing to listen."

I raise a brow and lean back in my chair, crossing my arms over my chest. "What does that mean?"

"It means," Derek interjects as he drops a black folder in my lap. "Had we all not brushed Janie off so quickly with her social media help, maybe we would've been prepared."

Looking at the folder skeptically, I root around in my bag for my glasses before opening the folder and rolling my eyes. "This is the shit she showed us over a month ago." As I go to close the folder, Derek's wolf's head hand tattoo covers the page as he stops me from closing the folder.

"Did you actually read her proposition, though?" He asks. I look from him to Ash and Atlas. Am I being ganged up on?

Taking my glasses off, I look back at Derek. "I thought we all agreed that changing the way we run the shop is a bad idea."

"Dude," Atlas shakes his head as if he is getting frustrated with me. I just watched him get yelled at for calling a girl Christine whose name was Katherine, but sure *I* am the frustrating one. "There are seventy-year-old artists here who are more put together than us." He again motions his hands to the old-timers milling around. "We look like amateurs right now! When I went and got our drinks, someone came up to me and asked for my QR code so he could see my portfolio. I don't know what that is! But you know who does? Fucking Janie." Atlas makes his point by taking the folder and flips the pages to show a box that you scan with your phone, and whatever you want will show up.

Okay, I have to agree, that could've been convenient.

"Also," Derek says, flipping through the folder. What the fuck? Were they all studying this over while I napped on the plane? I thought they were looking for strip clubs.

"If you look over this page, you will see that Janie actually made different sample itineraries for us for this convention. Different ideas for merchandise, different giveaways, she had everything organized down to us raffling off a tattoo. None of which was put into action because we never took her seriously. All of us stopped listening to her the moment she mentioned social media."

I hated how true Derek's words were. I remember how excited she was that day to talk to us. And then how hurt she was when we...when I brushed her off. Thumbing through the last papers, I stop on a piece of notebook paper with Janie's handwriting on it.

Ideas to run by Fox:
New Line of shirts depicting different female goddesses.
Convention Exclusive shirts that guys design themselves.
Explain idea for updated logo - have Fox sketch it out so it looks better than my scratch work.

'Than my scratch work?'

Had she drawn something that she was too embarrassed to show? I stare at her penmanship and wince. It wasn't smooth, you could see where the tremors were worse in some areas.

"You can't be a tattoo artist if you can't tattoo a fucking straight-line Fox!"

Flinching at the memory of Janie screaming that at me, I close the folder and sigh. "Yeah, I guess I kind of fucked up on that one."

After a silent minute, Ash and Derek decide to go off to look at other vendors since our table is completely dead. I look at Atlas, who keeps staring at me.

"Dude, I'm going to fucking hit you." I warn after catching him looking for the hundredth time.

Atlas looks me over and squints his eyes suspiciously. "Something is going on. You keep checking your phone. You're all mopey and Janie has gone silent. Did you two have a fight?"

God he is fucking irritating. "No, Sherlock, we didn't fight. One would have to be speaking to fight." I mutter the last part, but Atlas and his big ass ears hear me.

Atlas groans dramatically as he slumps back in his chair. "Fox!" He whines. "Come on, man! I really like Janie!"

I glare at him. "You what?" I growl. I don't know why what he said puts me into alpha-possessive caveman mode, but it does and I'm suddenly filled with the urge to beat his fucking face in for daring to *really like* my girl.

My girl? *Fucking hell...*

Atlas holds up his hands in mock defense. "As a sister, dude." I watch as a grin spreads across his face, and I know

I've stepped right into it. "You have a thing for Red, don't you Fox." His eyes twinkle...yes, fucking twinkle with glee.

I run my hand through my hair as I exhale harshly through my nose. I need some scotch.

"Atlas..." I warn through clenched teeth as I feel the heat creeping into my cheeks.

His grin just keeps widening as he points his finger at me. "Oh no, no no...I'm not scared of you, old man. Spill it. Did you tell her you liked her, and she turned you down? Is she not into the *"daddy"* thing?"

I can't help the laugh that escapes me as I lean back, feeling a little *too* smug. "Oh, she's into the *'daddy thing'*...oh fuck." God damn it, why can't I keep my mouth shut?

At's mouth fell open and his eyes go as wide as saucers. "No way," He half laughs, "You fucked Tony's daughter?" I lean over and whack him upside the head with one of the portfolio binders before telling him to shut the fuck up.

After a minute, he shrugs and rubs his head. "I mean, I guess it was bound to happen. You two have been living together."

"Didn't happen at my house." I mutter while tapping out a text to Janie.

> Me: I hope you're doing alright. Maybe you and I should talk more about you revamping Hel's.

"Where did it happen?" Atlas asks with honest curiosity and I just give him a small smirk. "At Hel's?" He asks the question even though I can tell he's growing concerned with what my answer will be. I give him a half, noncommittal shrug.

157

He groans, "Oh, come on, man...wait...where in the shop?"

Looking back up from the phone I see the look of fear, disgust and betrayal on his face. I smirk and lean back in my chair. "It would appear you already know where."

"You owe me a new fucking station!" He gags, and I can't help but laugh as he mentions something about old nuts hitting his table.

An older male voice interrupts Atlas' drama session. "Hey, there you boys are!" I look up to see a familiar man in his late sixties, bald with a beard that rests on his small gut, he wore a leather vest to show off his full sleeves that I am sure predate me.

"Arlo, hey brother." I smile as Atlas and I stand to hug the old-timer. Arlo was one of Tony's closest friends and initially helped Tony get Hel's started.

"Where is Janie? I heard she was helping run the shop now. I haven't seen her since she was about this tall." He says holding his hand level with his stomach.

I chuckle as I stuff my hands in my jeans pocket. "Yeah well, she hasn't grown much. But she stayed back in California."

Arlo lets out a wheezy laugh and pats my arm. "I wanted to apologize to her for missing her daddy's funeral. I had a damn heart attack the day before and the bastards at the ICU wouldn't let me out."

Atlas and I laugh as he shakes his head and I cannot imagine how his kids handle this old man. Stubborn as a mule. I have no doubt that he was raising ten kinds of hell trying to get out of the hospital to make it to the funeral.

Arlo sighs and looks towards me. "So, is she doing the business side or has she finally picked a machine up? I really would love to see some of her new artwork." Atlas and I exchange confused glances before I look back to Arlo.

"Artwork?" I repeat.

Arlo nods before his smile begins to fade. "Don't tell me she gave it up? Oh, she was amazing!"

She told me she wanted to be the next *"Pierce Tattoo Artist"*, but her disorder stopped her. Of course, I wasn't going to speak on that as I still am not sure who from Tony's past knows about it.

Arlo sighs and shakes his tattoo-covered bald head. "That girl came up with that drawing there when she was just ten years old." I look at the logo on my shirt that he is pointing to. Our shop's logo of the goddess Hel was Janie's sketch? We had all just assumed that when Tony said it was a *"Pierce Original"*, he was referring to himself.

I watch Arlo raise his shoulders in a shrug of disappointment. "She had such a passion for drawing. I am sad she didn't keep it up."

Arlo and Atlas' conversation becomes background noise when I feel my phone vibrate. I see it's a message from Janie and I nearly drop my phone trying to open it.

As I open the text, I see she sent me a photo of a white mug that says "World's Best Boss" on it.

Torch: I'm going to buy it for you, but you need to send me $9.25

Me: Why would I send you $9.25 if YOU are buying it for me.

Torch: ... BECAUSE you insolent fool! Michael Scott bought his own best boss mug.

"What's got him grinning like an idiot?" Arlo's voice

breaks my little bubble and I glance at the two men who were staring at me in bewilderment. A knowing grin crept across Atlas' face, and I feel a cold sensation wash over me.

"Oh," Atlas chuckles. "Fox here has turned his back on our bro pack and gotten himself lovesick."

It's a shame really, knowing that I'm going to have to murder my best friend. But Atlas is leaving me no choice. I silently threaten him with unimaginable pain as he continues to talk to Arlo.

"Yeah, he's got this fiery little pistol back home." He gives me a wink and it's at that moment I know that ripping his eyeballs out and shoving them into his over-sized mouth is the first thing I'm doing.

Arlo slaps me on the arm. "It's about time you start thinking about settling down, son! You're starting to get up there in years."

Atlas busts out laughing and shakes his head. "Don't worry about that Arlo, his girl has a 'daddy' kink apparently."

As I'm trying to figure out how I'm going to get away with making Atlas' murder look like an accident, Arlo's question nearly stops my heart.

"You got a name or picture of this pretty girl?" My wide eyes look towards Atlas who is showing zero mercy. An idea hits me, and I instantly relax causing Atlas to raise a brow.

Alright mother fucker...game on.

"Oh, sure Arlo!" I laugh as I quickly get on my phone and start scrolling through photos in my album before I show him the photo I was looking for. Atlas pales and his eyes narrow.

Checkmate.

The photo was taken last year at Ren's swearing in party

that she invited both Atlas and I to. Atlas had decided to go off and get drunk, so I went. Ren stood in the photo with her arms around my waist and an ear-to-ear smile behind her long blonde hair she had styled into curls that day.

Arlo let out a low whistle. "Damn Fox, now that is a piece."

Continuing to look at Atlas who is glaring at me, I grin brightly.

"Yeah man, Ren is amazing. She's a lawyer, super funny, and I mean...just look at her." My eye contact never broke from Atlas whose jaw continues to tick.

I give him a look as if to say *"done"*?

He gives me the slightest of nods before pulling Arlo over to our table to show him his portfolio. I let out a breath, I desperately need to get away from people. It's been a long, frustrating trip and we haven't even hit the weekend rush.

Deciding I want to continue my conversation with Janie in private, I head out of the convention room to text her. With my eyes focused on my screen, I walk around the corner to a quieter area and I smack into someone.

Instinctively, my hands go out to stop the person from falling, which is when I see the familiar overly bleached blonde hair and nearly burnt brown skin.

"Liza." I breathe as I steady her. "Are you alright? I am sorry."

Liza smiles at me as she adjusts her fake chest which was busting out of her too tight halter top.

She smooths her hands down her black leather skirt. "I think so. Ow!" She stumbles and falls against me. Fuck, did I really hurt her? I hate the woman sure, but I would never want to cause her, or any woman harm.

"Can I help you?" I ask while holding her up. "Can I get you some ice or a seat?"

"Actually," Her voice is soft and breathy. "I was just headed back to my room. I'm exhausted and wanted a nap... if you wouldn't mind helping me to my room?"

I look back towards the convention and sigh before nodding. I let out an *"oof"* of surprise when she all but leaps into my arms. This is a fucking bad idea, and I can already feel it. But I carry her through the lobby and to the elevator.

The elevator ride to Liza's floor is quiet and awkward, at least on my side since Liza stays in my arms, her arms hanging around my neck. If I stare down, I will see her entire chest, so I stare straight fucking forward. A shiver runs down my spine as I feel her nails scrape the base of my neck.

The doors to the elevator open and I all but run in the direction Liza tells me to. I stop in front of her room and lower her down gently. She leaves her arms wrapped around my neck and her breasts pressed against me with such a force I wonder if they may pop. Can fake tits do that? I mean, some are full of saline.

My thoughts are horribly interrupted when I feel Liza's lips on mine. As fast as possible, I push her off just as I feel her tongue begin to make its way into my mouth.

"Liza, what are you doing?" I ask in complete shock and a little - or a lot - disgust.

"I was trying to thank you for helping me. I mean, that is what you want, right?" I back away further as her hand grabs my dick through my jeans.

"Holy shit!" I nearly trip as I try to move away from her. "No! I got to go." I turn as I try to make my escape, but Liza grips the bottom of my shirt and holds me.

"What's the matter with you?" She hisses, as if *I* were in the wrong here.

I blink once, twice before shaking my head. "What's wrong with me?" I ask as I free my shirt from her grasp. "Liza, you tried to shove your tongue down my throat and your hand down my pants."

She rolls her eyes as she leans against the wall by her door. "And? You suddenly too good for us tattoo artist girls?" I shift uncomfortably as I rub the back of my neck. Liza gives me a knowing grin. "Oh I get it, twenty years can age a girl I guess."

"Don't." I snap and glare at her. "It has nothing to do with age. It was once a lifetime ago."

Liza laughs dryly and shakes her head. "Yeah well, had I known where you were headed, I would've dug my fingers into more than just your cock." She winks as she opens her hotel room door.

"Come on Foxy, for old times." She purrs and I feel my skin crawl.

I shake my head and back away. "Fuck. No. It was a mistake then and it sure as shit would be now." Her face darkens as she steps closer to me and I notice her limp is gone... figures.

"You're fucking Pierce aren't you." I pale and she knows she has me. "I knew something was off when you jumped to her defense that day. You hated Janie for years and then suddenly you chew me out over questioning her with the shop. You're fucking Tony's baby girl. Man...guess you only like them at a certain age."

"Fuck you Liza." I spit as I turn to walk away.

"That's a good move though!" She calls and God help me, I stop and turn to hear the rest of her statement. "You know, ensuring you get all the power over the shop. Keep her *satisfied* for the year and then she'll gladly sign it all to you. Hell, maybe the dumb bitch will fall in love with the unlovable Fox Simmons and just give it to you." Her cold laughter fills the hallway as I turn to head towards the elevators.

I need to get to my room, take a scalding shower, exfoliate, punch something and then drink...a lot.

AFTER CONSUMING my entire mini bar and scrubbing six layers of skin off my body, I lay in my hotel bed with The Office playing, though I'm not watching it. I'm staring at the unanswered messages Janie has sent.

> Torch: ... BECAUSE you insolent fool!
> Michael Scott bought his own best boss
> mug.

> Torch: Hello?

> Torch: FINE I'll buy you the mug without
> getting paid back for it. But I'm drinking out
> of it first.

The next message is a selfie of her holding the mug to her lips. She looks like she's sad even though she's smiling. Her eyes are red rimmed and her face is blotchy.

> Torch: You know, I have TONS of other
> people I could be talking to...but here I am,
> TRYING to converse with you.

> Torch: I forgot it's an hour ahead over there,
> maybe your ass is asleep.

Torch: Oh fuck maybe you found some *cat emoji* *fire emoji*

That message had been sent twenty minutes ago. I continue to stare at the screen as I think about what Liza said.

The unlovable Fox Simmons.

Most didn't know but Liza was latching on to artists back at the old shop I used to work at before I moved here. She was the "shop girl" at twenty-two and enjoyed hanging around to... well fuck or suck any artist that would have her. I was twenty-three and had just gotten my ass beat by my dad the morning before I headed into the shop. When I got there, Liza was the only one there. She took me to her car and sucked me off.

It never happened again, never went any further and when Tony showed up with her on his arm, I didn't even realize it was her at first.

Unlovable. I had told Liza that. I was in a weak spot and told her that my father had said that about me while burning me with his cigarette butt. Liza hadn't told me he was wrong, hadn't tried to give me any words of encouragement. She just said to pull my pants down. And I did.

Liza is wrong though; I would never take Hel's from her. The shop is ours together unless she wants to be bought out.

The love thing though.

I thought about how Janie asked if I found her attractive. The hints about dating, and how she lied about being cool with us having sex just that one time. I know that Janie doesn't *love* me. That is impossible. But I am beginning to worry that she might like me in a way I cannot reciprocate.

The thought makes my chest ache. I know that my feelings for Janie have blown way past friends. But acting on them could only hurt us both. What if I fuck up? Which is inevitable. What if she gets tired of me and moves on? Or what if something happens and she's no longer in my life and I'm left alone after trying to open up to someone?

I thought about my mom and how she looked at my father with all the love in the world, even after her beatings. She allowed him to beat her, my sister and then me, all because of love.

I was so happy when they were leaving and coming to live with me. Finally, away from him...I should've gone and got them instead of having them drive down.

I remember the ass beating I got at the funeral. I was nearly thirty and in the best shape as I had ever been. But when my father told me to get onto my knees, I listened. I allowed that man to wail on me for killing his wife and daughter. I allowed him to tell me that he hoped to God I would have a wife and daughter taken from me like he did. I allowed him to blacken both my eyes, break my nose and jaw. I allowed him to jab a lit cigar into my pec. All while screaming at me that I was an unlovable piece of shit that murdered his family.

A notification on my phone pulls me from the dark memories. I wipe my face, realizing it's wet before looking at the screen.

> Torch: What is the worst part of the convention?

I sigh and lean back against the headboard. I stare at The Office playing and smirk before sending out a text.

> Me: The worst part of the convention has to be the Dementors…

Torch: Dementors?

Me: Fuck yeah! They were flying all over the place! They'd suck the soul out of your body.

Me: Shit hurts!

The three dots appear, then disappear and suddenly a FaceTime call is coming through. I shouldn't answer it...

I hit accept and I see Janie's face appear on my screen and it fills me with a feeling like I'm home.

"I nearly pissed myself." She deadpans.

I raise a brow. "And what? You instantly think 'Gee, Fox is going to want to hear this'?"

I watch her blue eyes roll, "I meant you made me laugh so hard with that text dickweed."

I grin at her brightly, "Have I ever told you that your pet names for me make my knees go weak?"

She palms her forehead, "Why am I talking to you again?"

I give her a half shrug. "My guess is you missed my adorable looks and charm." I raise my brow as I notice how badly her phone is shaking. "Hey," I say softly. "How about you set the phone on the table or something."

I see her creamy cheeks go pink and she winces. "Yeah, sorry, my tremors are pretty bad today." She sets her phone down, propping it up against something before sitting in front of it. I can only see her from the waist up now and it's then I notice something on her arm.

"What's that?" I ask, gesturing to my arm. Janie looks at

the same spot on her arm and I watch her face scrunch up before she looks back at me.

"Okay," She says calmly and instantly my hackles rise. Something happened and she's about to lie.

"Do not," I growl as I stare at her. "Lie to me. What. Happened."

"She was jumped!" I hear Ren say as she flops on the couch behind Janie.

"What!?" I roar as I stand up trying to figure out what I need to do and who needs to die.

"Wait!" Janie says after punching Ren in the thigh. "I wasn't jumped! I just..."

"Spit. It. Out." If I didn't need this fucking phone to speak to her, it would be through the wall right now.

Janie takes a deep breath and shoots Ren one more glare before looking back at me. "I had to go to my apartment to talk to the landlord. Someone recognized me and shoved me. I stumbled off the curb and got scuffed up. I'm fine."

"I'm coming home." I state simply and hang up the phone. There is zero chance I'm sitting here talking to idiots for the next three days while Janie is over there, unprotected and getting hurt. My phone rings and I hit the speaker button as I continue to pack.

"What?" I ask.

"Fox!" Janie yells through the phone. "You are not coming back here! You are not my babysitter! I'm fine! I am going to the meet and greet tomor–"

"The fuck you are!" I yell into the phone earning a loud groan from her. "Your cute little ass is NOT going anywhere near those people."

"Fox, while the alpha male protective thing is very endearing, I am not your girlfriend, so it isn't going to work on me! You can't tell me what to do."

I chuckle lightly, "Baby doll, I have an easy one hundred and fifty pounds and damn near a foot on you. I will sit on you if need be, but you are not going anywhere."

There is a moment of silence before I hear a loud sigh. I smile, feeling victorious. "Fox?" Fuck...it's the Pissed Off Pierce voice. "If you come back here and try to stop me, not only will we only carry the vegan ink line, but I will scratch the finish off Vanessa."

"Okay brat that is too fucking far." I growl in annoyance. "Fine, but I want updates, got it?"

Chapter Nineteen

JANIE

"NAME...OH MY GOD." The nasally-sounding blonde woman who sits in the registration booth drops her pen as she stares at me in complete shock. I try to give her my infamous smile, but I'm sure it comes off more as a grimace.

"Jai." I state softly as I look expectantly at the rack of lanyards with name tags. To say I'm terrified to be here would be the biggest understatement ever. I rarely came to meet and greets when I was loved because of my tremors. So being here now, when a huge percentage of the internet hates me, is probably a dumb idea. But I need to get my life back.

The woman blankly stares at me as she hands me my lanyard. I notice my name tag isn't on the rack with the others, but tossed in a box on the floor. Apparently they didn't think I would show either.

I give the woman a small smile before walking away from the booth to head inside the convention area. I get to the loud entrance and instantly freeze, I can't do this. I run down several halls until I am in an abandoned area of the center and I see a bathroom sign. I walk in and walk over to the sink, gripping it tightly as wave after wave of dread and anxiety crash over me.

I don't want this. I don't want to go in there and do this. I look at myself in the mirror and scowl at the person staring back at me.

Jai.

Poker straight hair, perfect brows, not a freckle in sight. Highlighted and contoured cheeks with a smokey eye and a dangerously sharp winged liner thanks to Ren.

I wore an emerald green skater mini skirt, brown suede over the knee boots and a tight cream color long sleeve shirt.

I see Jai's bottom lip wobbling.

"Stop it." I snarl into the mirror. I look down at the sink and take another breath. I have to do this. I have to find a way out of Hel's. A way out of Fox's life.

I slump further as I think about Fox. The thought of leaving the guys, Hel's Ink and more importantly, Fox has put me into a depression. I haven't been handling it well since they left. I spend most of my time crying or searching for funny things to talk to Fox about that won't circle back to feelings, or *that* night.

That Night.

God, I ached for three days after. And I've ached for other reasons since. The way he looked at me...Calling me his girl...

His – if only.

"God damn it. Stop it!" I yell at my reflection before pushing off of the sink and yanking open the door and making my way back to the meet and greet. I am strong enough to do this. I am strong enough to deal with anything the people in there have to say. I am not, however, strong enough to deal with seeing Fox every day, knowing that I can't have him the way I want.

I SMILE AT THE TAN, blonde man in front of me as he goes over the company he works for - *Bliss Trips*. It's a travel influencer company based in Chicago. My social media experience has never been travel based, but maybe getting out of this city isn't the worst idea.

"This sounds amazing." I smile at him and notice he looks away and rubs the back of his head as if he were nervous.

"Y-yeah," He smiles and looks at me with his brown eyes. "I think you would be a good fit. I mean I will have to talk it over with my boss, but I have your email and I will get back with you as soon as I know anything."

I hear snickering behind me and quickly excuse myself from the man. I have been in the room for about an hour and Bliss Trips has been the only company willing to talk to me. I've been called a whore, a liar, and a snake. I was booed out of a panel I was supposed to sit in on and now I have a group of people behind me taking pictures and laughing.

I look at my phone and see all the notifications on the social media apps and a feeling of overwhelming dread consumes me. I get into my texts and go to the group chat I have with Stevie and Ren.

> Me: Girls, I need out. I can't do this.

Stevie: On the way babe, find somewhere quiet and we will text when we arrive.

Ren: If someone upsets you I will beat their ass.

Me: You're a lawyer, that doesn't sound smart.

Ren: Neither does someone messing with one of my people.

I smile softly as I head towards where I had entered earlier, when I am struck in the back of the head with something wet. I look at the liquid dripping off of me and hitting the floor, it's iced coffee by the smell of it and it's soaking through my clothes. I turn and look in time to get hit with some other drink. I sputter and move backwards, slipping on the wet floor and landing on my ass. I hear people laughing and the sounds of cameras. I haul myself to my feet, slipping as I run out of the room as everyone yells "Jai the Slut."

I continue to run until I am outside the convention center. Before hiding in an alley. I press myself against the brick building as I feel the tears coming. I don't know what compels me to, but before I can stop myself, I FaceTime Fox.

Two rings and he picks up with all the guys behind him. I look as their smiling faces go to scowls simultaneously.

"What happened?" Fox growls, standing up. I let out a sob as I shake my head, unable to talk. "Janie," I can hear Atlas in the background trying to get Fox to calm his voice down.

"Baby doll," He says softer this time. "Talk to me. What happened?"

I sniffle and look at the concern etched on his beautiful face. "Fox..." I let out a crackly sob. "I need a hug." I watch his face crumple as if I just broke his heart.

"Okay," He says and I watch him grabbing stuff from behind the table he's sitting at. "At, here is my key to my room. Bring my shit back with you." I furrow my brows together in confusion as he starts walking.

"W-what are you doing?" I ask as I try to stop crying.

"I'm heading to the airport, I'll catch the first flight out of here, and I'll come and give you a hug okay?" He said it like he was next door. Not in another state, hours away, at a convention for our shop.

"Fox..." I try to stop him. He *can't* do something like this for me when it can't mean anything.

"Baby doll, I'll see you when I land. I gotta go and get a ticket bought. Go home and stay there. I'll be there soon. You won't be alone, okay?" My lip wobbles and I go to speak but he ends the call.

"Oh my god!" Ren's angry voice catches me by surprise as she rounds the corner and stares at me. "I'll kill them." She snarls, nostrils flaring.

I grab her wrist and look at her, feeling completely exhausted. "Can we just leave?"

I SMILE SOFTLY as Stevie hands me a mug of hot tea before taking her seat on Fox's couch. Originally, I was going to have them take me to Ren's, but knowing that Fox would be insistent on seeing me when he arrives, I decided to just go back to his place.

I've showered and changed into a baggy blue hoodie and blue plaid pajama bottoms. I had to turn my phone off because the amount of notifications I had been getting was making me feel sick.

"Can I get you anything else?" Stevie asks and I can't help the laugh that escapes.

"Stevie, we aren't at the restaurant." I giggle as she smacks her head.

"Sorry," She says sheepishly. "Force of habit, I guess. One of these days I'll break it. But seriously, do you need anything?"

"A new life and identity." I mumble as I take a sip of my tea, allowing the warm liquid to fill me with a sense of calm, even if it's temporary.

Stevie gives me a sad smile and pats my leg. "Well, luckily for you. You can delete Jai and just be Janie. You can remove yourself from social media and within a year, you'll be forgotten. Some have to try much harder to get out."

"I don't want to delete Jai." I say probably a little harsher than I meant to. I take a breath before continuing. "I hate Jai, I think I always have. But she's been there through everything. She kept me safe and hidden and now, when the internet is trashing her, I'm supposed to just let her go? Not fight to fix it?"

Stevie shrugs before taking a sip from her own mug. "Janie, that part of you... you said it yourself, she's a lie. She's a mask that you used to hide behind. If you try to fix that online character...well look what just a couple of hours has done to you."

I glare at the floor. She isn't wrong, but that doesn't mean I want to hear her truth. If I give up on Jai, I have nothing but Hel's, and I can't have Hel's.

Before I can respond, the front door opens and Fox

walks in. I set down my mug before running across the couch and ottoman and jumping into his arms, not caring how it looks. I hear his bag drop to the ground before his strong arms wrap around me.

"Hey Torch," He says softly as I hear him inhale deeply. I squeeze my arms around his neck as tightly as I can as I feel his heart ramming against his chest. I smile softly to myself, for the first time in nearly a week, I finally feel safe and at home again.

Chapter Twenty

FOX

"I DON'T KNOW ABOUT THIS." Janie whines as she looks at the large swimming pool. My air conditioner went out last night. And while I am someone that can handle uncomfortable temperatures rather well despite my large size, Janie is not. About the time the house got to seventy degrees, she started bitching, and by noon when it was eighty-four in the house, she was losing her mother fucking mind.

So, since Ash and Atlas are still in Vegas, I told her I would take her to the pool in their building that is hardly ever used. I thought getting to cool off in a pool would make her happy, but she seemed antsy the entire time. And now that she and I are here, she is looking at the pool loungers like she's about to plant her ass into one.

"Torch," I sigh in annoyance. "Take off the dress and get into the water." I mutter as I remove my shirt. I glance over at her frozen body as she stares at me. I flex my chest, making the muscles bounce so that she knows I caught her staring before giving her a wide grin.

"Asshole." She mutters as she starts taking off her

yellow wrap cover up dress that goes down to her feet. I jump into the pool and when I surface, I nearly fall over myself. I quickly scan the pool area and sure enough, the men are looking.

Janie is standing at the edge of the pool, pulling her long curls up while her body moves and sways beneath that tiny turquoise bikini. I stare at her perfect fucking tits hidden behind those tiny triangles and my cock goes hard instantly.

The day we had sex, it was all so rushed, I didn't fully get to appreciate her form and fuck... everyone else was getting to right now.

"Torch," I growl as I walk to the edge of the pool. "Get in."

Janie frowns at me before crouching down and sitting on the edge of the pool, putting her small feet in the water. "Happy?" She asks as she splashes me with her foot.

I wipe the water off my face as I push my hair back. I swim closer until I'm in front of her knees. "I brought you here to cool off." I say softly as I drip water over her thighs, causing her to shiver. "If you were going to just stay in the sun, we could've stayed home."

"Fox," She groans and looks around as if she's nervous. I instinctively follow her gaze but see nothing besides a few men giving her looks that make me want to claim her right on the edge of this pool.

"What baby doll?" I watch the small quirk of her lips at my pet name for her.

She looks at me and sighs. "If you make fun of me, I will cry." She warns and pokes my chest.

I hold three fingers up. "Scouts honor."

"You were never a Scout, Simmons." She scoffs before sighing again. "I can't swim."

I raise a brow and have to force the laugh to stay back. "H-how? You live twenty minutes from a beach, most apartments and homes have a pool."

She shrugs and looks down at her feet under the water. "When I was about seven, my dad signed me up for swim lessons. The instructor was not the most observant and I was walking around the edge of the pool when I slipped and fell in. I was so scared and inhaled under water and began to drown." She lets out a shaky breath as she relives the traumatic memory. "Luckily, my dad was on the other side watching and got to me. We were back out of the water before the instructor even noticed. After that I didn't want to try again, I was afraid. And then I got older, Dad was busier, and I was too shy when my tremors started to be this close to someone. So, I always just dip my toes in."

I frown at her words as I stand so that we are near eye level. "You want to get in?" I ask as I press my wet trunks against her knees.

She shakes her head. "N-no, I know I could probably stand and be okay but, if I slip or..."

"Do you trust me?" I ask and her eyes shoot to mine. I watch as they flick to my lips for a second before coming back up.

"...yes." She breathes and when she utters that small word, I feel an overwhelming warmth rush through me.

I give her a smile as I press myself between her legs. "Wrap your arms around my neck, okay?"

She is hesitant, but only for a second. My heart aches at how bad she's shaking when she grips me. Once she is wrapped around my neck and waist. I lift her off the side and lower our bodies into the water. She lets out a small gasp and grips me tighter.

"Please..." She lets out a small whimper. "Fox, please don't let me go."

"Never, baby doll." I press my lips to her temple as I continue to slowly glide through the shallow end of the pool, which is still about four feet deep. After several minutes, I feel her shifting, her body loosening slightly. I press my back against the wall of the pool as I look at her.

"Hey," I smile softly. The first word spoken between us in at least ten minutes.

She doesn't speak, she just stares into my eyes. I wish I knew what she saw in them.

"What is it, baby doll?" I ask as I tuck a fallen strand behind her ear.

"Can you..." She struggles to find the words and I think she's about to change her mind, but she looks back at me and inhales. "Can you kiss me?"

"W-what?" I grip her hips tighter to ensure I don't slip and knock her off of me. "Janie, why would I do that?" I wince instantly. That came out completely wrong. "Fuck, wait." I say as I feel her body go stiff and she starts to pull away. "No, don't pull back, Janie, wait I'm sorry. It came out wrong."

Janie shakes her head and gives me that fake smile that I hate. "It's fine, it wasn't important. I just wanted the other guys around here to stop looking at me. Thought maybe by you kissing me, they might take the hint and fuck off."

That was a good lie, I'll give her that. She one hundred percent knows what to say to sidetrack me and bring out my possessive, jealous caveman side. And, if it weren't for the fact that it looks as though I've just slapped her across the face with my words, I would believe it that was her real reason.

"I think I'm ready to get out," She says, sounding almost

defeated. I nod and walk her to the edge of the pool where I easily set her down before pulling myself up and heading to the chairs to get dressed.

THE RIDE HOME is very quiet. So much so I annoyingly keep fidgeting. I cannot think of a single thing to say to her.

I wanted to kiss her. Holding her like that was so strangely intimate. Feeling her heart beating against mine. I felt that feeling again that needed to stop before it was too late, and I ended up destroying her life.

"Fox, stop!" I slam on the brakes at Janie's scream. I look around the empty back road but don't see anything.

"What the fuck Janie?" I yell but she ignores me and jumps out of my truck. "Son of a bitch." I growl, slamming my truck into park and getting out to see what she was doing. At the front of the truck, I see Janie half under it on the ground.

"What the fuck!" I get to my knees just as she comes out. Looking at her small hands I see the charcoal grey ball of fur. It was the size of Janie's hand and meowing like mad.

"Fuck." I groan as I already see it written on her face.

"We can't leave it!" She cries out and I scratch my neck.

"Alright fine, but we are taking it to a shelter tomorrow. I don't do pets." I watch as she glares at me before standing and getting into the truck. I follow suit and we take off down the road again.

There is a moment of silence before Janie opens her mouth to speak. "Can you take me to the pet store?"

"Why would I do that if it's going to the shelter tomorrow?" I ask as I continue to drive towards my house.

Janie huffs and sits back in her seat. "First off, you aren't the boss of me, if I decide to keep Winston, that is my decision."

I whip my truck on to the shoulder and throw it into park as I turn and glare at her. "Winston?" I ask.

She juts her chin out in defiance as she nods. "Yes, he looks like a dapper little gentleman. Winston suits him."

"You don't know if it's a male."

I watch her roll her eyes. "It's the energy he gives off Fox."

Did the chlorine in the pool fuck with her brain? What is happening?

"Either way," I say slowly. "*Winston* and his energy are going to the shelter tomorrow."

"No," Janie matches my slow tone. "I don't think he is. I think I'm going to keep him."

"Torch, you can't just... decide to keep a cat. You are the one that won't pick out curtains because it's too much of a commitment." I watch her face wince slightly as her shaky hands hold the fur ball close to her chest. The cat is eating up the affection, nuzzling into her warmth. The scene is fucking adorable.

"I don't care," Janie says firmly. "I'm keeping Winston. He needs me...he wants me." Her tone sounds almost broken at the end. She shakes her head and stares back at me, eyes determined. "I understand that I am staying at your place, and you don't like animals. So don't worry, I'll find a new place for him and me to live. I was going to have to start looking for apartments anyway, my landlord has, not so nicely, asked me to move out due to the complaints with the people outside his complex."

New place to live?

"No." I say as I put the truck back into drive and merge back into the lane, heading for the pet store. "You two will stay with me."

I STARE at the tiny fur ball as it sleeps in the crook of Janie's neck. It's purring so loud I can't believe she is napping through it. I took her to the pet store that had a vet office attached. We went ahead and got Winston, the male kitten, checked out and then Janie proceeded to load the entire cart with kitten food, toys, beds, dishes, a stretching post thing and some monstrosity called a "cat tree". When I saw the total I about shit, but...she was so happy. I had never seen Janie smile so brightly. She fought me on payment, telling me that Winston was *her* son, and she could afford him. But before I could stop myself, I was swiping my credit card and carrying the six-foot tall, heavy as fuck, blue and grey cat tree to my truck while Janie practically bounced the entire way out.

The two of them spent all afternoon together, playing, and getting better acquainted. Winston loves Janie's wild hair which, same little dude, he burrows into it every chance he gets.

Janie's earlier words run through my head for what feels like the millionth time – *"You don't like animals".*

Actually, I do like animals, I just choose not to allow myself to get close to anyone, animals included. It's safer that way, for everyone. I can't fuck up and hurt them, and they can't disappear from my life and hurt me. It's a win-

win. Though, glancing back at the two of them, sleeping on my couch, I no longer feel like not getting close is really such a "win".

"YOU KNOW you are allowed to like Janie." Atlas says as he continues the line on the large, sleeping man's head.

"How is he asleep?" I ask in amazement, completely choosing to ignore his comment. Janie and I were fighting because I wanted her to come to the shop today to help me with new displays and she said that Winston would think she abandoned him so unless she could bring him with her, she was staying home. I tried to *politely* remind her that having a cat in a tattoo shop would be against health codes. She then reminded me that me fucking her on the table was also against health codes and that if I found Winston to be so filthy, I must find her filthy too and she wouldn't want to "spread the filth" at Hel's.

Cats make women crazy. That is the conclusion I've come to after this weekend.

Atlas looks up at me with a cocky grin. "I got that tender touch man."

Ash scoffs. "Dude's a nomad biker with a metal plate in his head."

Atlas stops his line and glares at Ash. "You know, ever since your sister called you while we were in Vegas you have been sucking the joy out of my life. It's not appreciated."

Ash rolls his dark eyes before going back to sketching.

"Anyway," At looks back at me while inking his machine. "You are allowed to want her."

If he didn't have a very large, intimidating looking man *sleeping* on his table, I would throw something at him. Instead, I play it safe and flip him off. He only shrugs before continuing. "I'm just saying. She's not a little girl anymore, man. She's a grown woman. Hell, you've had younger."

"Hey now," I say defensively, but his raised brow and incredulous look stop me from lying to him.

"Our ages aren't the issue anyway." I mutter as I lean back against my seat and rub my hands over my face.

"Is it Tony?" Ash asks and I sigh, looking to the front of the shop, wishing like hell someone would walk in and make this end. I am going to kick the ever-loving shit out of Atlas for telling Ash and Derek about my night with Janie. Though I guess I can't blame him. When I ran out of the convention during her call, there wasn't much hiding it from them. After several quiet seconds, it's apparent that I am not getting out of this conversation.

"I don't know, alright," I say with only partial honesty, no way I am ready to delve this deep into my past with these fucks. "At first, yeah, that was my reasoning. Janie was off-limits. We all got that drilled into us when we started here. But...I don't know. Somewhere along the way, his words stopped being as big of a block, even though I still like to use that as my reasoning."

Atlas nods, but his face remains neutral. "So, is that the excuse you give Janie? That her dad explicitly said no one could date her that works for him, which is a complete lie, but whatever."

I jerk my head up and look at him. "You know damn well that is not a lie. We all got the same talking to, and we've had several come through here who got their asses beat for trying to break that rule."

Atlas shakes his head while wiping the spot on the man's head. The biker growls in his sleep and all four of us freeze and stare at him until he falls back into his deep sleep. Atlas lets out a breath before continuing the tattoo as well as our conversation. "The old man said that he didn't want any of us thinking that they were going to get paid just to look at his daughter. Not that no one could date her."

Derek walks to our cabinet and pulls out a fresh marker while muttering something.

"Say again?" I raise a brow at the man, and he stares at me with a scowl.

"I said," He speaks up though keeps a side eye on the biker. "You were the only one that didn't get the talk from Tony to not fuck his daughter."

Atlas and Ash both stare at me in shock and I glare at Derek in annoyance. "Maybe that's because it was implied." I grumble. "Or maybe he just knew out of everyone, I would be the one he didn't have to worry about."

"And yet..." Derek's voice is full of a smugness that makes me want to punch him. "You are the only one that fucked her."

Atlas groans, "In our sanctuary.... On my own table."

Guilt fills me at that thought. Tony did publicly go around telling anyone that worked here the rules about Janie, and while I had been present for many, if not all of those talks, never once had that conversation been directed at me. I had thought maybe it was my age, but Derek and I are the same age and when Janie turned eighteen, you best believe Derek got a talking to, even though I don't think the man has said more than ten words to the girl his entire time here.

Tony never did talk to me and maybe it was because he trusted that I wouldn't betray him in that way.

"Stop looking so guilty." Atlas' voice cuts into my thoughts.

I stare up at him and sigh. "Tony was the only person that gave a shit about me! The only fucking person that didn't make me feel like a useless waste of space! I came to apprentice here and within days I lost my mom and sister. A year later, I had to start financially caring for a father that spent his entire life using me as a punching bag, as an ashtray, he reminded me every day that I was worthless! Including on his fucking hospital bed where he reminded me ***with his dying breaths*** that no one ever loved me and that I cause nothing but pain."

My eyes go wide, and I look up to see the men all staring at me with shocked expressions.

"Fox..." Atlas' voice sounds laced with some kind of pity that makes me feel angry. I'm about to tell him as much when the biker sits up, startling us all.

He looks directly at me, and I feel like I may have to fight this man.

He opens his mouth, and his massive body deflates. "That is a reflection on your father, son. Not you."

O.... kay? I give Atlas a look that says, "What the actual fuck" and he just stares at me and shrugs.

The biker continues. "I don't know you, or this girl. But if she has you this conflicted, son you are already in it too deep. You ain't getting out unscathed."

His words hit me unexpectedly. I give him a polite smile mostly out of fear. I may or may not be able to take him, but even if I win the fight, I am going to wish I had died after the ass beating, he will deliver. I excuse myself and head to the break room to get away from the overwhelming emotions happening in the tattoo area.

Before I can take a breath, there is a ding from my phone and I feel annoyance rush through me. I get ready to chuck my phone across the room but the name on the screen catches my eye.

Torch

I open the message and I feel myself visibly relax and I feel the corners of my mouth pull into a smile. She's sent me a selfie. It's of her and Winston, she's holding him, and they are pressing their faces together. Her smile is so big, her dimples are popped, and her nose and eyes are wrinkled. No filters, no make-up. Just her and that cat, happy as can be. And she sent it to me.

"Son, you are already in it too deep. You ain't getting out unscathed."

Fuck.

Chapter Twenty-One

JANIE

"HERE." I look at Fox, who is holding a bag out to me as I'm sitting on the floor playing with Winston. I raise a skeptical brow as I stand up and take the bag before plopping onto the couch.

"What is it?" I ask. Winston lets out a meow that is far larger than his tiny body as he tries to climb up the couch. Fox walks over and helps my son up and I can't help but smile. Fox loves Winston, even if he acts like he is an annoyance.

"Just open it." He grumbles as he puts Winston next to me. I untie the shopping bag and pull the item out. I look at it in confusion for a moment until I realize what I'm looking at. It's a tablet with a pen. I look from the tablet back to Fox who has a shy smile on his face.

"I umm..." He rubs the back of his neck, "I know you mentioned missing drawing and thought maybe you would like to try digital drawing because it's a little more forgiving with the lines— Why are you crying?"

I ignore his panicked question as I hold the tablet tightly to my chest. He got me a present... a sweet, thoughtful present. I set the tablet to the side and place Winston on the floor before moving to the ottoman where he sits and straddling his lap.

"J-Janie..." He breathes as my hands hold his jaw.

I stare into his eyes and then down at his lips. "Fox...not one more fucking word." I growl, repeating his words from our last physical encounter.

I press my lips to his and a whimper escapes me. God, he feels so good. His mouth hesitantly opens, and I force my tongue inside his eagerly, earning that growl that goes straight to my core. I pull back for air and look at his hazy eyes, full to the brim with desire, I would bet my eyes were matching.

"I need this." I pant and grind against him. He groans and his hands grip my thighs.

"Janie..." It sounds like a desperate plea.

I notice the pained look of his face. "Fox?" I whisper, feeling the rejection again, just like at the pool.

I feel his strong hand on my cheek and I rest into it, enjoying the warmth. "Baby doll," He says softly and I deflate.

"Okay." I force a smile and move off of him while trying to avoid brushing against his raging erection.

"Baby doll, listen." Fox stands up but I scoop up Winston and start towards my room.

"It's fine Fox, I would really rather not listen to this." The feeling of embarrassment is becoming overwhelming. If he doesn't want me, why does he keep doing nice things?

"Janie!" His demanding bark of my name stops my progression towards the door. Turning to look at him, I see the battle on his face and I soften my rigid stance.

"Okay," I breathe, allowing him to speak if he wants.

Fox nods and rubs his hands together anxiously. "I care

about you Janie, but you've got to realize how bad of an idea it is for us to be physical."

I set the sleeping Winston up in the hammock of his cat tree before turning back to Fox. "We've already been physical." I state, crossing my arms.

"Yeah, and look at where we are now," Fox huffs. "You are a stay-at-home cat mom, living in my house and you're trying to fuck me again, meanwhile I'm full of anxiety and guilt."

I glare up at him. "Don't bring Winston into this," I snap, "And you told me to live here. I've told you several times now I will move out. You asked me to stay. You want me gone? I'll leave."

"No, I don't want you gone!" He runs his hands through his hair in frustration. "I just...I can't be your boyfriend, Janie. I won't be and I need you to understand that because when you kiss me like that, when you look at me the way you did in the pool the other day. It makes me feel like I'm in a boyfriend zone."

Huh. Well, that hurts far more than getting turned down for sex. I look at his pleading face and I have the urge to punch him. Hard. But how can I? Fox has said several times he is not getting into a relationship with me. If I went ahead and caught feelings, that's my own fault. He looks like he's about to speak again when my phone rings.

I see the look of annoyance on his face when I grab it but what do I care? Not my boyfriend, not my problem.

"Hey Ren." I say when I put the phone up to my ear, Fox doesn't move, he continues to glower at me with his intense hazel eyes.

"Janie..." Ren's sad tone grabs my attention.

"What's wrong?" I ask and Fox blinks and comes closer,

I shove him away, not wanting his intoxicating presence near me.

"Can you come over, please?" She cries into the phone, and I instantly head towards the door, slipping on my flip flops.

"I'm coming over now." I say before hanging up the phone.

"I'll drive you." Fox says and I hold my hand up to stop his progression.

"Fox, I can go to Ren's by myself."

He looks genuinely confused as he crosses his arms over his chest. "Ren is my friend too."

"She didn't call you." I say definitively as I walk to the door. "Besides," I sigh as I open the door and look back at him. "Some distance might be good for us. Make sure you feed Winston in an hour if I'm not back." I shut the door without waiting for a response and head to my car, eager to put all the distance I can between him and I.

"THAT SON OF A BITCH!" I yell as Ren opens the door and I see her swollen, split lip.

"Please," She cries, and she curls into me. "I know you're tiny but just wrap me in your massive dick energy." I give her a forced laugh as I pat her back and walk with her to her couch where her blue-eyed husky, Bruno lays, eagerly wagging his fluffy tail while awaiting his mandatory pats.

"So, what happened?" I ask while scratching Bruno's ear.

Ren looks away, almost as if she is embarrassed. "I went out on a tinder date, it was going so well until...his wife showed up."

"Oh no..." I wince and she nods as if confirming where I believed the story to be going.

"Yeah," she sighs. "She called me a fat slut and then back handed me." She forces out a laugh. "Her engagement ring busted my lip."

"Oh sweetie," I pat her thigh. "You know..."

"Save it," she groans. "I know, I'm a catch, I'll find my perfect man one day blah blah blah."

"Well, it doesn't seem like I'm needed at all." I laugh and she groans as she lays her head in my lap.

"Janie, can't we just be in a relationship together?" She whines and I laugh.

"You and I both know we enjoy certain people of the opposite sex far too much to do that." I groan as my gut twists at the thought of Fox.

Ren scoffs, causing Bruno to jump. "Speak for yourself. You're the one in love with Fox."

"Hey now!" I playfully shove her away. "Don't be throwing that word out there. It's a crush and he made it brutally clear right before you called that he has zero interest in anything to do with me."

Ren raises a brow. "Really? *Brutally*?"

I over emphasize my nod. "Yep. Here is a direct quote," I clear my throat to do a terrible impression of Fox. "I can't be your boyfriend, Janie. I won't be and I need you to understand that."

Ren's lip curls and she stares at me for a moment before shaking her head. "What a douche. Well fine, he's dead to us."

I whine as I fall back on the couch. "Why does he do

nice things if he doesn't want me? He just gave me a fucking drawing tablet because he thought I might like to start drawing again but knows it's impossible with my tremors."

Ren holds her hands to her chest. "Oh my god! How sweet!"

"Right!?" I shriek. "Then I kissed him because he just did the sweetest thing anyone has ever done for me in a long list of sweet things he's done and he tells me he doesn't want me! I thought we were the confusing sex."

Ren shrugs, "The only people who say we are the confusing sex are men, and obviously we can't rely on them to have coherent thoughts."

Bruno, evidently annoyed by the lack of attention he's receiving snorts and then howls at me. Ren rolls her eyes, "Again, men."

I giggle as I scratch Bruno's belly. "Leave Bruno alone, he's not a man, he's a prince." I say in my baby talk as he licks my cheek.

"Yeah yeah, my little service dog flunker." I laugh as I remember Ren telling me about Bruno while I was staying here during the convention.

Ren has Type One Diabetes, and three years ago, her father made her get Bruno to help track when her sugars were not stable. Apparently, after getting Bruno and taking him to all the classes, they couldn't certify him because poor Bruno has an anxiety disorder. So, according to Ren, every time her sugars would go too high or drop too low, Bruno would have a panic attack.... or the dog equivalent to a panic attack. It was so bad that she couldn't rely on him to tell her if she was high or low, just that something was wrong.

So that brings us here, three years later. Bruno still has panic attacks but has grown accustomed to Ren's diabetes and can alert her to check her sugars if he senses it's out of whack. I don't know too much about her diabetes, the only reason I found out was because while I was at her apartment, her blood sugar dropped too much too fast and I had to be walked through how to help her. She said no one in her life besides her family knows. She doesn't like to be seen differently and because she is plus sized, people hear she is a diabetic and, due to the lack of education, think it's due to her being bigger.

Ren wears an insulin pump and some kind of monitoring device but keeps it hidden under her clothes. I couldn't say anything. I kept my disorder hidden, people suck, and they love to try and explain to you what you are doing wrong and how to fix it. It wears on you.

"Will you sleep here tonight?" Ren's voice pulls me out of my thoughts. "There is this dance class tomorrow I thought you and I could go to, and I could introduce you to my friend, Sunday. I think you'll really like her. Then maybe we could go back to your place since Fox will be gone still and gush over Winston?"

I grin brightly, "That sounds amazing. Let me just text Fox so he can take care of Winston and then I'll go back to ignoring him."

I stare at my phone and see that I have multiple missed texts from Fox.

> Fox: You didn't really just leave without me
>
> Fox: Janie! Come on girl, talk to me!
>
> Fox: Winston is not happy with waking up and finding you not here.
>
> Fox: He thinks I have something to do with your disappearance. He keeps bouncing sideways and hissing at me...then tripping.

Fox: He just pissed in my shoes…

Fox: Please come home. I didn't mean for what I said to come out shit. I really didn't.

Fox: Winston misses you and thinks you should forgive Uncle Fox for being an asshole.

Fox: He says Uncle Fox might miss you too.

Ren let out a laugh. "Yeah, can't and won't be your boyfriend. Janie, if that isn't a boyfriend then I have no idea what one is."

I sigh while scratching my head, "According to him, this isn't a relationship." I mutter as I tap out a text.

Me: Spending the night with Ren. She's fine, bad date. Tell Winston I love him and miss him.

I go to turn off my phone but Fox replies instantly.

Fox: Just Winston?

Me: Yeah, no one else should be missing anyone else as per our previous conversation. Good night.

I don't wait for his response as I power my phone down and head to the bedroom with Ren and Bruno.

"LAUREN..." I breathe as I stare at the dance studio and the large metal poles fixed to the floor and ceiling. "I thought you said, dance class."

"I did." Ren shrugs as she walks up to a pole. "This is dancing."

"This is a stripper class!" I hiss as I feel the redness creeping up my face.

"Pole Dancing, actually." I jump at the buttery soft feminine southern accent from behind me. I turn, and holy lady boners. This woman is a goddess. She stands tall and straight, tone, lean muscles everywhere. Her silvery-white hair is expertly braided and flipped over her shoulder, resting on her small, toned chest, the ends tinted a bright turquoise. Her skin is a light tan, freckles over just the tops of her cheeks and her slender nose. I have to admit; I'm jealous. She has the perfect number of freckles. The freckle pattern that girls - and guys - were drawing on their faces or using filters to create. Not like me, who is covered in them head to toe.

Her honey-color eyes glitter under the lights in the dance room. A smile graces her full lips, nearly weakening my knees. I don't know whether to hate her or if I want to fuck her at this moment.

"Hey Sunday!" Ren's voice pulls me out of my trance. I watch as Ren pulls the beauty into an embrace.

"Janie, this is Sunday Sutton. She runs this dance studio. Sunday, this is Janie Pierce." Her eyes widen, and her smile falls the slightest bit.

"Pierce? As in Tony Pierce?" God, I could listen to her read the ingredients in a shampoo bottle. I wonder where she is originally from.

"He's my dad...was my dad." I still am not sure how to respond. Wouldn't he always be my dad?

Sunday gives me a soft smile. "I'm sorry for your loss; Tony was such a character."

I raised a brow. "How did you know him?" I probably said that with a bit more hostility than I meant, but I am beginning to fear that this beauty may be one of my dad's old flames.

Sunday turns and removes her white crop T-shirt to reveal her strappy blue sports bra and a massive black and grey dragon tattoo that takes up her entire back with pink cherry blossoms scattered around. It is a beautiful piece, but not one that my dad did. It looks more like Ash's work.

"Ash?" I ask, and when she gives me a slight nod, I can't help the pride I feel in myself for being able to differentiate between my guys' work.

"Yes, ma'am, I spent a little while in that shop. Your dad was amazing. Now, I am so excited you decided to come with Ren! I've been trying to get her to come for, at the very least, a private class for a year now."

I scratch the back of my head nervously. "Well, I'm here for moral support, but that's all I'm good for. I have zero upper body strength. There is no way I can jump on that pole without busting my ass."

"Oh, you'll bust your ass," Sunday says while tossing her shirt off to the side and walking to the front of the class where the front pole is. "Can't learn to walk without falling a couple of times. Falling is important."

I raise my brow and look from Ren to Sunday. "And why on Earth would I want to fall? I would much rather do things the right way the first time."

Sunday swung lazily around the pole until she was looking at me. "How do you know what the right way is unless you experience the wrong way? Falling teaches you what not to do."

AN HOUR AND A HALF LATER, Ren and I are panting on the dance studio floor. Sweat rolling off of us. Sunday, the pole dancing queen that she is, is near the top of her pole, in a pose that I've learned is called the *Remi Hold*. She told us this after Ren and I...okay, mostly I, failed at the much easier version called the Pole Sit.

Ren was excellent, and I told her she was never allowed to doubt herself again. She has an impressive amount of strength and had very little trouble holding herself on the pole, unlike my weak ass.

"You ladies ready to shower and go out to get drinks?" Sunday moves down and off the pole with a grace I will forever be envious of and squats in front of us.

"Better idea," I pant, still unable to breathe correctly or move. "We go shower and then eat pizza and drink at home."

Ren weakly slaps her hands together in agreement, and Sunday laughs.

"Alright, well, are you two going to be able to get yourselves home?" I roll my head to look at Ren, who is giving the same painful look that I am sure is on my bright red face.

"Uh..." I breathe. "Maybe give us five minutes."

"OKAY, SO WAIT," Sunday shakes her head as she takes a sip of her beer. "So, do you want him or not? Because it sounds obvious that he wants you."

I groan and hide my face in the couch cushion. "I don't know! I mean, I have feelings for him...I think? Those feelings typically go between irritation and horniness but still...feelings."

Lauren shakes her head as if I am disappointing her. "Still cannot believe you've only fucked the lumberjack once."

Stevie, who we invited over after she got off work, laughs as she plays with Winston. "True, I thought for sure there would've at least been a blowy in there."

Sunday's mouth drops, and she stares at me in disbelief. "You live with that god, and you've only done it once?! My word, maybe mama was right, and I am a whore because I would've made damn sure that man's dick was ruined for anyone else." She laughs and grabs a slice of pizza.

Sunday Sutton is a charming, twenty-five-year-old Alabama girl who was a professional ballerina until three years ago. Sunday has epilepsy, and years ago, her seizures were becoming too frequent, and after having them at several events and dances, she decided it was time to retire. Instead of returning home to Alabama, Sunday flew from New York to California and opened her dance studio with the help of her father.

"I don't know what to do." I sigh as I pick a slice of pepperoni off my pizza. "I can't be around him because all we do is fight, and I am sure the main reason we fight is that I'm emotionally and sexually frustrated with him."

"What are you going to do Friday?" Ren asks, looking up from kissing Winston's head. I quirk a brow as I stare at a complete loss in her direction.

CHAPTER TWENTY-ONE

"Friday," She repeats slowly. "You know, the party?"

I sit in confusion until it hits me. We are having a celebration of life party for my dad. Atlas is renting out his apartment building's clubhouse, and a bunch of dad's old tattoo artist friends are getting together. I'd completely forgotten about it. And I have no way of getting out of it.

"You think I could tell Fox he can't go?" I cringe at Ren's warning look. "It's a joke!"

"What if you take a date?" Sunday asks while her mouth is full of pizza.

"That's a good idea!" Stevie beams as she stares at me, a smile forming on her lips. "You bring a date, and then you won't be alone or have to worry about him."

"Plus," Ren says, tapping her chin. "We get just the right guy and Fox will get jealous as fuck. Maybe it'll snap him out of whatever inner struggle he is having."

I chew on my bottom lip and sigh. Bringing a date is not something I feel comfortable doing. Hell, did I even know anyone that would be willing to be seen with me after getting canceled?

"I don't know. It's kind of hard for me to get a date since everything with Brody." Ren rolls her eyes at the mention of Brody. Sunday makes a small "Hmmm" while tapping her beer bottle against her lips.

"Oh! Luca!" She squeals, and Ren starts cheering.

"Luca?" I ask, suddenly wary of the girls. I look at Stevie for help, but she is at just as much a loss as I am.

"Luca is an exotic dancer. He's been coming to my classes for two years to up his stage game." Sunday grins. "He is gorgeous and one hundred percent gay, so no worries about having to fuck him afterward. But he looks like...my lord..." Sunday starts fanning herself with her hand while Ren is nodding furiously and scrolling through her phone.

"Here is his Instagram." Ren says, and oh shit. Okay, this black-haired, tanned Italian Adonis is almost too much to look at. All those perfectly sculpted muscles –

"Is that an eight-pack?" I ask as Sunday nods and raises her hand in praise.

"The Lord gave to this man, and it was good."

"Are you even sure he would help? I mean, he looks way out of my league. I doubt it would be believable that he and I are dating."

"First off, if he were straight, Luca would most certainly not be out of your league. And second, he is an escort. He does this shit all the time. I'll see if he's free." Sunday grabs her phone and starts tapping away. I looked nervously at Ren and Stevie. I don't like new men. But Ren seems to be okay with it. I'm sure he's nice, and it would be fun to have someone dote on me all night to help with the awkwardness of Fox and then the fact that I didn't want to go and feel the overwhelming grief I knew I would from talking about my dad's passing.

"Yay!" Sunday squeals. "He said he'd love to!"

Chapter Twenty-Two

FOX

"STOP LOOKING IN THE MIRROR." Atlas hisses while handing me a glass of bourbon. I glance at the spherical ice in the glass and raise a brow at Atlas while pointing at the bougie ice.

"Dude," Atlas groans knowingly. "Ash is extra, okay. Don't ask me." I snort and drink the liquid while looking around the room. To say I'm uncomfortable would be an understatement. I'm in a new suit, in a crowd, talking about my mentor's death, and I'm waiting for Janie to show up. She's thirty minutes late, not that there was a set time to arrive. I need to see her; it's been too long. I thought I would see her after work after she spent the night at Ren's. But I was wrong. She and Winston were gone when I got there and when I sent her a text, she said she needed space and would be staying with Stevie while apartment hunting and she would be working on our online presence from there.

Coming home to my empty house the last few days, no smiles, no laughs, no fights, no Winston. It's been the absolute worst feeling. All I could think about was that creepy ass biker and how he said I was already in it. He was right, I'm in and there is no going back. I decided then that I needed to tell her that, even though I am not sure what it is, I am feeling something for her. I also wanted to be honest and upfront about why I had been so hesitant. For the first time in my life, I wanted to be open with someone. But the realization of that had me going back and forth no less than a hundred times on the decision.

As of right now, I am ready to tell her. I just hope she comes through the door soon before I lose my nerve. Again.

I hear the door open and watch as a man walks in that I don't recognize. He's about my height, has dark tan skin, and is obviously very built under what appears to be a costly suit. His black hair is pushed back, and he has a calm smile on his face. I am about to ask him if he's in the right place when I see who is on his arm.

My heart stops.

Long, poker-straight red hair, smokey dark makeup, dark nude lips, and a short, tight halter cocktail dress, black...and backless. I forget how to breathe, and all my blood rushes straight to my cock, leaving me light-headed. Her blue eyes meet mine, and she smiles before pulling on the guy's arm and pointing my way. You've got to be kidding me. There is no way they are together. This is a dream...a fucking nightmare.

"Fox," Janie smiles as they walk up to me. "This is my date, Luca." I stare as the man smiles and holds out his hand. For a second, I am still while I try to decide if I should shake his hand or deck him.

Deciding calmer heads will prevail or some shit, I stick my hand into his. "Nice to meet you." I say crisply, though in my head I am screaming — *I will kill you and everything you hold dear.*

"It's so great to meet you as well." Luca's voice is deep with an Italian accent that I'm sure gets him all kinds of women. But not mine. Janie wouldn't go after him...would she?

"Janie has spoken so much about you and the men at the shop." Why are his teeth so fucking white? It's annoying. He is annoying.

"Funny, because she has never once mentioned you." I say and take a drink of my bourbon to hide my smirk as I see Janie's face heat up.

Luca's smile doesn't waver. "Well, you know how it is when things are new. But, of course, we are still trying to see where we fit in each other's lives, minus the bedroom." Had I known I would be committing a murder tonight, I would've worn a t-shirt instead of my nicest outfit. Oh well.

As I go to explain to Luca, in great detail, how I plan on skinning him while he watches, Janie speaks up.

"Luca, could you get me a drink? Atlas knows what I like." I watch as she twists her fingers together nervously.

Luca leans in and kisses her temple. *My temple.* "Of course, pet."

Pet?

I watch as this fuckers lips move to Janie's cheek, the cheek that I want to stroke and kiss. The rage going through me is too much. I need to punch something right now. I watch as Janie completely ignores me and talks to some asshole that may or may not have known Tony. At this point, I've realized everyone is suddenly an old friend of his.

I watch as she smiles at the man, it's fake, but he

doesn't care. I stare at how her dress hits just below her perfect ass, and it's almost too much to think about.

Luca, the golden retriever he is, comes bouncing back to Janie and hands her a drink. As Janie rests her head on Luca's arm, I slam my empty glass down and turn to walk down the hall of the modern clubhouse to the private bathrooms. I run my hands over my beard in frustration.

Why is she doing this to me? Is she purposely trying to make me insane? Does she want me to gut that man in front of this entire party? Because that is where we are heading, fast.

I hear high heels clicking on the hardwood floors; I know it's her before she speaks.

"Get tired of your new puppy?" I sneer as I turn to face Janie. When I see her face, all the anger leaves me as concern takes over.

"What's wrong?" I walk up to her trembling body and grab her shoulders. "Did he hurt you?" I growl, my anger hitting a dangerously high level.

"W-what? N-no." She whispers, her bottom lip quivering. She looks up at me with watery eyes.

"Did you really put my old sketches on my dad's urn?" I still for a second, trying to readjust my emotions.

"Oh, right. I forgot Atlas picked it up today. Yeah, I found them in The Office right after we picked up his ashes and thought that maybe they could print them on the urn like a collage."

Janie shoves me into the open bathroom before shutting and locking the door. I stare down at her, but before I can speak, her lips are on mine. Her tongue in my mouth, and fuck yes, she tastes like the sweet alcoholic drink that fucker brought her, and sunshine, and Christmas morning.

I growl against her mouth, earning a moan as I slam her

against the door. I feel her release my hair from the band and run her fingers through it, gripping and tugging as she presses harder against me like she can't get close enough. I understand the feeling.

I press my rock-hard cock against her belly, and she inhales a sharp breath, breaking the kiss. No way I am stopping this. No one is going to come to their fucking senses right now. I grip the back of her neck with one hand and put the other one on the back of her thigh, pulling it up to my hip.

"Jump," I demand in a gruff voice. She obeys and wraps her legs around my waist, her dress bunching up her hips. Then, using the hand on her neck, I find the clasp on the halter straps of her dress and easily unclasp it, sending the top half of her dress pooling between us.

I feel her grind her hips against me, and I roll my eyes back and moan. "Fuckkk."

My lips capture hers again as I palm one of her bare breasts. She lets out a needy whine as she continues to grind against my dick.

I pull back and glare down at her. "What about him out there?"

She is in a lust-filled daze but shakes her head. "Don't stop." She orders as she puts her feet on the floor. I watch as her dress slips completely off of her, revealing her naked breasts and black lace panties. I stare in shock as I look her up and down, only minutely aware that I am palming myself through my pants.

"Do you have any idea what you do to me?" I ask slowly as I slip out of my suit jacket, tossing it to the side. "Do you have any idea how badly I've wanted to fuck you since the moment you walked in tonight? And then you're with that happy son of a bitch, and I want to murder him and fuck you on top of his dying body." I wrap her hair around my fist and jerk her to me.

"Jealous?" She asks between shaky breaths. I let out a small puff of air before pulling her closer to my face.

"Dangerously." My voice is low, and I lick her bottom lip, causing her to shudder.

"Your fault," She breathes against my mouth. "I could've been yours tonight." I stare into her eyes, her pupils wide. I slide my hand down her stomach, over her panties, and between her thighs. I slip inside, and a smirk forms as I feel her. She's dripping.

"Oh, baby doll...." I purr as I slip a finger inside her. Curling my finger before pulling out and slipping it into my mouth. Fuck her taste is so fucking rich, sweet and tangy. Warm and wet and the most addictive thing I've ever tasted. "You were always mine." I slip my fingers back inside her hot, tight entrance, rougher this time. She grips my shoulders as a gasp escapes her. I press the heel of my palm against her clit while I pull her face to mine.

"Make yourself cum on my hand." I order, my voice low. Once I feel her moving against my hand, I capture her lips and begin fucking her mouth with my tongue. I swallow every one of her moans and cries and I pump my fingers into her faster and her hips grind and buck harder. I feel her movements become jerky and I feel her walls spasming around me. She's going to cum. I break our kiss and watch as her pale pink nipples become tighter and her abdomen tenses.

"Oh god..." She pants and rolls her head back. She begins to cry out and I slap my hand over her mouth and watch her eyes roll back as she violently bucks against me.

Once she stops her movement, I remove my hand from inside her and my other from her swollen mouth. I need to be inside her, now. I stare at her as she pants, her eyes, and body begging for more. Then it hits me.

"I don't have a condom." Why? Why did I stop carrying fucking condoms?!

"I don't care." She pants as she stares at me. "I am on birth control."

That's all I need her to say. In an instant, I slip off her wet panties, stuffing them in my pants pocket before spinning her around, so she is gripping the sink and looking into the oversized mirror. In record time, I pull my cock out and press the crown against her now extra tight, dripping entrance.

Staring into her lust-filled eyes in the mirror, I grip her hip with one hand as I guide her to my cock.

"Did you fuck him?" I have to know before I enter her. I have to know.

"No." She breathes. "Just you," I smirk in satisfaction as I force myself inside her to the hilt. I watch her body tremble as she tries to adjust to my size, shaking and gasping in the process. I groan out a strangled breath as I too need to adjust to the extreme tightness. The sensations without the condom are almost more than I can handle. When was the last time I had sex without a condom? High school? I can't remember.

I feel her grind against me, and I release a low hiss. Fuck she feels terrific. I pull out several inches before pushing back in, causing a small cry to escape her. I pick up the pace. As much as I crave to give her hours of pleasure, a public bathroom at a party while her date is waiting on her puts a time constraint on us. Although, a part of me likes the thought of that perfectly tanned fuck seeing his date getting bent over, receiving her pleasure from me.

"Yes! Harder! More!" She cries out as I continue to slam

into her dripping pussy. Fuck she's so tight. And warm. And mine. This is it, I refuse to let anyone else experience her. I stare at her reflection in the mirror, her head down, and I am not too fond of it. Moving one hand from her hip but continuing with the same speed and force, I run it past her bouncing tits to her neck and grip her delicate throat.

"Look in the mirror," I growl. She doesn't obey at first, and I squeeze the sides of her throat slightly, getting her attention.

"I said to fucking look." I bark. Her head whips up, and our eyes lock, and fucking shit. Her face is red from arousal, her eyes have a hazy look, and her mouth is open as she pants and moans.

"You feel so good, Janie." I groan as I slide my other hand from her hip down to her swollen clit. Her knees buckle as my fingers rub her.

"Stay up, baby doll. I'm not done with my pretty girl yet."

"Yours?" She whispers, and I stare deep into her eyes. I glance at my face and barely recognize the animalistic caveman looking back. Eyes dark, lip curled, a light sheen of sweat over my face.

"Yes," I grunt, shoving myself deeper inside, earning a cry. She's close. I can feel her already tight walls becoming tighter around me.

"Mine. Say it, Janie, I want you to say you're mine, tell me I'm the only one that can give you this kind of pleasure. Say it now!" I drive into her over and over as my fingers continue around her hardening bud.

"Ah! Fox! I-I'm yours!" She presses her back into my chest as her hand wraps around the back of my neck, gripping my hair.

"You're it." She forces out between moans. "No- no one

has ever made me feel like you. Oh god! Oh god! Fox!" She screams my name, and I move my hand from her throat to her mouth to silence her orgasm again, as tragic as that is.

"God fucking damn it!" I growl as I chase my own release, her tight walls contracting around me.

"You are so fucking good. Such a good fucking girl." I whisper as the sounds of her pleasure and our skin slapping fills the bathroom.

"Good girl, milk my cock baby. Take what belongs to you." I watch fire light in her eyes and before I realize what's happening, Janie fucking Pierce bends in half at the waist, allowing me deeper access to her contracting cunt. It's too much. I grip her tight fucking ass as I ram her against me over and over while I feel my balls tighten. Groaning, I throw my head back and let out a guttural sound as I fill her with spurt after spurt of my hot load.

After a moment, I remove myself from inside her and start putting myself back inside my pants. I watch as Janie stands there, hands gripping the sink again.

"Are you alright?" I ask as I offer to help her get cleaned.

She pushes me off. "I'm fine. I need a minute to get situated." I feel uneasy in my gut as I watch walls going up. I can't let this happen.

I grab her wrist and pull her to me. "Baby doll," I cover her opening mouth with my finger so she can't interrupt. "I want to go back home, and I want to talk to you about us. And I fucking want you to bring my cat back."

She lets out a small, sad laugh before looking up at me. "I don't want to go there and get hurt."

I kiss her forehead, "I never want to hurt you, please, I want to open up and talk to you."

She looks at me and gives me a sweet smile before kissing me on the lips. "Okay. I'll meet you there."

"With my cat-son." I insist and she presses her face into my chest to quiet her laughing.

She looks up at me with her eyes as bright and clear as a summer sky. It makes my heart pound and I try to breathe through the anxiety. I can do this. I *want* this.

"I'll wait for you outside." I say, figuring she will want privacy to get cleaned up, plus I need to make sure the coast is clear for her. Though, I am completely fine with everyone, including the golden retriever, knowing what we just did.

Janie looks around the bathroom and frowns. "Where are my panties?"

I smirk as I pull out the garment and wave it in front of her.

Her eyes widen. "Fox!" She hisses as she reaches for them, I move them out of her reach.

I grip her by the back of the neck and bring her closer to my face. I make her watch as I inhale her scent from her panties. "Do you have any idea," I growl as I inhale deeper. "How fucking intoxicating your scent is?"

I watch her cheeks go crimson as she mutely shakes her head side to side. I fall to my knee as I slip her feet into the holes of her panties. I slowly slide them up her legs and a wicked grin creeps onto my face as my hands run over her soaked inner thighs. Our mixed juices running out of her pussy.

I slip the panties all the way up before pressing my nose into the front of her pussy, inhaling again and letting out a growl. "Baby doll, you are driving me insane." I stand up and grab her hand placing it on my hardening cock.

"I'm ready for you again." I whisper and she chuckles lightly.

"We need to get out of this bathroom." She pushes on my chest lightly and I groan in annoyance but obey. "Knock so I know it's clear and I can come out. I will go and get Winston and we will come to your house." She says as I head to the door. I give her a small smirk, shutting the door behind me.

Once I am sure that no one is around, I tap on the door, signaling to Janie that she is free to come out when she is ready. I look at the party and let out a sigh. As much as I want to stay here, and just talk to her about everything now, I will wait, allow her to go get Winston and come to my house as she promised, and we will discuss everything then. I want her in my life, and if that means I have to pull back the curtain and show her some of my scars so she understands why this is harder for me than it would be for others, then that's what I will have to do. It's worth it... she's worth it.

Chapter Twenty-Three

JANIE

"YOU LITTLE SLUT!" Luca teases as he drives us to Stevie's apartment.

I groan and hide my face in my hands. "I'm so sorry, Luca! I don't know what's wrong with me!"

"Oh, honey, you are thinking with your lady dick. It happens to us all." I groan again and rest my head against the seat of his Range Rover.

"He wants me to go to his place so we can talk."

"Do you want to?" He asks and I shrug while staring at the raindrops hitting the windshield.

"Yes. But I'm afraid to. I really like him, but every time we get close like this, he ends up pushing me away. I'm afraid–"

"That you'll go to his house, open yourself up and he will do it again?" He smiles knowingly and I nod grimly.

"I really like him, but I don't know if there can ever be a real future with him given how he acts like a cornered rat every time I try to show him any closeness or affection. I don't know if it's just him, or if it's something to do with me..."

Luca laughs dryly. "Honey, trust me on this, that man cares about you."

I roll my eyes, "You spent all of ten minutes with the man. How would you know?"

He gives me a half shrug as he pulls up to the bakery parking lot where Stevie's rather tiny apartment sits over-top. "Believe me," He chuckles. "That was eight minutes longer than I needed to come to that conclusion. He was ready to murder me tonight the moment he saw me enter with you." I blush as memories of Fox fill my mind. Him fucking me, his jealous snarls and dark eyes, making me tell him I was his.

"Hey!" Luca taps my forehead. "No nasty thoughts on the expensive leather. Now, go get your feline and then go get your man." I can't help but laugh lightly as I reach over the console and give Luca a hug.

"Thank you for everything." I whisper as I kiss his cheek.

"Yes, yes, I am wonderful. Now off you go, there was a man at the party that I really would like to get to know better."

Raising my brow, I pull back and cock my head. "Who? No wait, I don't want to know which of my father's friends you're about to bone."

Luca gives me a grin and I climb out of the car to head inside and grab Winston.

I RUN through the downpour with Winston's covered carrier in my arms as I head up the steps to Fox's porch.

Knocking on the door several times as I try not to shiver from the rain soaking me. The door opens, and Fox is standing there, shirtless with black pajama pants sitting low on his hips.

"Holy shit, you came." He breathes out as if in shock at my presence. "Shit, you're soaked." Shaking his head out of whatever trance he is in, Fox lets me into the house. "Go take your clothes off and grab one of my shirts, and I'll throw these in the dryer for you." He gestures to my soaked black leggings and purple shirt that have become like a second skin.

I drop my backpack while setting Winston's carrier down and opening the small door to let him out. Instantly he meows happily and rushes out, running straight to his cat tree.

Turning to stare at the man, who was already scratching Winston's head, I tilt my head to the side. "Did you burn all the clothes I had here?"

Fox looks at me, equally as confused. "No, why would you think that?"

"You told me to go get a shirt of yours, like my own clothes aren't in the closet I was using." I watch as he lets out a breath and turns to give me his full attention.

"When you are cold, you put on my hoodies. You're soaked, I figured you were cold. If you would rather your clothes, go for it." He sounds tired and anxious as he speaks. It makes me wonder if he was going to shut down on me again.

I don't verbally answer him, I just nod before walking down the familiar hallway to his room. I proceed to strip out of my clothes, including my wet bra and panties, before grabbing a towel and drying off.

I run my fingers over all his shirts, landing on a blue

216

hoodie. I slip it on as well as a pair of boxers before running the towel through my hair one last time to ensure I'm not dripping. My long, thick hair loves to hold water, and the last thing I need is to make a puddle somewhere and then slip on it. It's happened several times.

Walking down the hallway, I smell the heavenly aroma of hot apple cider. Walking into the kitchen, I grin as I see Fox pouring said cider into two mugs.

"My favorite." I muse before tossing my clothes into the dryer myself and starting it.

I walk over to him and take one of the mugs before inhaling the warm apple and cinnamon scent.

"I also have pumpkin muffins over on the table." I raise a brow when I notice them in a Tupperware container instead of store packaging. "They're from Stevie." He says casually as if he noticed my confusion.

"When did you see Stevie?" I ask while taking a sip of the hot drink, enjoying the way it warms up my entire body.

Fox rubs the back of his neck, his nervous tell. "I've been going by in the mornings on my way to Hel's."

My mug pauses at my lips, and I stare at him. "Why?" I ask nervously, afraid that the man I have feelings for may be trying something with my best friend.

Sensing my discomfort, Fox's eyes widen. "Oh god no!" He waves his hands. "Not like that, I mean I really like Stevie but..." He shifts uncomfortably. "I was coming in to see if I could get her to tell me how you and Winston were doing."

My eyes soften at his confession that obviously makes him uncomfortable. I watch as he stuffs his hands into his pajama pants pockets while leaning against his counter. I marvel at his thick, strong, tattooed body and that trail of hair under his belly button that I still haven't had the plea-sure of running my fingers over.

"Are you mad?" His voice pulls me out of my completely inappropriate trance. "If you're worried, Stevie is a fucking vault. She wouldn't say anything besides you and Winston were alive. I think she gave me the muffins this morning out of pity." He laughs dryly and I can't help but smile gently.

After a moment of awkward silence, I take another sip of my cider before clearing my throat and motioning for him to follow me to the living room. "I wanted to show you an idea I had for new merchandise." I say as I reach into my backpack and pull out the tablet, he bought me. "And if you hate it, it's cool. Just remember I'm new to digital art and I'm rusty to art in general." I open my drawing app and nervously open my saved drawings. It took me some time to figure out exactly how to work with digital illustration, but after a couple of days, I finally caught on. But even so, I'm rusty as hell, and showing an artist of Fox's caliber my sketches makes me very nervous.

The image pops up, and Fox instantly snatches the tablet.

"Holy shit, Torch!" His lips pull into a smirk as he studies the image. The drawing is of Hel in half-color, half black and white. The colors I chose for the human side of her face were deep and rich which contrasted well, at least I thought, against the black and grey skeletal side.

When Fox looks at me, I don't know what I see on his face, but it squeezes at my heart. "This is amazing," He smiles. "I'm so proud of you. And I would be proud as fuck to wear that design."

Oh. The look is pride. For me. I place a hand over my

chest and squeeze my eyes shut as the familiar stinging starts.

"What's wrong?" I feel his palm on my knee, and fuck, he is so warm. I shake my head, unsure of what to say. Or what I could say without sobbing.

"I just..." Nope here they come. I take a shaky breath and look at him as I feel the tears rolling. I see the panic on his face and realize he thinks he is causing the tears. Well, he kind of is, but not in a bad way. I force a smile. "I think that is the first time in my life that someone has said they are proud of me."

Fox's face falls as he stares at me in what I guess is disbelief. "I find that impossible to believe. What about your dad? He was always bragging about you." Now it was my turn for my face to fall and to stare in disbelief.

"My dad never said he was proud of me once." Fox scoots closer to me and wraps his arm around my shoulders. The gesture makes my already aching heart ache that much more.

"Well, he said it to us all the time." His voice feels like a warm hug I didn't realize I needed. Before I understand what I'm doing, I twist my body until my face nuzzles his chest. It's now that I remember his lack of shirt. I feel my face heating up, but I don't pull away. Instead, I run my hand up his stomach to his broad chest. My fingernails run back and forth through his chest hair. I smile as I hear his heartbeat quickening.

"Fox?" I murmur. My voice is unsure. Just hours ago, his hand was around my throat while I was gripping a bathroom sink for life as he railed me. But somehow, this right now seems more intimate.

"Yeah?" I notice the nervous tone in his voice as well. Is he afraid of us fighting again? Of me telling him my feelings? Is he going to run? I let out a sigh. I know we have to talk, but I'm terrified. I'm terrified that I'll be rejected by him. Again.

I lick my dry lips as I bury myself deeper into his chest, oddly finding comfort there even though he's the one I am uncomfortable with.

"I have feelings for you." I'm unsure if the words actually came out because Fox isn't speaking. After what feels like an eternity, Fox shifts to sit me up, and the oncoming rejection fills every part of me. I can't believe this. Again? I was stupid enough to have sex with him and think he would want something more with me...again.

"Hey, hey, calm down. What is it?" Fox places his hand on my face, and I feel my tremors worsening.

"Nothing, I think I need to back up." I smack his hand away and stand up, trying to think how I would get away from him. It's dark, there's a thunderstorm outside, and driving back to Stevie's right now doesn't sound safe.

"W-what?" Fox's face turns to panic as he stands up and goes to stop me, but in his haste, he slams his shin into the corner of his coffee table.

"Ah! Fuck!" He cries out before looking back at me. "Where are you going?"

"I don't know!" I groan through my embarrassment. "Insane apparently! I mean I keep doing the same thing over and over again, expecting a different result..."

"Janie!" He limps towards me and grabs my shoulder. "Baby doll, you didn't let me speak. I...have feelings for you too."

"But?" I sob out as I hang my head low, waiting for the blow.

Fox sighs and rolls his neck. "Yeah, there is one of those...I need to talk to you about some shit that has happened to me in my life. Maybe it can help us work things out better." He lifts my chin to look me in the eyes, "Will you listen to me? Please?"

I nod and allow him to lead me back to the couch. I take a seat next to him and watch as he rubs his hands over his thighs. "I am not very good at this," He says weakly. "So um... If you could just bear with me, and know that during this conversation, nothing I say should be misinterpreted as a shot against you, okay? So please, just let me get this out."

I grab his hand and give it a squeeze. "Okay, I'll listen."

Fox nods and stares over to Winston, who is snoring in his hammock, the scene makes Fox chuckle.

"I like animals." He says after a moment. "You said when you found Winston that I didn't like animals, but I do. I just didn't want to get attached and have to watch them go. Or worse, they need me and I am unable to help them. So I figured it was better to not bring that kind of worry into my life, that kind of pain."

I bite the inside of my cheek to stop myself from speaking. I need to let him talk, and I need to really listen to him.

His gaze makes its way to his hands that are resting in between his bobbing knees. It is weird seeing someone as confident as Fox so nervous.

"Janie," He breathes my name and I want to hold him to me, to kiss away whatever was causing him this much mental anguish. "My dad, I've mentioned he was a shitty person. But I need you to realize that, maybe he was right about some things." He runs his hands through his long hair before resting them back on his knee.

"He beat my mom and sister for a long time. Until I was about twelve or thirteen. By then I was hitting puberty, and I was pissing him off so that he would hit me instead of them. He'd beat me with a belt, or whatever was handy. Punch, kick, put his smokes out on me..." I watch as his hand absently went over his chest, and I begin to wonder what he has hidden under all of his tattoos.

Fox takes a breath before continuing. "The physical abuse sucked, but I took it, hell I preferred it over the mental shit. The yelling, the belittling. Telling me I was stupid, worthless, a waste of space. All while my mom and sister would stay in their own world, ignoring him. Which, I get, they were probably just relieved that he was onto someone else after the years of abuse they suffered before I stepped up."

Oh my god. How could a father do that to his child? How could a mother see it happening and not stop it? Relieved that your husband was beating your child instead of you?

I cover my mouth with my trembling hand to hide the wobbling of my bottom lip. I *have* to keep it together. Fox has been holding a past back that needed to come out and I know that if he feels that it's overwhelming me, he will stop.

He will stop to protect me, even if it hurts him. Just like he did for them.

"As I grew up, in my teens and even early twenties, I couldn't leave home. I couldn't move out or go to college, not that I was smart enough to make it there anyway." His self-deprecating laugh breaks my already shattering heart. I wonder if younger Fox had dreams about college, about doing something else with his life, but his dad made him feel like he couldn't make it.

"I had to stay home," He continues, "At least until my mom and sister left. I couldn't leave them alone with that man. But they wouldn't leave. I don't know if it was fear, or love, or what it was but I could not get them to leave him." I hear the frustration in his voice as he speaks through gritting teeth.

"I was working at this tattoo shop as an apprentice. And no, not like the apprenticeships Tony had." He laughs and I can't help but smile softly. My dad was known for being a lot more kind to the apprenticing artists than most shops.

"So, I was getting beat down at work and then going home to get beat again. It was just a constant, never-ending stream of shit. I never felt good enough, I never felt like I would get out." His eyes have a slight sheen over them as he continues to speak, voice cracking slightly.

"Then, I met Tony. He was doing a guest chair at the shop I was at. Everyone was so excited because he had just gotten the title as the *"Good Luck Tattoo Artist"*. My boss made a huge deal about Tony coming in and how nobody better even think about talking to him. The last morning, he was there, I was the one that was supposed to let him into the shop, and I was late. I had gotten beaten by my father and when I tried to get him off...I shoved him too hard, he fell down the stairs and broke his leg. My mom..." His voice cracks and I watch as his hand balls into a fist. "My mom kicked me out. Told me I was a monster and to leave. So, I got to the shop and your dad saw me and took pity on me I guess because my drawings back then were atrocious. But he told me to pack my shit and come work for him here. I don't know why I agreed, but I did."

He rubs his hands over his face, and I can tell this next part is the hard part for him. "I'm there for only a couple months, the best months of my life, and I get a call from mom. Dad beat her so bad she had to be in the hospital for days. No one had told me. The guilt I felt for not being there, for not protecting her...I told her that she and my sister needed to come down here. They could live with me in my shitty apartment and things would be tight, but we would get by. She asked me to come up there, to go get them...Janie had I known...you have to know I would've gone." Fox chokes out a sob and it's then I remember, his mom and sister died in a car crash while moving here.

I can't fight it any longer. I pull him against my chest as he silently shakes for a moment. I feel the wetness on my shirt but say nothing. He needs to let it out, he's been holding it back for far too long.

"At the funeral," He whispers, his head still resting on my breast, his hand gripping my hoodie. "My father beat me within an inch of my life. Told me it was my fault, that every one that got close to me would be in danger. I was more to blame for their deaths than the truck driver that hit them." He grabs my hand and guides my fingertips over his bare chest to a tattoo over his heart of a broken pocket watch. I run my fingers across the tattoo, and I notice the center is not smooth skin. "He drove his lit cigar into my chest here. Told me to remember that pain because that is the pain I would cause to any one I let in."

He sits up and looks at me, I'm sure my expression is everywhere. I feel so much. So much for the young boy trying to protect his mom and big sister. For the young man just trying to feel worth something. For the man now, finally opening up because he does feel something for me, but he is scared that if he lets me in, we will both only get hurt.

"I'm sorry your dad hurt you." I finally say after a long stretch of silence.

Fox huffs out a laugh, "Baby doll, it was a long time ago and you don't need to be sorry. I just, I need to tell you so that you would understand why this thing between us is so hard."

I give him a soft nod. "So, what do you want to do?" I wince inwardly as I prepare myself for the blow. I want him, I want to be with him. But after hearing what he said, I understand now why he is scared, and I don't want to push him into anything he's not ready for.

"Well for starters," Fox cups my cheek as he stares into my eyes, his lips forming the softest of smiles. "I'm going to kiss you the way I've wanted to for far too long." Before I can reply, Fox's lips capture mine.

The kiss is nothing I've ever felt before, even from him. It isn't as demanding, or lust filled as it has been in the past. He's tender and careful as his mouth explores mine. His hands cup either side of my face, and I let out a soft whimper as his tongue slips between my lips. He tastes like apple cider, adding to the overall sweet and warm kiss.

Fox breaks the kiss and looks down at me, our foreheads pressing together, his hands staying firmly planted on my face.

"So," He starts, his eyes dancing with humor. "Are you sure you want to try this boyfriend girlfriend thing out with my old ass?" I laugh loudly and wrap my hands around his neck as I press my body against his, melting into his embrace, feeling, for the first time in I don't know how long, at home.

"Yes, I am more than sure."

Chapter Twenty-Four

FOX

THIS ISN'T HAPPENING. There is zero chance that what I'm experiencing is real life.

"Oh my god," Janie breathes as she grips my arm. "That cotton candy is bigger than my hair...I must consume it."

I laugh as I watch my tiny redhead bounce over to the line where they do in fact sell cotton candy that put all other cotton candy to shame. I watch as Janie eagerly hops from one foot to the other as the worker makes her cotton candy. As she takes her treat, I pay the man behind the counter before she and I go back and join our group.

Atlas had mentioned last week about the fall festival coming up. As usual, I ignored him because festivals are not my scene. Too many people, everything is a scam and there is zero chance that a machine that is constructed and then deconstructed that many times is safe to ride. But apparently, those are all thoughts that *single Fox* was allowed to have. *Boyfriend Fox* should've already known about the festival and had tickets to present to his girlfriend, according to Atlas.

Regardless of whose idea it was or who would rather

shove a hot stake up his dickhole than be here, Janie's entire body lit up when he mentioned that he and Ash were going, so how could I not get tickets for her and I?

I look at Atlas, who is currently trying to hide the fact that he is miserable being here without a date, and Ash, who is here with some woman that I shouldn't even waste my brain cells trying to remember her name. The girl was beautiful, as were most of the women that he dates, and I'm using the term 'dates' loosely. I think this one's name is Autumn. She's tall, thin and covered in tattoos. Her edgy purple hair and leather attire don't scream family festival, but she makes it work.

Janie on the other hand, looks like the excited kid entering Disney World. Her hair is loose and wild, the way I love it. She wears no makeup, allowing every one of her freckles to show. And she has on a shirt that is tied in the back, it is blue, and, on the front, it read:

"That's what." - She.

When we first met Autumn at the entrance of the festival, she read Janie's shirt and didn't get it. Janie then decided that Autumn was dead to her.

"Fox!" I look down at Janie who is pulling on my arm.

"What baby doll?" I can't help but smile and wrap my arm around her small waist. The last two weeks have been the greatest of my life. Getting to be Janie's boyfriend, there is no greater gift, and I can't believe I almost let that go. Am I scared that one day she'll want too much? That there may be a line I can't cross? Yes. But that is a problem for another day because this, here, now. It's magical, and I never want it to end.

"Ferris wheel." Was all I heard, and my face fell. Well, I

guess the magic is over. I look over at the giant round monstrosity and my stomach feels sour.

"Yeah Torch, I don't know..." I groan as I peel my gaze from the structure of doom to my girl, who is pouting. Fuckkk. That bottom lip of hers, she pushes it out and wrinkles her forehead and I feel like I'm becoming putty.

Atlas laughs, "Fox is afraid of heights, Red, but I'll ride it with you if you want."

I glare over at Atlas, is he seriously trying to take my girl on a Ferris wheel ride?

"I'm not afraid of heights." I growl defensively. "I just have a completely healthy, rational fear of the machine collapsing due to a rusty bolt."

Janie giggles and hugs me around my waist. "It's okay, I'll ride with Atlas, here you can hold my cotton candy." I go to protest, I would've ridden the fucking ride. I may have been white knuckling it the whole time but...I deflate some as I watch Janie run up to the cart with Atlas and slide in. She waves at me, and I put on a fake smile and wave back as I stand there feeling like a fucking moron. Atlas and I are going to have a serious talk after his little ride with *my* girlfriend. If he wanted someone to ride with him, he should've brought a date, but he won't be stealing my girl again.

"HOW LONG ARE you going to stay mad?" Atlas groans at me while he rests his head on my shoulder.

"I will kill you." I growl as I shove his face off of me. "Why would you take her on the Ferris wheel?"

Atlas scoffs, "If I had known it meant that much to you, I wouldn't have offered. I wanted to go, she wanted to go, and you hate heights."

"It's not the heights..." I mutter as I glare at him.

Atlas rolls his eyes, "Whatever. Anyway, it's not like she gave me a blowy or anything. We sat in the cart together."

I feel my right eye twitch at his statement. "Next three men that want ass or dick tattoos, you're getting...no I changed my mind. The next thirty."

His jaw drops as he stares at me in disbelief. "I said it's NOT like she blew me."

"Forty." I state casually and Atlas grumbles something I don't understand, except for one name at the end – **Ren**.

"That's who you should've invited." I mutter as I see Janie making her way back to us with a mountain of funnel cake and a corndog in her mouth. I feel all anger rush out of me as I stare at the adorable spectacle in front of me.

"Fox!" She squeals and shows me the corndog. "Three dollars and I already crammed like four inches down." I hear a couple younger guys snickering and I shoot them a warning glare before turning back to her.

"Baby doll," I chuckle and kiss her head. "I think you've consumed your body weight in fair food."

Beaming up at me she holds up a piece of the funnel cake and feeds it to me. The act is very foreign to me, but I really enjoy it. It's so sweet, she is so fucking sweet.

"Awww..." The guys from earlier mock. "That's so nice of you to help feed your grandpa!" I stiffen and look at the guys. They are probably around Janie's age. Sometimes I forget about our seventeen-year age gap. Did we really look that out of place together?"

"When you get done feeding gramps," One of them

smirks. "Maybe I could feed you." He grabs the crotch of his jeans and I see red. I start to charge them, ready to beat his face into ground meat, but Janie stands in front of me and places a hand on my chest to stop me.

"Sorry boys but your mini wieners aren't going to satisfy my appetite." She flips her hair over her shoulder before grabbing my wrist and tugging me away. "Now come on Daddy, your baby doll is hungry." I smirk as I follow her away from the crowd. We walk in silence for several minutes before hitting the tree line where the festival ends.

"Are you taking me somewhere to murder me?" I joke as she pulls me a few feet into the wooded area before she whips around and pushes me against the trunk of a tree. Actually, she didn't move me at all even though I felt the amount of force she tried to use. I threw her a bone though and "fell" back, throwing in a small grunt just to boost her confidence.

She steps up to me, her face almost completely covered in the shadows with the lack of sun. She reaches up and grips my beard, pulling me down to meet her eager mouth. She tastes of the ninety pounds of sugar she's consumed this evening. Slipping my tongue deeper into her mouth, I reach around to her luscious ass and grip both cheeks in my hands. I hear her moan against the kiss, and I go to turn us around so I can press her against the trunk, but she stops me, breaking the kiss.

"No." She says firmly as she removes my hands from her denim covered ass.

"No?" I repeat and raise my brow. "Why no? What's wrong?"

"Nothing," She whispers and kisses me again. "I just have a plan and it doesn't involve you pinning me to that tree." I chuckle and go to ask her what her plan is, but I don't have a chance.

"Oh, holy shit…" The guttural noise I let out as her hand runs over my erection that is screaming to break out of my zipper is anything but manly. I roll my head back against the tree as she lifts my shirt and begins planting hot, wet kisses down my stomach. She reaches my navel and I notice her pause. Looking down, I watch her clear the ground with her sneakers before dropping to her knees and unbuckling my belt.

I watch in complete shock and amazement as she unzips my jeans and I feel her hand reach in and free my cock. I hear her small gasp and I can't decide if I'm annoyed or more turned on over the fact that I cannot see her that well.

"Baby doll…" I whisper as my hand runs through her hair, gripping her at the back of her head. A shudder runs through me as I feel her wet tongue lick the underside of my tip.

"I want you to fuck my mouth." She whispers while running my tip over her soft lips. Holy fucking shit is this real?

"Baby doll…" My mouth is bone dry. I try to tell her we don't have to, but she slips the head of my dick into her sweet mouth and my knees feel weak.

"Janie…" I breathe as she slides me further in, inch by inch. My hip involuntarily twitches causing a small thrust, it makes her gag slightly and I shouldn't get turned on by that. "Sorry." I whisper but she moans deeply, and I feel it through my cock.

"Fuck." I pant out as I grip her hair. I feel her moving back and forth on my cock. She's timid and unsure of herself as she tries different angles and I begin to wonder how much practice she has doing this.

After a couple moments, I can tell she's getting frustrated by how badly her hand is shaking on my shaft as she tries to stroke me.

"Okay," I breathe pulling back, I don't want to embarrass her, she is in the woods after all, and on her knees trying to make me feel good. "Baby, you feel amazing, you're doing a great job." I praise as I find her cheek and stroke it.

"I've only done this once and it was a long time ago. I'm sorry. I should've googled it." She mutters and I can't help but chuckle.

"Okay, you got this. I'll help you, just use your tongue a bit more." I whisper as I guide her back. I feel her flick her tongue over my tip and I groan. "That's my girl." I breathe out. "Good, now suck." She obeys and begins to suck as I grip her hair and begin to slowly move her head back and forth. "That's it," I pant, and I grab her hand to place it at the base of my shaft. "Stroke..." I growl out, trying like hell to keep myself under control.

Something clicks inside Janie. She begins hitting the right stride, the right angle and she is turning me into melted butter. "Fuck!" I hiss as I grip her tighter, my hips thrusting, I try to stop myself, but she urges me to continue by grabbing my ass and pulling me towards her.

"Whatever witchcraft you are doing with that tongue..." I pant as I roll my head back and let out a deep moan. "Don't stop." My good girl doesn't stop. No, she intensifies the pleasure I'm feeling by reaching her hand into my boxers and cupping my balls. She's so gentle but the intense pleasure of that mixed with her taking me down her fucking throat, it's too much.

"Let go," I barely manage to get out, my balls tightening and my cock going rigid. "Move or I'll cum in your mouth." She doesn't move away. Instead, she forces me in as far as I can go, and I feel myself let loose down her throat. "Fucking God! Janie fuck!" I growl out as I finish inside her. A gasp escapes me as I feel her licking and sucking me clean before standing up and trying to buckle my belt. I don't let her though, I crush my lips against her, slipping my tongue into her magical fucking mouth that now tastes like me. Fuck... she tastes like me.

I pull back and press my forehead to hers. "Wow." I breathe out, causing her to giggle.

"Sorry, I need more practice." She says shyly and I kiss her again, this time with more urgency. I turn her around, backing her up against the tree as I drag my teeth over her bottom lip, causing her to whimper.

"You," I say, my voice low and thick. "Are phenomenal. So, stop doubting yourself." She goes to speak but the ringing of my cellphone startles us both. I growl in frustration as I look to see it's Atlas calling. "Needy fuck." I mutter as I grab Janie's hand to help her get back to the festival grounds.

"He does seem kind of clingy." Janie mutters as we blend back in with the crowd. I send Atlas a text saying we will meet them in the center of the festival.

"Yeah," I sigh while sticking my phone into my pocket. "I have no idea what's up with him."

Janie snorts, "Probably the fact that Ren is dating someone, you know they got a thing for each other."

I stop walking and look at her. "What? She is actually dating someone?" Janie gives me a half shrug and nods.

"Tonight, is like the third date. I'm not a huge fan of him but whatever makes her happy." Nodding, I follow

Janie as we meet up with Atlas and Ash, who is now dateless.

"Where's your girl?" I ask as we stand around the bar top table next to the dance floor. Thankfully, the music isn't playing considering we are right next to a speaker.

Ash shrugs and takes a swig from his beer bottle. "Left, I guess. I don't know, I got bored with her like two hours ago when she asked if I would give her a free tattoo after this."

Janie laughs. "Yeah, don't you just hate it when women use men just to get that one thing they want. It's disrespectful really."

Ash deadpans and gives Janie the finger. "Listen, I am a very generous lover. I would've given her at least eight of the best orgasms of her life to my one."

Janie wrinkles her nose. "That is physically impossible." Atlas spits out his drink and I freeze, eyes wide as I watch Ash's mouth form an evil grin. Fuck.

"So Janie," He beams. "How many orgasms would you say is physically possible for a woman to experience in one night?"

Janie lets out a breath. She's really thinking about this? She looks at me and then...oh my god she's holding up her fingers.

"What constitutes a full orgasm? Like is there so many minutes in between?" I groan at her question as my two dickhead now *ex friends* burst out laughing.

"Fox!" Ash shakes his head in disbelief. "You better do right by her. Having to ask such questions."

"Hey fuck off." I growl as I feel embarrassment creep up my body. Janie and I have yet to have a night where we just had sex. Our times were quick and wild, and while they were still some of the best sex I've ever had, I do feel shitty that I haven't given my girlfriend the kind of night she deserves.

"Quit being dicks and go get us some beers." Janie snaps at the two, who both say a "yes mom" before walking away. I hear the music starting up and people heading to the middle dance floor, and I shift uncomfortably. Janie is on her phone, but I see her swaying back and forth to the beat. Fuck, am I supposed to ask her to dance? I look around and notice other men taking their partners out to the dance floor and I want to run. I don't dance. I'm not coordinated in that way. I'm old, giant and covered in tattoos, nothing about me screams "slow dance".

Janie is staring out at the dance floor, and I see the look of longing on her face, and I groan inwardly.

"You uhh...you don't want to do that, do you?" I ask her nervously as I motion my head towards the floor. She smiles shyly and fuck...she looks so pretty. I feel shitty that if she says yes, I'm just going to embarrass her out there.

"Nope." Her answer is short and her smile fake.

"Liar." I smirk and watch the panic on her face appear.

"Okay," She sighs. "Maybe a little, but I'll survive without it."

"I could... dance with you if you want." God was this t-shirt always this fucking tight? I see her expression brighten and shit, I'm going to have to dance.

"Really?" She asks, her voice full of hope. I give her a nervous smile as I stand up and offer her my hand before taking her out to the dance floor.

"I'm not very good at this." I admit as I place my hands on her hips. She smiles up at me as we continue to sway back and forth.

"I think you are doing amazing." She beams and I can't

help but lean down and kiss her softly as we continue our little dance that I am sure is less dancing and more rocking.

"I like you." She whispers softly as she rests her head on my chest. I feel my heart constrict and I kiss the top of her head.

"I like you too, baby doll."

Chapter Twenty-Five

JANIE

"WAIT," Ren says as she sets her coffee cup down and stares at me in shock. "You got Fox to dance?" I can't help the smile pulling at my lips as I shyly nod and remember the festival two nights ago.

Ren, Sunday, and I came to *Nuts About Dough* to hang out with Stevie on her break and they all are dying to hear how mine and Fox's first official date went.

"It was so sweet." I say excitedly. "I mean he is absolutely the worst dancer. You get that man doing more than a little sway and he is stepping all over you. But he tried, and that meant so much to me." I sigh dreamily as I hold my hands to my chest.

"It's so adorable," Stevie says slowly. "That I may vomit." I playfully hit her before sipping on my drink.

I turn my attention to Ren, "So...how was date number three?" I watch Ren visibly stiffen as she fidgets with her mug.

"Fine." She says quickly. "I'm going out with him again this weekend."

Frowning at her statement, I look at her quizzically.

"Was that your decision?" I ask. Something with this man is off and I can't put my finger on what it is. I just know that my sleaze ball gauge is never wrong.

Ren gives a half shrug, still fidgeting with her mug. "I was actually hoping to rest this weekend. I don't know, I've been feeling really run down lately. But Andrew has some party he is going to on behalf of the firm, so he tol– asked if I want to go with him."

Stevie, Sunday and I all exchange knowing looks, Ren slipped, and we heard it. I looked at my usually brighter than the sun friend. The last couple of weeks, she's looked exhausted. Dark circles under her eyes, worry lines and even her hair looks dull.

"Babe," I say softly as I reach over the table and hold her hand tightly. "You know that if you need to tell us anything, you can. We love you."

Ren's eyes snap up and she recoils from my touch as if I burnt her. "Don't use that crap on me." She hisses while scooting her chair back to stand up. "I'm not some dumb, helpless little girl. I am a fucking lawyer for Christ's sake. My mother is a skilled surgeon, my father is a judge! You don't get to look at me with pity like that. I got to go."

Sunday goes to walk after Ren, but I stop her and shake my head. I had backed Ren in a corner accidentally and she saw no other way out. Going after her now would only cause her to lash out more. Once I saw Ren's Rav4 peel out of the parking lot, I let out a breath. "Do we think it's physical?"

Stevie takes a sip of her drink. "Maybe a shove but I don't think he's physically hurting her yet, at least not enough to where she feels the need to hide her body." I nod, that's true, Ren had been wearing a halter tunic top and capris.

"Who is he again?" Sunday asks while crossing her toned arms over her chest. I can see the fury in her eyes, Sunday is a take no shit girl. I am sure she will gladly take a bat to him if need be.

"Andrew Cambridge." I spit his name out like it's poison.

Stevie furrows her dark brows. "As in Cambridge, Prescott & Sons?"

I press my lips together and nod. "Yep, he is one of the 'sons' and Ren's boss." The girls both groan and I nod again. "Yeah, it's an absolute mess." I look down at my phone when it vibrates and sigh as I see the text.

> Ren: I'm sorry, and I love you and the girls very much. I just can't talk about all of this right now. But I need you three to do me a favor.

> Ren: Whatever you talk about between yourselves is fine. But if you care about me AT ALL you will not tell the guys at Hel's. None of them can know who I'm with.

> Me: I'll stay quiet as long as I feel you're safe.

I slide the phone to the middle of the table to allow Stevie and Sunday to read it. They both shoot me worried glances and I let out a long, tired breath. I will stay quiet as long as she's safe. Too bad I don't feel like that will be for very long.

FOX SCOWLS at me and the anger rolling off his giant body is almost too much. "I need to punch something." He growls and I give him a nervous smile.

"How about a big hug instead?" I try but only get the same glare.

Atlas slaps the shirtless Fox's back. "I think it's a brilliant idea Red!" He beams as he rips his shirt off. "So do I get to pick who greases me up?" He asks while looking at the people behind me who are setting up for the photoshoot.

"No," I snap while poking his chest. "Ow." I mutter waving my injured digit.

Atlas smirks and makes his pecs bounce. "Like a fucking rock, right?"

Fox smacks him upside the head before glaring back at me. I match his glare and raise him by sticking my tongue out. "You agreed to this." I smile brightly.

"Your hand was on my dick, I would have agreed to anything." He grumbles in my ear so Atlas doesn't hear and I can't help the laugh that escapes me. It's true, I had asked him if he would be willing to do a photoshoot to introduce the guys and everything on social media, while preparing to suck him. He was very eager to say yes.

"Who is greasing me up..." Atlas whines and I roll my eyes.

"Because you won't shut up, Gale is." I snap and point to the seventy something year old woman who is struggling to open a jar of something.

Atlas huffs. "Jokes on you, I wanted it to be Gale." I give him a look that tells him to shut up before walking over to check on Ash and Derek. I see Ash flirting with the photographer. Ash is the smallest of the four men, which doesn't mean much considering he is still over six feet and has a toned swimmers build. He and Atlas are the only two without neck tattoos. Ash's Traditional Japanese tattoo work covers nearly every inch of him. Beautiful colors and scenes of warriors, dragons, and koi fish decorate his arms, back and chest.

"Ash," I say after staring too long. It's hard not to, the work done on these guys is some of the best work you will see. Which is why I thought this photoshoot for social media and the website would do well. Not to mention they are all attractive as fuck. "You're up first." I smile and then turn around. "Derek, you're...holy shit."

So it's now that I realize I've never seen Derek shirtless. He might be more built than even Atlas. I look over his tight abs and rock-hard chest. I cock my head at his artwork, and I feel a heaviness as I stare at everything. It's all black and grey and everything is dying. Wilting flowers, realistic skulls, rotting fruit, a broken hourglass. His tattoos were... so sad.

"You know," Fox's low growl from behind me sends shivers down my spine. "I don't share. And I don't like it when my girl is staring at other men." I roll my eyes and turn to him.

"I wasn't staring at other men. I had never seen Derek's tattoos. They're really sad." Fox frowns and glances over at Derek as if looking over the man's art.

He smirks and looks back at me. "Baby doll, that's just the type of art he puts on his body. Like Ash is strictly Traditional Japanese and your dad was ninety-nine percent Traditional American. At and I are the only two in the shop that collect different tattoos."

"Well," I look up at him and cock my head to one side. "What is Derek's called? Because 'rotting fruit' is not one of the traditional styles."

"It's Memento Mori Art." Derek's gruff voice says from his spot at his station. Crap, had he heard everything? His dark eyes meet mine and I give him an apologetic look.

"They're really pretty." I say and then hide my face as all four men start laughing. What a dumb thing to say.

"Alright!" I grumble after a minute. "Enough giving me shit. Let's get you boys greased up and flexing."

Chapter Twenty-Six

FOX

"FOX!" Panic fills me as I hear Janie's scream from across the shop. I stand to run to the front showroom, but before I get there, my tiny redhead runs into the work area. She runs to me and jumps, her legs and arms wrapping around me. I wrap my hands around her as I steady myself.

"I did it! I did it!" She repeatedly squeals, completely unable to stop wiggling from excitement. I don't know what she's talking about, but I can't stop smiling. The last few weeks she and I have spent together as a "new couple" have been the best weeks of my life. And moments we get to share like this matter to me more than I thought they would.

"What did you do, baby doll?" I chuckle as I set her down. Her blue eyes sparkle, and her dimples are front and center, a rarity I treasure each time I'm lucky enough to see them.

"Okay," She says, taking a short breath. "So remember last week when I said I uploaded a short video introducing you guys, and it went viral? And then the shirtless pictures?" I nod and notice Atlas, Ash and Derek are around us now.

"Yes," I mutter. "I think we all remember, and I seem to remember we all agreed not to mention it again after we were manhandled by Gale." That old woman was so unsuspecting. Coming up to us with her shaky old lady hands, until she grabbed the oil and started her very personal rub downs that left all four of us feeling very filthy.

"Yeah yeah," Janie waves her hand dismissively. "Well, I announced pre-orders on the first of the new design merch for the shop, the picture I drew, we sold out with just pre-orders." I watch her bouncing up and down, squealing. "They love my drawing, Fox! I did it!" I smile as I wrap my arms around her tightly and squeeze her.

"That's amazing, baby doll! I'm so proud of you!" I release her, and she takes turns hugging each of the guys.

"This is just the beginning! So Atlas, we will get this one out, and in two weeks, you guys have the convention in Florida, so we will be doing teasers for that design to get people ready and interested in the convention. And since we are doing that and have a great following now, the convention center is comping your rooms. Meaning, be on your best behavior." She says the last part in her scolding mother voice as she stares at Atlas and Ash, who both give her round-eye innocent looks.

"What?" Atlas asks, earning a slap on the chest.

"No strippers, no parties. I heard about what happened with you guys in Vegas after Fox left."

"What happens in Vegas, sta-" Ash's mouth slams shut at the warning look Janie gave him.

"Good, now I have to go to dance class with Ren." She stands on her tiptoes and gives me a soft kiss, causing the guys to make kissing noises behind us.

"So, what kind of dancing are you girls learning?" I ask as she grabs her bag.

"Pole dancing." She says simply and gives me one last kiss before walking out, leaving me flabbergasted.

"Wait..." Atlas looks from the door that Janie just walked out of back to me. "Pole? As in strippers?"

I blink several times and shake my head. "No." I chuckle hesitantly and look back towards the door.

"There is no way she and Ren are taking stripper classes...I mean, she's gone to four of these classes since we've been together. She would've told me...right?"

Derek shrugs as he grabs a water bottle from our mini fridge. "She's an adult. Maybe she doesn't feel like she needs to tell you."

I roll my eyes at his remark. "Obviously, she doesn't need to tell me. I just feel like I would've known by now."

"Oh?" Atlas snickers. "You mean she's not asking you to put a pole in your bedroom?" I punch his arm before hearing the bell chime.

"I'll deal with you later." I mutter as I go out front to help the customer.

"SO, things with you and Janie seem good." Atlas muses as he and I clean up the shop. Derek and Ash were already gone so it was a rare moment he and I had alone.

"Yeah," I can't help the smile forming on my face. "She's really great."

Atlas makes a gagging sound before sitting on his chair.

"I am really happy for you. I'm glad you two finally admitted you're in love."

My whole body goes rigid, and I feel cold sweat wash over me.

In love?

"I never said anything about love, brother." I state softly as I feel my anxiety rising.

Atlas laughs, "Okay right, you look at every girl you fuck like that then?" I glare at him which only seems to solidify his point. "So what? You just haven't told her yet?"

"Nothing to tell." I grumble as I sit down on my own chair. "Love is not a part of what she and I have. I like her, I like being with her, and that has to be enough. Love, marriage and all that are not in the cards."

I see a serious look wash over Atlas' face and it is kind of startling. I wasn't used to seeing anything besides his relaxed, happy go lucky expressions. "Why? Because you're so old and you'll be a senior before your kids are in elementary school."

My face falls. "No, you fucking prick!" I throw a pillow wedge at him before sighing. "I just don't have it in me to fall in love. To allow love anywhere near me again."

"Oh my god." Atlas groans as he looks up towards the ceiling. "Dude, how fucking broken are you behind all of that flannel and hair?"

"Fuck off!" I yell defensively.

Atlas shakes his head. "Just because you refuse to admit it, doesn't mean it's not true. You want to be a coward with Red, that's your choice. It's just sad because she's going to expect you to, at the very least, love her at some point, and if you say that weak ass excuse to her, you'll break her heart."

"You're one to talk about refusing to admit things." I mutter more so to myself, but Atlas hears me.

"If you're going to say it, say it with your chest bitch." He states nonchalantly while staring at the tiles on the floor.

"Fine," I breathe out. "You have a thing for Ren, I don't see you acting on it."

"No, it's not like that. Lauren is just –" He pauses as he looks off into the distance as if he is admiring something he could never have. He lets out a sigh and I watch his shoulders slump as he speaks again. "She's brilliant, a lawyer, and classy. She and I could –" He stops, looks up at me, and my grin widens.

"Could never what, At? Could never be in love? Get Married?" Atlas flips me the finger and shakes his head.

"The difference is, Ren and I are not a thing. Have never been a thing. Will never be a thing. I'm not into her *that* way." His eyes go distance as he mutters "Besides, she's with someone else."

I roll my eyes. "Yeah, a fucking waste of space dickhole."

Atlas' head snaps up so fast I can't believe it didn't break. "What?" His voice is low, almost murderous.

"Chill out, it's just that I know she's dating that Cambridge guy at the law firm." I watch as Atlas' expression doesn't change.

"The fucker that made her cry last year for calling her porky pig? THAT is who she is dating? What the fuck is the matter with her? How have none of the girls said anything to her?" Atlas is up and pacing now, nostrils flaring with every angry breath he blows out.

"At," I say, trying to calm him down. "Ren is an adult.

And she is a tough girl, if that douchebag is dating her, I am sure he did a lot of groveling."

There is silence between us for a brief moment before Atlas sighs. "So, when you two do get married, talk her into a fall wedding because I am definitely not wearing a tux in July."

Chapter Twenty-Seven

JANIE

Ms. Pierce,
My name is Brandon Stephens; I am the manager of
"Bliss Trips" - the largest travel influencers in the United
States. We spoke at the meet and greet a couple of months
ago. We have seen your work with the company "Hel's
Ink" and are familiar with your past social media
presence as Jai. I am emailing you to offer you a position
as one of our travel influencers. I have already shown your
photos and work to the CEO at our last meeting; she was
as impressed as I was. You have the exact look we are after
and the fun personality that we believe will match our
other influencer that would be your travel companion.
We would love to meet you if you would be interested in
setting up an interview. Our CEO is old school and
believes in "in-person" interviews, our location is in
Chicago, if this is something you feel you would be
interested in pursuing, we would love to have you and will
gladly take care of your hotel expenses.
Please feel free to call me anytime with questions or to set
up a date for the interview.

Sincerely,
Brandon Stephens
"Bliss Trips"

I AM NOT sure how many times I've read the email. Double digits for sure. Earlier this year, receiving this email from Bliss Trips would've been my dream come true. So why did I continue to read over it, feeling queasier each time?

"Have you mentioned it to Fox?" Sunday asks from her spot on Ren's couch. She, Ren and I were going to head to some community outreach program that Ren was the head of, but before we could head out, I received the email and needed them to tell me what to do.

I shake my head. "No, I just got it five minutes before I told you guys."

Ren lets out a short laugh. "She meant, have you mentioned this to him at all. Like that you had shown interest in doing this?"

"Oh." I whisper as I chew on my thumbnail. I feel my tremors picking up as my anxiety begins to build. "No, I...I mean I filled it out at the meet and greet and then kind of forgot about it."

Sunday sits up and looks at me. "Well, what are you going to do? I mean a travel influencer...does that mean you would be gone a lot?"

"Typically, three weeks a month," I whisper thinking to the travel influencers I've met in the past. "Sometimes longer depending on where I would be going, what the piece is on and whether they need me to go back to Chicago for any reason."

Ren whistles for Bruno to go over so he can eat his food. "Well," She sighs and turns her tired eyes to me. Is she losing weight? She looks terrible. "Those travel influencers make great money if you can get signed with an agency like Bliss Trips. Plus, you would get to see the world, build your social media presence back up."

"But you wouldn't have Fox." Sunday counters and I wince. Not having Fox would kill me, and I know why, it's because I'm falling in love with him. I've known it for a while but the night of the festival, him dancing with me...it just set everything into place.

"I'm not leaving Fox," I say, more to myself than the girls. "Nothing is worth me leaving him."

I GRIN WIDELY as I sit on the bed and watch Fox running a towel through his freshly showered hair.

"What?" He laughs as he looks over at me, giving me a full view of his bare chest and torso, the rest of him covered with a blue towel.

"That one is my favorite." I laugh as I reach out and poke the small tattoo of a Japanese cat eating a bowl of ramen on his ribs.

Fox groans as he sits down and rests back on the bed. "Out of all the badass tattoos in that fucking gum ball machine, I would end up with that one."

When I was around eighteen, Dad and Fox had a friendly competition, and the loser had to get a tattoo out of the dreaded gum ball machine. Dad had an old gum ball machine in which he dropped a bunch of plastic containers with tattoo stencils. So you would pay fifty bucks and get whatever was on it. It was a neat idea but never got much use, which I'd said was because it was all old-school tattoos. There was nothing to appeal to other people.

"Yeah, about that," I grimace as I stare at him. "I might have changed those out the night before you were due to lose."

Fox had lost the bet against Dad, and after Fox left that night, Dad and I stayed at the shop and emptied the machine, replacing all the balls with super girly or inappropriate art.

"Be happy you got one of mine. Dad drew one of a cat holding a magnet."

Fox cocks his head to one side before it clicks in his head. "Pussy Magnet?"

I laugh loudly as I kiss his chest before making my way down his stomach. His stomach is solid, not ripped, but still muscular. I run my tongue over the hair that goes from his navel to where the towel rests and smile when he hisses out.

"Fuckkk, Janie."

I smirk as I untie his towel, exposing him completely to me. I stare at his hardening cock and lick my lips. As I kiss the tip of his crown, Fox inhales sharply. I smile as I swirl my tongue around the tip, earning a low groan. I straddle his legs as I grab the hair tie from my wrist and wrap it loosely over my curls before wrapping my hand around his cock and giving him a tight squeeze and slow pump.

"You're going to kill me with this teasing." He whispers while running his hands over my thighs. I bend back down and give his tip another lick before slipping him past my lips.

"Shit!" He gasps and grips my thighs tighter as I slip

more of him in. I begin pumping the part of his shaft that I can't fit in my mouth as I bob my head, sucking his cock and swirling my tongue around his head. His groans are turning into short cries, he is no longer holding my thighs, but instead, his hands are lost in my curls as he begins to guide me up and down his length.

"Stop." He breathes out and tugs my hair. The pull causes his dick to pop out of my mouth, and I growl in annoyance.

"I was about to cum." He says between pants.

"And?" I ask, still very much annoyed that I didn't get to finish him off.

"And," Fox locks his legs around mine, and in one swift motion, he is on top of me as his hand makes its way down my neck and over my breast, rubbing my hard nipple through my tank top. "I need to feel you." Letting out a whimper, I arch my breasts further into his large hand.

"Fox," I whisper as I wrap my arms around his neck and run my fingers through his hair. "I want it soft this time." I let him finish sliding my pants off. He stares back at me and furrows his brow.

"What do you mean?"

"I want..." *You to make love to me.* I can't say that, he will bolt. Chewing on my lip I ponder the correct words before locking eyes again.

"I want it, softer...sweeter this time." He has a look of apprehension on his face, but he nods as he parts my slit and angles his throbbing cock against my entrance. Once he is level, his eyes find mine again, I stare at him and let out a loud moan as he fills me completely.

I watch his expression go into something like shock as he takes in every part of my face.

"What?" I breathe as I rock my hips up against his. I

watch the almost pained look on his face as he leans down to kiss me.

"You are so fucking beautiful." He groans against my lips. "I see it every day but watching the lust and pleasure swim around in your eyes, the way your mouth opens with every thrust I push into you." To emphasize, he pushes into the hilt several times. "But really, it's the way you are looking at me. It's...it's almost too much." He lets out a small laugh before thrusting into me again, he growls loudly as I squeeze my walls around his cock and meet his thrusts.

"How," I pant out and arch my back. "How do I look at you...oh— right there." A whimper escapes my mouth as I dig my nails into his firm shoulder blades.

He doesn't answer, he just continues to stare at me, and I am okay with it. The way he's staring at me, like I'm a priceless treasure is overpowering. I can feel him in my mind, body and soul.

"Fox," I manage as I feel myself getting closer. Am I really going to say it? I open my mouth to speak. I see the look of almost panic in his eyes and in an instant, he captures my lips. I let out the most passionate moan as he fills me with his seed. His rough movements send me over the edge, and I cry out as I find my own release while gripping him tightly to me.

As we come back down, lips still together, tongues dancing – I decide to leave what I was going to say unspoken. This, right now, us...we are perfect, and I just want to enjoy it.

GROANING, I wake up and smile softly as I feel the familiar weight of Fox on my chest. I look down and see him nuzzled into my bare breast, his hair fanning his face. He looks so peaceful. I hate that I have to move, but...I need to pee, desperately.

I slide out from under him just in time for Winston to climb up the bed and stare at me. I pet his head to stop him from letting out a loud meow before walking towards the bathroom.

"Where are you going?" Fox grumbles, still half asleep. My body freezes and I clutch my heart as I turn to stare at him.

"I just need to pee, though I just about wet myself thanks to you." He lets out a sleepy laugh that would be super adorable if I wasn't about to wet myself. "I am getting hungry, so you should think about feeding me." He gives me a lazy wave as I walk out of the bedroom. Just as I sit down, I hear my phone go off and groan. "Can you answer that and tell them to hang on a second?" I call out and smile as I hear him grumbling about having to get up.

After washing my hands and grabbing a shirt that was hanging on the bathroom door, I slip it on and walk back to the bedroom to find Fox sitting on the edge of the bed, staring down at my phone. The muscle in his jaw is ticking like mad.

"Who was it?" I whisper, unsure as to why the room suddenly feels so heavy.

Fox's stare meets mine, and... why does he look hurt? I stare at him and then back to my phone.

"Fox?" I say again feeling my anxiety rise.

Fox shakes himself out of whatever thoughts were going through his mind before holding his hand out and offering me my phone. "Brandon Stephens called," His voice was hoarse and distant.

My heart falls to my stomach. And I watch in fear as Fox stands and begins to put clothes on.

"W-what did he say?" I ask cautiously as he roughly yanks his jeans up.

Running his hands through his hair, Fox grabs a hair tie off his nightstand and pulls his hair back. He lets out a dry laugh. "Well, he wants to know if you have a preference between window and non-window seats for your flight to Chicago."

Shit.

"Fox..." I say calmly as I hold my shaky hands out. "Wait, the guy is jumping the gun, okay? I never confirmed that I was going to Chicago to meet them."

His hazel eyes fix on me, and they look...hurt. "But you knew about the job, you were thinking about going and you didn't bother to mention it to me?"

"God," I groan in frustration. "No, alright just...stop talking for a minute. Look, when you were in Vegas and I went to the meet and greet, Bliss Trips was like the only company that gave me five minutes. So yes, I did talk to them about a possible job. But Fox, that was before you and I..." My eyes go soft and grab his hand. "I never heard back from them, I completely forgot about them until this morning, he sent me an email while I was with Sunday and Ren."

Fox stares at me for a moment before exhaling a breath. "Do you want to go?"

I look at him and I smile as I place a hand on either side of his face. "Fox, I have real feelings for you, and the last thing I would want to do is jeopardize our future over some silly influencer job. I want to be with you."

The look on his face isn't one of relief, but almost guilt. It is there, only for a second before he shoots me a smile and kisses the top of my head. "Come on baby doll, let's get you something to eat."

Chapter Twenty-Eight

FOX

"ALRIGHT, BOYS, SMILE!" Janie says as she holds her phone out to take a photo of Atlas, Ash, Derek, and me as we stand in front of baggage claim at the Miami Airport. She seems unsatisfied with our half smile, half grimace but chooses to stay quiet. It has been an exhausting day. The plane ride took about six hours, and I white-knuckled the armrest for two of them as we went through a 'mild thunderstorm,' as the pilot called it. Meanwhile, our plane was shaking and dropping. Everyone said I was overreacting when I declared I was driving back to Los Angeles, but I wasn't kidding.

Besides the flight from hell, Florida is three hours ahead of us, so while it's six our time, it's now nine here. We are all hungry, but Janie refuses to eat airport food, saying it's a recipe for food poisoning. But at this point, I'm so fucking hungry I will eat right out of the trash.

"Mama J..." I roll my eyes at the whine coming from Atlas. He walks over and rests his head on Janie's shoulder, which takes some crouching and bending to reach.

"Yes, Atlas, I know you all are tired and hungry." She

lets out a sigh as she looks up from her phone. "Alright, our Uber is out front. Let's go to the hotel, and I already placed orders with the hotel to have food in our rooms." The three men and I all exchange looks as if we are thinking the same thing, Janie is precisely what has been missing every time we ever have gone to a convention. I rub my chest as the ache returns. This ache I've been feeling all week. At first, I thought it was heartburn, then a heart attack. Actually, I'm still convinced it's an attack on my heart. Just not in the medical sense. I'm going to make Janie go to Chicago, after this convention is over, I'm going to explain to her that she should take the job there because there is no way I can keep her from that if the only reason she is staying in California is her hopes of some romantic future with me.

"Come on, boys," She gives us a tired smile. "Let's head out." We grab our bags, and I hold Janie's as well before heading out of the airport.

Janie and I are not talking much, not because we were fighting or anything, but I think I've been distancing myself to prepare for the inevitable and she's probably picked up on it. I've been staying late at Hel's or falling asleep on the couch instead of our bed.

Fuck, when did I start calling things 'ours'?

I want her to stay. God knows I do. But I can't make her. This job is an amazing opportunity for her, and I won't be why she doesn't take it. I won't look at her and see her resentment. I've experienced that enough in my life. I can't have her stay with me hoping that I can love her the way she deserves to be loved.

I do love her...I think. But that just means I've got to cut this off. What if I tell her I love her, and she stays with me and then I fuck everything up, which is a given. If that happens and she gave up her future and has to start all over, again...how would I be any better than that purple-haired fuck face, Brody?

I turn my head to glance at Janie. She is explaining to Ash the different merchandise that she's brought for the convention. I can see how excited she is to talk about it by the speed her hands are moving. God, I am in love with her, and doing what I need to do to make her happy in the long run is going to fucking destroy me. But I am willing to suffer that pain if it means she's able to be happy.

JANIE USES her key card and lets us into our room. I set down our bags and look around. It is a nice suite. Clean, and modern with a balcony that I am sure overlooks the ocean, though right now it's black outside, so I will have to enjoy that view in the morning. I eye the single bed and partially wish there were two of them.

"The food should be here soon," Janie's voice is soft and small, the complete opposite of how she was with the guys. "I was going to head to the shower unless you wanted to take one first."

I desperately want a shower, but I shake my head. "You go ahead. I am going to check my emails first." Lies. I don't have any unread emails. I had been glued to my phone most of the trip when I wasn't afraid of falling towards the Earth in a tiny sardine can.

I can tell she knows I am lying when she smiles softly and nods. "Okay, thanks."

Once I hear the bathroom door shut and the water turn on, I let out a massive breath as I walk out to the balcony. I may not be able to see the ocean, but I can hear it and smell it and NOT smell Janie, which is very important at the moment. I inhale the salty air as I sit on the chair outside. Staring at my phone, I look at the photo I have on the lock screen. It's Janie and me. She is on my back and grinning over my shoulder like the happiest kid on Christmas while gripping my face with one hand to squeeze my lips together in a fish face. It's probably my favorite photo in existence. Every time I look at it, I can't help but smile. I want more of those pictures. I want more memories of her... with her.

I hate that it has come to this, and so quickly. I spent so much time denying my feelings, pretending to hate her that I wasted so much between us. I think back to her birthday at the club, when she asked me to dance.

"Not even if there was a meteor heading straight for us and the only way to save all of mankind was to dance."

God damn it, why didn't I dance with her then? Why didn't I kiss her the first time I felt the urge? Why am I still not telling her everything going on inside me?

I hear the bathroom door open and quickly shove my phone into my pocket before standing up.

STEPPING out of the bathroom after a much-needed ice shower, the smell of hot wings hits my nose. I raise my brow as I look at Janie.

"You hate wings?" I say as I grab my shirt and throw it on before taking a seat next to her on the loveseat.

"I know, but you like them, and it's been a rough day, so

I thought you'd enjoy these. And look!" I stare in disbelief as she opens the small refrigerator and pulls out a container.

"They had peanut butter pie!" I watch as her smile drops slightly. "It's... your favorite, right?" It is my favorite. My favorite meal, dessert, and she has my favorite beer - Modelo - sitting next to my food.

"Why are you doing this?" She flinches, and I realize that might've come out harsher than I intended. She lowers the container with the pie back to the fridge.

"I'm your girlfriend. Girlfriends do nice things."

"Janie..." Another flinch. Except it is more than a flinch, her eyes go glassy, and her bottom lip begins to tremble.

"I – you never call me Janie unless it's bad." There is a tremor in her voice, and I hate myself for putting it there.

"There is a ticket in your bag for Chicago." I say as I take a long swig of the beer.

"I am aware." She whispers and I freeze, my beer bottle still at my lips.

I look at her and raise a brow. "You know? When?"

"Brandon called me to confirm yesterday. I was confused at first but silly you, you used Hel's email address for the confirmation from the airlines. So, I saw it." Her arms wrap around her midsection as if she's trying to hold herself.

"You're going to Chicago." I say as even toned as I can, though on the inside I am anything but.

"Not if you tell me to stay." She whispers, not looking at me.

"What?" Her whole body is trembling now, and all I want to do is wrap her in my arms and calm her down. But I can't, I need to get this done so she can move on. I never will. I will forever be cemented in this feeling of having to give up everything because I am not enough.

"Tell me not to go, Fox." Her small, cracking voice pleads. "Tell me that you want to stay with me and that I have to return to California with you. Tell me that I'm not the only one falling in love here. Tell me you see the possibility of an amazing future for us. Tell me and I will go home and never mention Chicago again." I must look like an idiot. I can feel my slack jaw. I am hot and cold at the same time, and I am pretty sure I'm starting to shake at this point.

She is falling in love with me. Janie Pierce, the brat determined to stay my sworn enemy and make my life a living hell – is sitting beside me, tears running down her cheeks, begging me to tell her that I feel the same and that she can't go.

Tell me not to go.

"I can't, Janie." I manage to get out, though I feel like someone is squeezing my throat. "I can't tell you not to go –"

"You can!" She forces out through a sob. She clasps her tiny hands around mine and presses my palm to her chest. I feel her poor heart beating as hard and rapid as my own.

"You can tell me, Fox! You love bossing me around. Just tell me that you are fall –"

"I can't," I say sternly, removing my hand from her heart. "Janie, I can't say what you want me to say. I can't say I'm falling in love with you, and that you need to stay." Her being this close to me is suffocating. I stand up and put some space between us.

Turning back, I look at her face and God, please let me take back those words. But I can't. You can't un-ring a bell. The look of devastation and rejection taking over her features is enough to make me want to beat my own ass for causing her this pain.

"Oh," Her voice is so small that I can't be sure if she actually speaks the words or if I imagined them. I can see her trying to smile, but her mouth won't cooperate. "Well, that changes things then, doesn't it?" I watch as she wipes her palms on her leggings before standing and heading to her bags.

"What are you doing?" I ask when she puts her backpack on.

She refuses to look up at me as she grabs her stuff. "I'm going to get another room."

"What? No! Janie, wait –" I stop myself as she finally stares up at me with shattered eyes. I didn't know eyes could shatter, and it is something I could've gone without knowing.

"Good night, Fox." She walks out the door, and once it clicks shut, I begin to shatter too. Hurting her now is best, though. She will be better off to leave now before I ruin her life completely. But still, even knowing I am doing the right thing, it doesn't stop the tear that runs down my face.

Chapter Twenty-Nine

JANIE

THE LOUD SCREAMING of my alarm pulls me out of my thoughts... okay, not thoughts, more like staring blankly into nothingness because my mind, body, and heart are too exhausted from sobbing to do anything else.

I grab my phone and turn the alarm off. But once I do, my scheduled- *"do not disturb"* turns off as well, and notifications start pouring in. This is too much. I should not have to handle this right now. My brain cannot seem to remember how to make the phone silent, and every new notification is an added level of anxiety. I can't take it anymore. It's all too much. I stand up and have to brace myself to keep from falling. Grabbing the phone, I walk to the balcony door and open the curtains, wincing at the very bright sun. Stepping out onto the balcony, the smells and noises become too overwhelming. I place my phone on a lounge chair and go back inside, shutting the door.

Ding
Ding
Tweet

Boop

I can still hear them. I can still hear everything.

"*I can't say I'm falling in love with you.*"

I march outside and grab my phone before falling to my knees and slamming it repeatedly against the balcony.

"Why. Won't. You. Shut. Up." I sob out with each impact. The phone finally silences. I look down at the broken, mangled device. The screen is black. Standing up, I leave the dead thing outside for good measure before walking back into my room, closing the blinds, and laying back down in my bed.

I DON'T KNOW how much time has passed when a knock on the door pulls me out of my trance. Why is someone knocking at my door anyway? I have the **"*do not disturb*"** hanger on the door. The knocking continues, and I growl as I throw the sheets off and walk to the door. I rip it open and nearly slam it shut when I see Atlas.

"Hey! Hey! Hey!" His large hand grips the door to keep me from shutting it.

"Go away, Atlas! This has nothing to do with you." I growl as I use my entire body to shove at the door. Atlas' big giant stupid body doesn't budge, and I wind up letting out a slew of curse words as my ass collides with the floor.

Atlas comes into my room and shuts the door.

"I didn't invite you in!" I yell and hit his knee.

"I'm not a vampire, Janie." He helps me up and turns

the light on. Flinching at my appearance as he stares at me, Atlas rubs the back of his neck. "So...rough night?"

Did he really just ask me that? I shake my head in disbelief before turning and crawling back into bed.

"Okay, that was dumb." He says as I throw the covers over me.

I let out a sarcastic "HA." "Good looks and a brain? Look out, ladies!"

I hear him sigh, and even through the covers, I know he's staring at me. I rip the covers off me as I sit up and turn to give him all of my frustration. "What do you want, Atlas?"

He appears to not be phased by my rage. Foolish man. He clears his throat. "Fox is —"

"Don't care." I interrupt. I can't deal with anything revolving around him, and there is no way I can handle hearing his name or acknowledging that, yes, he is still alive and in this hotel at the convention downstairs. I would rather pretend he never existed.

"Janie!" His voice is a desperate plea, but I'm not answering today.

"You are all very, very grown men. Handle your shit yourselves. I'm leaving soon anyway. I am catching an early flight to Chicago."

He lets out a frustrated growl. "Janie, you can't. Listen, I don't know what happened, but you must know that he cares about you." I laugh coldly as I stand and start packing. I can't be around the guys, and now that Atlas knows which room, I'm in, **he** won't be far behind.

"He doesn't," I mutter as I shake my backpack to make more room to stuff the rest of my belongings in there. Shit, I would have to get a ride to get a new phone. Damn it.

"He doesn't what?"

"He doesn't care!" I snap as I grab my broken phone off the balcony. "I told him my feelings last night. I told him that I would stay. I **stupidly** told him I was falling in love with him! He said he couldn't tell me the same! So leave me alone!" I grab my bags as I shuffle out of the room and down the hall to the elevator. Maybe I will get lucky, and I can get to Chicago tonight.

Chapter Thirty

FOX

"OH MY GOD!" The excited young redhead squeals as she bounces up and down. "I follow you guys! I am like obsessed! I am so hoping to win one of your shirts!" I give her a small nod and turn the tablet towards her.

"Just fill out the info below and if you win, someone will contact you." I mutter and then I am being wheeled away from the table as Derek and Ash take over talking to her and Atlas takes me to the other side of the room.

He sits in front of me and sighs. "You look like shit."

I glare up at him, though it's hard to do when my eyes feel like sandpaper is being rubbed against them and I have this enormous weight over my entire body.

"Oh fuck..." Atlas' eyes go wide. "You've been crying."

"Fuck you." I snarl as I shove away and head out of the convention, Atlas hot on my heels.

"Dude, if you are this fucking upset, go apologize and tell her you made a mistake." Atlas words stop me in my tracks.

"You don't think I've already tried that?" I growl as I

continue walking until I am outside the hotel. I inhale the salty air deeply as I try to calm my brain.

We leave tomorrow, we go home tomorrow. Janie is in Chicago as we speak, and I can't get to her. I've tried calling and texting, but she won't answer. I called Ren and Stevie, both have decided I'm dead to them. I was able to find out through Instagram that Sunday is on her way to Chicago for a "Girl Emergency". So my hope is she is with Janie. Not that Sunday would spill anything to me anyway. I know her less than any of the girls and what I do know is that she would sooner rip my dick off and shove it down my throat than help me if I hurt Janie.

I hurt Janie.

It's been playing on repeat for two days. I hurt her. I hurt the woman I'm in love with...because I didn't want to hurt her. Fuck, even trying not to be a fuck up, I end up fucking up.

I lean against the wall of the hotel as I look at the picture of us on my phone's lock screen. I think about everything, the looks, the smart-ass remarks, the flirting, the donuts, the kissing, her holding me when I took her in the pool...saying she trusted me.

"I need a hug..."

When she said that to me and when I got home, and she leapt on me...I think I knew then somehow that I was in love with her. Even if I couldn't admit it. She was willing to stay with me, all I had to do was tell her that I could be falling for her too.

The truth was I had already fallen long before. How could I not? She's smart, and funny. She is beautiful and the biggest pain in the ass. Everything is met with an argument, with a question...there is no blind faith. If Janie decides she trusts you, it's because you had to earn it. I had earned it...and then I set it on fire right in front of her.

I was so terrified of becoming my father. Of trapping a woman that was in love with me. Hurting her and not leaving her with any options. And in trying to not become him...I ended up hurting the woman that is in love with me.

Chapter Thirty-One

JANIE

"JANIE, we are just so thrilled that you are here!" Brandon is brimming and practically levitating out of his seat as he and his boss, Patricia Humphrey, sit across the board room table from me. Patricia would've been my *"hashtag goals"* last year. The woman is close to late sixties, though I guarantee that ninety percent of her parts are younger than I am. She's elegant with her long, thin body that is wrapped in an oxblood power suit that for sure cost more than my car. Her raven hair is pulled tightly in a french twist with zero, and I do mean **zero** fly aways. Her midnight black, coffin shaped nails tap on the conference table as she reads over my folder.

I give him a smile that I do not genuinely feel as I continue to twist my fingers under the table, hoping that they don't notice my tremors. Something that until last night, I hadn't realized I had stopped worrying so much about it. Over this year, I stopped hiding, stopped wearing baggy clothes year around, I stopped shying away from making friends due to fear of judgment. Now I'm right back where I started. I actually thought about bailing on the interview, but with Sunday being here, that was not possible.

I had texted her and Ren while at the airport and filled them in on everything, and when I told them I had no idea where I would be staying since I was showing up early and I would figure it out once I got there, Ren booked me a room, Stevie went to Fox's and got Winston back and Sunday booked herself a flight.

I have never had real friends before. I had co-collabs that I would exchange favors with. The idea of any of them doing a fraction of the shit that Stevie, Sunday and Ren do for me is laughable.

Sunday has spent the last two days detoxing me. She took me for massages, pedicures, facials, and to this one salon that only specializes in washing your hair. But the best part of it was that Sunday taught me you could ask for a "silent service." Meaning there was no chit-chatting, no having to force a fake smile. It was all just about the phys- ical moment. I hadn't realized how therapeutic that would be.

And this morning, Sunday got up and flat ironed my hair for me, so perfectly straight and sleek you would think she had been doing it for years. She dressed me in a power suit, black, with an emerald green camisole and the sharpest pair of stilettos I've ever seen. I scream power and business. But inside – I miss my Hel's T-shirt and leggings. I miss my freckles, I miss my crazy hair. I miss my giant tattooed lumberjack.

I bite the inside of my cheek to hold back the sob trying to break free.

"I'm delighted to be here." I say elegantly, using the voice I always used with my brand deals. Funny how I spent years mastering this fake persona. Creating "Jai". Now I

273

can't stand her. Her voice is like nails on a chalkboard. I don't know when it started, all I know is at this moment, I hate Jai more than I've hated anyone.

"I don't know how much Brandon has told you about the job," Patricia says as she closes the file she had read. "So, what we are looking for is a co-host."

I blink and stare between Patricia's pore-less face and Brandon's...why is he so excited?

"I'm sorry?" I shake my head, giving them an unsure smile. "Co-host?"

Patricia nods. "You would be co-hosting a vlog channel with Brandon where you two will find yourselves growing closer in your travels, relationships blossoming in the most beautiful places, along with cute banter."

A fake relationship for views.

My mind immediately goes to Brody, and my stomach churns. "I'm sorry, I thought this was a solo job, and it would be photos, not a vlog."

Patricia laughs as if what I had said was the most absurd notion ever uttered in her presence.

"Janie, did you really believe I would pay to fly you worldwide for Instagram shots? Come on now. You've been in the social media world long enough. You were influencing before it was a big thing."

I turn my gaze towards Brandon. His overly eager smile, short, wavy blonde hair, and tanned skin that undoubtedly came from a bottle or a bed - all of it screams fragile ego. Yeah, he won't last a month in a vlog. Someone will make fun of that fake baked color, and he will crumble. I give a small smile and continue to listen as the two of them continue to talk about the job and all it will entail. Though I am only partially listening. My mind keeps going back to Fox.

Why? Why would he even start a relationship, and then continue a relationship with me if he didn't see love as a possibility? Had it been too soon? I didn't think so. We were well over getting close to ending the first year since Dad's death. I don't feel like that is an absurdly short amount of time to decide if you are in love with someone.

I wanted to stay with him. I wanted to stay at Hel's. But I wanted him, no I needed him to tell me that is what he wanted. We agreed that we would go our separate ways after the year, but we didn't speak on the subject since we'd become a couple. I didn't want to stay there if he wanted me gone. But I really did not want to be here either.

I listen to Patricia drone on and on about what would be expected of me and Brandon. Speaking of...The man's eyes haven't left mine and this small conference table is too small. The man keeps *bumping* his foot into mine and I am three seconds from throat punching him. That would make for some great banter.

I smile at the thought and Brandon must take it as a sign to keep going because I feel his foot trail up my calf.

My thoughts go to Fox. One word and Fox would snap him into two. Fuck... I really miss him.

Chapter Thirty-Two

FOX

I SIT on the bench outside the building where Bliss Trips' headquarters are stationed. My leg continues to bob up and down rapidly as I watch everyone walking out of the building, waiting to see my girl.

Yes, *my girl*. I was an idiot, and I am ready to admit that to her now and every sixty seconds for the rest of my life, just as long as I get to be near her.

Hearing the rumble of thunder from the darkening skies above, I curse and shake my head. I had been in hot, sunny Miami for three days and was supposed to return to warm, sunny California. Instead, I'm in Chicago, in a T-shirt, freezing and seconds from getting drenched.

It doesn't matter though, I will not leave this spot. I need to talk to Janie first. I made a mistake, and I refuse to let her go, not like this. She is too important to me.

Miami

Two Days Ago

"You are the biggest fucking idiot that has ever fucking existed." Atlas snarled once he caught up to me outside the hotel. He shoved me against the wall. I don't even try to fight back. I don't care. He can beat me, belittle me. It was nothing compared to how I feel over hurting Janie. It's nothing I don't deserve.

"She's in love with you! And you tell her no?" I looked at the ground before glancing up at him. My face must've said something my mouth couldn't because Atlas instantly softened, and he stepped back.

"I am in love with her." I choked out, my mouth extremely dry. When was the last time I drank anything?

"Then why... Oh, Fox..." Atlas smacked his head.

I gave a partial shrug. *"She can't give up that opportunity because of me. If she wants this, I need to let her go. I can't have her stay with me and me end up fucking everything up between us."*

"So what! Fucking go with her sometimes! Take vacations! You know this will only be a temporary job. Most of these travel influencers last a year or two! You're giving up something real. Something good. Something amazing, Fox."

"You don't think I know that?" I snapped, pushing myself off the wall. *"I am over forty, have no family, no education past the tenth grade. All I have is my job. And that woman came in here, and fucking found something inside me that she..."* I laughed in disbelief. *"That she loved.... about me. She's young and smart, fast and funny. She is so goal-oriented and passionate. She's warm...."* I rubbed my chest where the now-familiar ache resided. *"She is everything good and decent, and I am so fucking in love with her. I'm in love with her enough to let her go so she can find her way."*

I harden my gaze as I head to the front entrance of the hotel, but Atlas' voice stops me.

"But do you love her enough to go after her and find your way together?"

ATLAS HAD that dumb look on his face after those words left him. But I had to agree with him. She was willing to give up something for me. Why hadn't I offered the same in return? That day at the convention, I made travel arrangements to fly out the next morning. And while sitting at the convention, I noticed, well, all of us guys noticed how much Janie has gone from being the annoying brat there to make life harder, to a vital part of our group. The shirts we designed were a hit. Our booth was constantly full of fans and customers, and new clients making appointments to fly out to have our tattoos on them. She set it all up without our help. We could carry on Tony's dream of Hel's Ink because his daughter was here making it happen. I couldn't let her leave, thinking that none of it mattered. But more importantly, I couldn't let her leave thinking that it was because I wasn't in love with her. That I was rejecting her. I need her to know that I am so in love with her.

A flash of red catches my gaze, but I almost brush it off because that suit-wearing woman is not my Torch. But she is. She looks like a corporate CEO on her way to a meeting. It doesn't suit her. She is stunning, of course, but the sharp angles of her clothes and makeup make her look cold and unapproachable.

I cuss while running across the street as the skies

unleash what can only be described as a monsoon. Janie, of course, has an umbrella, as does everyone else on this godforsaken street corner, except me.

I run up behind her, my body starting to freeze from the rain.

"Jesus Torch, already in a man killer suit?" I watch her body stiffen. Her head whips around, and her body follows. She stares at me in complete shock as I try to blink the rain out of my eyes.

"What are you doing here?" She calls out over the loud rain and busy street.

"I love you!" I say just as a loud boom of thunder shakes the Earth.

She shakes her head. "What?"

"I said!" I close the few steps between us until I am standing under the umbrella with her. I take the umbrella from her hands and hold it higher over us. "I love you, Janie."

Her bottom lip quivers, and she moves her head away. "Stop it." She snaps and grabs the umbrella back before walking away.

"Janie, I mean it!" I yell as I run after her, she spins around, and I nearly run into her.

Her lips are pressed into a thin, hard line and her blue eyes are hard and filled with electricity. "So what? Now that I'm here, you want me to drop everything and go back with you? What about the last three days? What about three days ago when I told you my feelings, and you let me leave, broken?"

"I didn't want to be your reason for staying in California and giving up on this if it's what you wanted." I say as I will my teeth to stop chattering.

"And now?" She raises her brow and looks around.

"What are you doing here now?"

"I can't be your reason to stay," I say, walking closer to her again. "I refuse to be that selfish. Now, Atlas, Ash and Derek? They are absolutely that selfish and want you back at the shop immediately." I watch as the corner of her mouth quirks despite trying to keep her scowl firmly in place.

"I can't make you stay, but I will go with you sometimes, and you can come to visit me when you can. We can figure it out if this is the life you want, baby doll. I just, I want to be a part of it. I am terrified to fuck this up Janie, but I...fuck maybe I am that selfish because I am willing to risk fucking it up if it means I get to keep you." I wince at my comment. "It sounded way better in my head, sorry."

There is a long silence between us, and I am thankful my body is going numb, so I don't feel the cold rain anymore.

"The job is for a vlog show," Janie states as she starts to turn again. "They want me to go with another man. We will travel and have an on-camera relationship."

Suddenly, I am not feeling so cold as my boiling blood runs through me. "Well, I don't know how they will expect him to have any sort of relationship with you when he is in a fucking coma."

She forces her lips to stay down. "Don't make me laugh." She pleads, her eyes brimming with unshed tears.

"Do you want the job?" I ask, feeling suddenly very heavy. Was coming out here a mistake?

I watch as she stares from me back to the building. She bites her lip and shrugs. "It's something I know how to do. You would get the shop to yourself, and we could both move on."

"I will never move on." I snap. She flinches, and I hold

my hands up to apologize. I sigh and look around the crowded sidewalk.

Fuck it.

I fall to my knees in front of her.

"Fox! What are you doing?!" She hisses, looking around at the passersby as they slow and murmur.

"Janie Hel Pierce," I say as loudly as my shivering voice will allow. "I am wholeheartedly in love with you! Please! I am on my knees begging!" I watch her uncomfortable smile and red face as she waves at the crowds.

"Stop it!" She grinds out as she futilely tries to pull me up.

I continue, even though I am sure I look like the biggest idiot. I don't care, I am the biggest idiot for ever letting her think she wasn't worth the risk. Never again. No matter what she decides, she will always know that she is worth everything and more. "Tell me you don't want me. Tell me to leave, and I will. But I won't stop loving you. And I'll never stop showing the world how much I love you as long as I live. Even if that is only a few more days because I am certain pneumonia or hypothermia is going to sink in soon."

She lets out a small laugh as tears fall down her cheeks. I go to stand up, but she goes to her knees as well, her petite body trembling.

"I want you, and I want to go home with you." She smiles, and I pull her to my chest, ignoring my drenched shirt.

"God damn, you're an icebox!" She hisses and tries to pull away.

"Nope, you're not moving, Torch."

Chapter Thirty-Three

JANIE

"THIS REALLY WASN'T NECESSARY." I sigh as Fox and I walk into the room to the suite he got for us. Apparently, going to the hotel Sunday and I were staying at was not on his agenda.

"Stop talking Torch." He lifts me up over his shoulder and carries me into the suite.

"I can't even see the room!" I squeal as he continues to march his ass to wherever he is going.

"It's a suite, there is a room, a bathroom and a bed. Oh hey, now there is something."

Fox drops me on the bed, and I follow his gaze. "It's a balcony," I state dryly. "Surely you've seen one before."

He glares at me but it has zero effect. I'm far too busy staring at his absolutely soaked body. His clothes cling to him like a second skin. Part of me wants to put him in a hot shower, the other wants to put him in the bed, naked.

"I'm going to thaw out in the shower." Guess he made that decision. "I will be no more than ninety seconds." He leans down and kisses me in such a passionate way my toes curl in my shoes. I watch as he walks away, removing articles of clothing as he goes.

I hear the door click shut and the water turn on. It's then that I decide to get up and move around the room. It's actually very nice. A king size bed, massive flat screen tv and a couch. I peer in the closet and pull out a robe. Fuck it's soft.

I slip out of my shoes and the rest of my clothes before wrapping myself in the plush, navy-blue robe. God, it smells amazing, fresh, clean and maybe vanilla?

Padding over to the sink that is on the outside of the bathroom, I begin to wash my face with the face wash they have in little bottles. Usually, I would be leery, but this place actually looks like it may have better facial products than I do.

I squeeze and scrunch my wet hair, it had gotten completely drenched before we'd been able to hail a cab.

As I step onto the balcony, I can't help but smile.

He loves me. Fox loves me.

I feel his hard chest against my back as he closes his hands on either side of the railing. "You know what I want to do?" He inhales against my neck deeply and I feel my core begin to tighten.

"Hmm..." I manage as his teeth nibble on my ear. I watch one hand move from the railing and slip under my robe, straight for my pussy.

"Fuckkk, you're already getting wet for me baby doll?" I whimper my response as his fingers circle my clit.

"Fox," I breathe, throwing my head back against his chest. "We are outside."

"I know, and the thought of fucking you over this railing in broad daylight has my cock so fucking hard I can't think straight." It's then he presses his erection against my backside that I realize he is completely naked, not even a towel.

I'm nervous to be out in public during the day. But we are in one of the top floor suites and no one can see us on either side. Doesn't mean someone might not see us with a telescope.

Really? A telescope?

I have to admit though, I'm dripping at the thought of getting fucked out here. I bite my lip, nervous before bending forward on the railing and rubbing my ass over his cock. As I bend forward the rain begins to hit me, and it somehow adds to the excitement. Fox wastes no time, after all, fucking in downtown Chicago on a balcony in broad daylight isn't meant to be slow and sweet. Besides, I feel like he might have some anger from me leaving that he is holding on to. Hell, I still have anger from Miami. Angry sex sounds like a great way to start working through it.

Fox's hands slide up my waist, lifting my robe over my ass. I feel him press against my entrance and I cry out as he shoves himself inside me. My knuckles go white as I grip the railing, moving back to meet every one of his angry thrusts.

"Tell me how much you missed this." He grunts as he grips my hips to thrust harder. I look over the railing at the figures below, they look like small ants. I wonder if they can hear my cries.

"I missed your cock!" I moan loudly. Fox swiftly spins me around and I wrap my legs around his waist as he presses me against the railing. The only reason I am not terrified of falling is his massive hand holding me tightly to him as he pounds harder into my pussy. His free hand goes up to my throat and gives me a squeeze and I roll my eyes back in my head at the sensation.

Fox's voice is low and almost dangerous as he growls in between each forceful thrust.

"You." *Thrust.* "Are." *Thrust.* "Mine." *Thrust.*

His grasp tightens and in doing so, pushes me that much closer to my orgasm.

"Oh godddd!" I manage as I dig into his back while my head hangs over the edge. I can feel his cock throbbing inside of me as he lets out the sexiest noise I've ever heard, I cry out his name as I explode around him.

We stay like that, still, connected to each other, both panting and shaking. Fox runs his palm over my forehead, brushing my hair out of my face. The way he stares at me, it makes me want to cry.

"What is it, baby doll?" He asks as he kisses the tip of my nose.

"Why are you looking at me that way?" I ask softly as he nuzzles into my neck.

"Like what?" He pulls back and looks at me the same way, the corners of his mouth hitch upwards. "Like I've won the lottery?" He kisses my lips. "Like I've found the lost treasure?" He kisses me again. "Like I was just given the greatest gift ever imaginable?" He takes my bottom lip into his mouth and nibbles on it softly, causing me to let a moan escape. "Is that how I'm looking at you Torch?" He slips his tongue into my mouth in a deep, claiming kiss. I feel his dick hardening again inside me and I break the kiss to look down.

"Really?" I laugh and he shrugs.

"Listen, I have zero idea what's happening. Up until this very moment, I thought I was too old to go back-to-back."

I wrap my arms back around him and smile. "Well take me inside, we definitely shouldn't waste it. I hear that *some* people receive up to eight orgasms."

Fox snorts as he carries me back into the suite and lays me on the bed. "He's lucky I didn't beat his ass right there for that snarky comment." I watch his eyes dance all over me. "But I guess if that's what my girl wants, I will have to deliver or die trying."

I giggle and kiss the tip of his nose before staring into his warm eyes. They look so happy. "I love you." I say while grabbing his face in my palms. "You are my treasure too, Fox. I love you so much."

His eyes mist slightly, and he looks away before taking a breath. "I'm going to lose all sex appeal if I start blubbering so knock it off." He jokes. I pull his face back to mine and kiss his lips while raking my fingers through his beard.

"Not possible."

Epilogue

FOX - SIX MONTHS LATER

"I DON'T KNOW ABOUT THIS." Janie groans nervously as she chews on her lip. I watch as she slips her leggings over the curve of her ass and hips. I stifle a moan while trying to stay professional.

"You'll be fine." I mumble as I slip my glasses on while she lies on my table, fuck this woman and her constant pull she has on my cock! I am too fucking old to be this hard this frequently.

"Hang on. Cut!" Ren growls, and Janie rolls her eyes as she sits up from the table.

"Fox," Janie pats my forearm. "Baby, I love you, but I will kill you in the most gruesome of ways if you mess this video up one more time." She reaches over and kisses my stunned lips. "I've told you, act like she's not here."

I look from the redhead to Ren and back. "I don't know why we have to do this." I whine.

"I told you she will stop filming after the first line! But if you want to be the one to tattoo me, you have to do it! This is going on the website, I'm trying to show people how gentle you are with first timers." Her eyes drop down and I watch her eyes roll and her cheeks redden.

"Really?" She hisses and I give her a sly smile.

"Was I gentle with you the first time?" I waggle my brows suggestively causing her to flick me on the forehead.

"Where is Derek? I'll have him do it." My demeanor darkens and I glare at her.

"I was promised the first tattoo." I grumble, feeling slightly wounded.

"Then put your boner away and do it!" She growls and it's kind of hot.

Ash, Derek and Ren all groan and I roll my eyes.

"Don't be jealous." I roll my neck and dip my needle in the ink. "Alright Torch, let's do this again."

Thankfully Ren gets the shot she needs, and I can finally work on Janie's tattoo, her first one.

After Chicago, Janie returned to LA, we retrieved our cat-son, Winston, and Janie turned down the job with Bliss. I also threatened Brandon, gruesomely, when he started trying to stay in contact and Janie let it slip about his "happy feet".

Once Janie and I made it to the end of Tony's twelve-month arrangement, we had to make a decision. Fifty-Fifty partners, or one of us buys the other out. It pained me for about half a second, but I told Janie I wanted to give up the rights of ownership and I didn't need to be bought out. She, the stubborn brat she is, said I was an idiot and we were doing a split. She and I went back and forth in a battle that lasted nearly a month. I ended up giving in, only because she decided to abstain from sex until I did so while simulta-neously embracing the nudist lifestyle at home. I made it three hours before waving the flag in surrender.

There was one stipulation though, I own forty-nine

percent of Hel's, not fifty. It was important to me that Janie held the primary ownership of the shop.

Hel's has been busier than ever the last few months. So much so that we had to hire two new shop hands and a "marketing assistant"- whatever that means. All I know is, Janie took this place and made it better than her father or I ever could've.

"Where is Atlas?" Janie asks while looking over at Atlas' empty station. "I cannot believe he's missing my cherry getting popped."

I stop my machine and stare at her over the rim of my glasses. "Really?" She gives me an innocent smile.

"He should be getting ready for court," Ren mutters, not looking up from her phone. Atlas got into some trouble a few weeks back. Though he hasn't told any of us what had happened, all we know is Frank is the one representing him and Ren and At have been at odds with each other since whatever incident happened. I figure when the case is over, At will finally come around to talking to us. But I think right now he is embarrassed by it and trying to keep to himself.

The weird thing is, he left his loft that he shared with Ash. When Ash questioned him as to why, he just said he needed a change and Ash could use the extra space for when his sister moved in. Nobody knows where he moved to as he refuses to talk about it.

It's been hard though, not having my best friend around as much as usual. I just hope if he's in any real trouble he knows that we got his back, like he's had mine so many times before.

"Alright, baby doll," I say as I wipe down her thigh. "She's done." I watch as Janie hops off my table and walks to the full-length mirror. She stares silently at the tattoo, her hands over her mouth.

It is a tattoo of Hel. The living side is the colorful one she did last year, while the black and grey skeleton portion was the original drawing she had made years ago.

"Fox," I watch as the tears spill. She turns and presses a kiss against my lips. "I love it. And I love you." I smile as I press my forehead against hers and stare into her big eyes.

"I love you too."

The End

What's Next

Fox & Janie were book one in the interconnected Hel's Ink series. Book two will be out early 2023 and will feature Atlas' story so make sure you are following for release dates!

Also, Fox has been turned into an audiobook thanks to the talented Narrators - Paige Reisenfeld and Christian Leatherman. Available now on audible.

Acknowledgments

Cover - Kate Farlow - Y'all That Graphic

Editor & Personal Assistant - Raeleen Nelson - Book Witch
Author Services

Narrators - Paige Reisenfeld & Christian Leatherman

All of my Beta & ARC readers

About the Author

Author & Artist

Sarcastic potty-mouth, neurodivergent hot mess, full-time author.

When DJ isn't fighting off the annoying side effects of ADHD or the worst case of imposter syndrome known to writer-kind, they're weaving contemporary romance stories filled to the brim with imperfect alphaholes and witty females whose love conquers every hurdle thrown their way.

In her books, representations of the imperfect sides of life are not hidden in the shadows, they're front and center, a reminder that everyone deserves a happy ending.

Also by DJ Krimmer

Closing the Distance

Chasing Noelle (Winter 23)

Must Love Cat - Sapphic Novella

Remnants - Dark Sapphic Novella

Atlas - Hel's Ink Book Two

Ash - Hel's Ink Book Three (June 23)

Derek - Hel's Ink Book Four (Summer 23)

Stevie - Hel's Ink Book Five (Fall 23)

Jackson - Rowe Brothers Ranch Book One (Winter 23)